Deadly Shades of Blue

Tanis Cordes & Sharon Phillips

Deadly Shades of Blue

Copyright © 2005 Alexa & Ernesta Publishing

All rights reserved. No part of this book may be reproduced or utilized in
any form or by any means, electronic or mechanical, including photocopying,
recording, or by any information storage and retrieval system, without
permission in writing from the publisher.

First Edition

Editor: Kenya Zappa

Cover Art: David Beeson

Library of Congress Control Number

ISBN: 0-9768376-7-6

Printed in the USA

This is a work of fiction.
Any resemblance to persons living or dead,
places or events is purely coincidental
and based on the imagination of the authors.

To Karen, Kelly and Russ with my deepest love.
Tanis Cordes

For my sons Daniel and David with special thanks to David
for the artwork on our book cover.
Sharon Phillips

PROLOGUE

Rain spattered the windshield just like the girl's blood had when she cut her. *That was not my fault,* she thought. *That dumb hag made me do it. Tried to make her be quiet but no she just started to scream and wanted to run. She had to die.* She smiled as she remembered the knife glistening in her long fingers as it slashed the struggling girl's pulsing, black throat.

She had never before felt the surge of power that she experienced when she watched her prey cease to struggle. *Your life is mine and so is your man.* She had always known how to hurt someone either with hex, spell or potion, but she had never killed anyone who crossed her. Not unless you count the animals she practiced on.

This new power and danger were exhilarating, a high that she knew she would never give up now that she had found it. She had been waiting all of her life to experience this moment; to take whatever she wanted. She pulled into her driveway, parked her car and watched his seductive shadow in the window.

Chapter One

March

Savannah slowly raised her eyes from the report that she had been struggling with for hours. As the Director of the Atlanta Women at Work Center, she worked most evenings and weekends just to keep up with the volumes of paperwork. As she massaged her aching forehead, she rued the fact that the Center's success created even more work for her. *At least*, she mused, *taxpayers won't lose another wink of sleep worrying about tax dollars going to indigent mothers.* She had removed twenty women off of welfare in her January report alone. That four hundred dollars – more or less - a month per woman would now be diverted overseas to help with the war effort and more homeless, hungry children. What a business, suffering. There seemed to be a never-ending supply, especially when it came to children.

While pondering this thought, she suddenly heard a noise in what was supposed to be her empty office. Someone was standing in front of her desk. Savannah's eyes widened as she focused on Nefertiti reincarnated, or a vision that was certainly an amazing look- alike.

"What the …"? she said out loud. "Harold, Harold,…" Nothing from Harold their big lumbering security guard who looked and acted like an over-fed Basset hound.

"What are you doing in here?" Heart pounding in her chest, she asked this strange woman standing in front of her. She was staring at a tall, slender-necked, black woman who appeared to pop out of nowhere. Composing herself, Savannah grilled the intruder, "How can I help you?" *Now that you scared the living shit out of me.*

"Why, ma'am. I'm here for the interview," the woman replied, seemingly nonchalant at the fact that she had illegally entered a women's center at 6:30 p.m. on a weekday night, evidently walking right past a guard and sauntering up to the director's desk without pause

Pissed off at herself and the stupid, slovenly guard, who was absolutely the most worthless piece of shit, Savannah demanded "How in the hell did you get in here? Didn't you see the guard at the front desk?"

The inept guard had cost a bloody fortune. But given their location and the nature of the business itself, she felt it was money well spent. She had, unfortunately, opted for the economy, no gun-carrying package. She should have known that you get what you pay for. He spent seven hours of his eight-hour shift pouring coffee out of his gallon thermos and talking lasciviously low on the phone to some bimbo who evidently liked to hear a man go on for hours about his undying desire for her. Nevertheless, up until today, she had felt safer just knowing someone was there when she was working late at night. She had let this guard problem slip along with many of the other things she needed to take care of at the women's center. She needed to focus. The woman was trying to explain something. *Maybe if I listen for a minute I can find out why she's actually here.*

"Why, ma'am, don't you remember? We set up this interview two weeks ago. I talked with your office manager, I think her name was Aisha, who said you really needed someone right away and she said to come in tonight." The woman looked at her watch, "Six-thirty, right? I was supposed to meet with Ms. Hart?" She stared at the nameplate on Savannah's desk as if to remind Savannah that she was apparently Ms. Hart.

Savannah couldn't find the words to explain to this woman that Amelia, not Aisha, probably forgot to tell her about the appointment. Too late now she had gotten her throat cut, murdered in cold blood. Dead office manager, dead husband, and complete stranger staring at her in the middle of her office, *wow what a fun year this has been.*

For starters, Savannah couldn't think of Amelia, without tearing up. She had, according to the police, secretly returned to working the streets. Evidently she was hooked up with some of her old friends, the kind that got her in trouble in the first place. Office scuttlebutt was that she had been dating some lowlife. Amelia had paid the ultimate price for returning to her former life. Someone had cut her throat and left her lying dead in a deserted alley. The media had just loved it. Murder sells.

Of course, Savannah could have forgotten the appointment. After all, she was a mess just like her office, which looked like it had been recently hit by a scud missile. These days, she could barely keep from drooling in public, let alone keep track of every single event during the day. Right now, the center was running on automatic pilot, because all she could manage to do was show up, do the budget, and rely on her co-pilot Peggy to gather together all the loose ends.

Add to that the recent death of Tommy – her young, beautiful, chemically dependent husband, dead as a doornail. Her heart ached just thinking about him. Her working late had increased since his death. Anything she could do to avoid her empty house she did.

Never mind the fact that she had a caseload, which required heavy-duty interventions. The women she ended up with were at the end of the line. They were the rejects from her staff, who had given up on them and just couldn't stand to meet with them one more time.

Last but not least, she had a spring fundraiser, truly impossible to fathom, which would require her to be at the top of her game in her little black dress and high heels, so she could entice the local corporations to be socially responsible. It would be particularly tricky this year since the Center had a murder take place practically in its own back yard. She would be fielding questions about the efficacy of the Center and its ability to truly rehabilitate these wayward women, especially ingrates like Amelia who had the gall to get themselves killed. Donors might tighten their purse strings over this mishap.

Given all that was going on right now, her mind was a junk drawer so full of clutter that it was impossible to sort out where anything belonged. This too *might* pass, she thought, but for right now, she apparently needed to talk to this apparition, while trying to figure out what quirky, little message the universe was sending her now.

Gathering her strength, Savannah looked at the woman the way she imagined a sane Director of a Center would talk to a woman who evidently had an interview appointment. Although the woman's eyes were kind of ominous and a little fierce, she did seem to know what she was talking about. She looked at Nefertiti, or maybe more like a young Lena Horne, "What can you do?" She asked bluntly. *...and make it quick.*

"Why, Ms. Hart, I can do just about anything." Looking at Savannah's clutter, she continued, "I can start by cleaning up this mess. How do you ever find anything, ma'am?" she was seriously wondering, you could tell.

Hey don't stand on politeness, dear, Savannah thought. *My kind of person. No fuss, no big deal, just come in and clean up this frigging mess.* Savannah relaxed into her chair, folding her hands in her lap, and let her carry on.

"If you don't mind, Ms. Hart, I'll sit down here." Savannah watched Nefertiti in action. She made quick work of the crap on the chair in front of Savannah's desk and leaned over Savannah's desk, a pool player lining up her shot.

Don't mind me, Savannah thought as she observed the woman's obviously buff body. The woman was in extraordinarily good shape filling out the little Danskin number. She looked like an ad for Ebony, front page, with her body–clinging black knit pants, very tight Tee and matching jacket. *Wow, I must be in the wrong business,* Savannah thought, as her eyes landed on a very fine gold necklace. She was fascinated by the diamond ring on her right hand, which looked pretty expensive, if real, especially for someone who ...

The woman diverted Savannah's attention, "Ms. Hart, I've been an administrative assistant in South Carolina for the last 3 years. I've never been an office manager, but it can't be that hard. I know I can help you, cuz I'm not afraid of hard work. I have two daughters, and I need to get real busy making a living. I can't waste any more time." Opening a leather folder, she quickly produced a resume for Savannah.

Savannah cleared a path on her desk and placed the resume squarely in front of her, meeting the woman's earnest stare. Her features were refined, lips slightly full, beautiful, high cheekbones and a perfectly, painted face highlighted with bronze. Her eyes had light shades of lavender on the lids and she smelled faintly of expensive perfume. Her dark eyes were perfectly lined in thin, black liner, as were her arched eyebrows.

She is truly a vision except when she opens her mouth, Savannah thought. The voice had sort of a high, quacking quality to it, which Savannah thought over time would probably drive her absolutely crazy. At this point, the journey was a short one. Savannah suspected that men would ignore the voice to get to that body. Like many women, she probably used a more seductive, resonant voice when she spoke with men.

She rattled on, "Ms. Hart, I really need this job and by the looks of things you could use someone like me to help you. I'll work as many hours as you need me, and I'll get my childcare all set up for my girls." Savannah was taken aback when she came around the desk and asked if she could sit down. Savannah gave her the chair as she parked herself in front of the computer. She minimized the budget report window and brought up a blank document on the computer screen. She eyed a letter on Savannah's desk and typed up the first paragraph in seconds with no errors. Savannah salivated at the thought of someone actually coming in and knowing what in the hell they were doing. *Sold to the woman, in the back row, with the dirty hair and circles under her eyes.*

The woman returned to the seat in front of Savannah's desk. "Ms. Hart, I need this job real bad. Franklin, that's my husband, my ex-husband, is in South Carolina and I need to stay here away from him. I have my two daughters now, but if I don't get a job, he'll get custody of them. I'm scared to death cuz he's real mean. I have a restraining order on him, but I gotta get work. Please help me out?"

Savannah took the resume and stalled while she figured out the earliest day Ruby could start, "Your name is Ruby, Ruby Ebota. It says here you were working in Beaufort." In a way Ruby reminded Savannah of a high-priced hooker. Nothing cheap about her, but she did have a "come fuck me quality" to her. Savannah sighed as she thought how jaded she had become.

"Let me show you what I've done." Ruby's fingers pointed to each line on the resume and she quickly covered the information ending up in a breathless, "So you can see I can do this."

This woman could sell paper to a pulp mill, Savannah thought. In the back of her mind, Savannah knew Ruby's high voice racing along on every subject would ultimately drive her even crazier than she felt today, but nothing could stack up to the last few weeks of sleepless nights, bizarre nightmares and the never-ending truckload of work responsibilities. After all, the woman looked okay, and she typed at the speed of light.

Upping the ante, Ruby said, "I have some pictures," She dug around in her small, leather shoulder bag, stood up and walked around the desk, leaning over Savannah, "This is Jasmine and the little one is Faith. Jasmine is six years old and Faith is two." Ruby skootched down next to Savannah to point out each of the girls in their glossy snap shots.

Savannah turned to see the pictures *–so maybe I've misjudged her* -and could feel Ruby's body inches from her. She noticed small beads of perspiration above Ruby's lip as she smiled and talked. Ruby stood up, laid her hand on Savannah's shoulder, and looked down at Savannah, "Is there anything more important than children?" Without skipping a beat, she added, "When are you looking for someone to start? We're staying at a real cheap motel and I have to get a job and get us an apartment right away."

It had all happened so fast that Savannah, even with a few red flags waving in her mind, was basically only aware that right in front of her, only an arms length away, was an immediate solution to her problem. God knows who she really was, and God knows that right now she didn't really care. What she needed was someone to haul the crap out of her office, set up her appointments, take care of the teetering stacks of paper, and maybe even find a decent guard who in the future actually stays awake while on duty. She took a deep breath and looked at the resume again. *They're staying in a cheap motel – Eek! Oh, what the hell,* "You can start on Monday."

Ruby lit up like Saks at Christmas. "Oh, ma'am, I'm so grateful. I'll work hard for you, you'll see. I can't wait to tell Jasmine and Faith, bless those little babies. I have to go to South Carolina this weekend and get some stuff. I'll be back first thing Monday morning. I'll leave you my message number at the motel in case there is any change in plans. Otherwise, I'll be here at 8:00 on Monday." Ruby wrote down her number and held out her hand to Savannah.

Savannah shuddered as she shook Ruby's hand. She was astonished at how cold Ruby's fingers were. They were hard and wrapped around her hand like a claw. She quickly forgot this as she realized that Ruby could get her kids into a decent apartment and get started making a safe home for them. Desperate herself for help, she knew this was truly a spur of the moment decision. Normally, she would have gone through the whole process, but nothing at this time was normal. Life isn't always perfect or certainly predictable. She would take what she had and run like the devil with it.

Chapter Two

As she sat alone listening to Ruby leave the building, Savannah flashed back to the day she had found out about Amelia's murder. *God what a nightmare that had been,* Savannah thought as she remembered the morning Amelia had not shown up for work. She had been pissed off at her at first because she had forgotten to call in. By that afternoon, Savannah's frustration escalated giving her a throbbing headache and a tense knot at the base of her neck. She had even tried calling Amelia at home herself. As she rubbed her neck to get some of the pain moving along, Savannah heard voices out in the lobby. Vivian, her temporary receptionist, came into her office. "Ma'am, I'm sorry to bother you, but there are two policeman here to see you and they say it is very important."

" Just send them in, Vivian." Savannah stood up behind her desk and prepared to greet them. She straightened out her skirt and looked up to see two men enter her office. Now what?

The first one walked over to her and extended his hand. "Detective Al Benson," offered the taller of the two men, "and this is my partner, Detective Ed Stanton from Atlanta Police, Homicide, Central. Could we speak in private, please?" asked Detective Benson, a gaunt, thin man about 40 with prematurely gray hair and a mustache.

"Of course." replied Savannah. "Thank you Vivian, would you close the door on the way out?" Vivian nodded solemnly and closed the door quietly behind her.

Savannah quickly removed the clutter from the only two available chairs in her office. "Please sit down," she said with growing concern at their solemn manner. Both men, unsmiling, were clean cut, and dressed in dark suits and conservative ties. Detective Benson motioned his younger, well-built, partner to the chair nearer the window. Benson sat directly across from Savannah.

One look at the detectives' faces told Savannah they were dead serious. Savannah got right to the point. "What is the problem?" she asked in a pleasant but curt tone. In the past, the local cops spent a lot of time at the Center, sometimes for reasons that eluded Savannah. She was convinced that they could use their time going after some real criminals. Not that the women at the Center were angels, but usually they were guilty of petty theft, fraud, prostitution or drugs never anything murderous. Most of their criminal activity was wrapped around the need to get some money coming in. *This time is different*, she sensed as these men were from the homicide division.

Detective Stanton sat and fixed his clear gray eyes on Savannah. In fact, he seemed to be staring through her silk blouse. He stuttered as he shifted from looking directly at her breasts, to looking at her, "S-s-s sorry to interrupt your busy schedule, Ms. Hart, but I am afraid we have some bad news."

Detective Benson butted in, "Amelia Brown was found murdered last night."

Suddenly the room became unbearably close as horror spread over Savannah's face, "Not another death." she whispered as the word *murder* echoed in the room.

"What do you mean?" countered Benson, who looked like he certainly hadn't expected her to say that.

Realizing he must have thought she was talking about other murders at the center, Savannah quickly explained, "I lost my husband in December and now this. Please just tell me what happened."

She watched Detective Benson take notes. *He probably thinks Tommy's death is an important clue to the murder. I can't believe I said that out loud.* Detective Robot continued in his *monotone voice.* "We are sorry for your loss and we know this is a shock, however there are certain questions we need to ask. I will also answer any of your questions that I can." Meaning, as she well knew that he would give out only a few, if any details, keeping the revealing pertinent evidence to himself.

Savannah's body filled up with immense sadness when Benson announced that, "Amelia Brown's corpse was found in an alley in Midtown. The area in which the body was found and the way she was dressed suggested that she was one of those prostitutes you find down there, we see them all the time. Probably involved in a trick gone wrong or a bad drug deal."

Where do they get these guys, Savannah wondered as she railed from the "one of those prostitutes" remark.

Looking at Savannah's face, Benson backed off of his remark. "Sorry, ma'am, didn't mean nothin'. It's just that you know these women just don't use common sense. Why…" Savannah held up her hand to stop him. She caught a glimpse of Stanton out of the corner of her eye who was now checking out the slit in her skirt where her legs were crossed. Benson recovering from his mistake started over.

"Ms. Hart, it's just what the evidence suggested at first." Benson continued. "She's got a record, you know. We talked to her mother, who said Amelia had been working here over a year and that her girl wasn't in trouble any more."

Savannah flinched; *they'll bring up everything and it will be in the paper for everyone to see. Her poor mother.* She made a mental note to contact Amelia's mother as soon as the police left and offer her help in any way possible. She knew how financially depleted the mother would be without Amelia's income. She could only imagine how devastated she must be as Amelia was an only child. Amelia had been a beautiful young African-American woman, light brown skin and eyes, short black curly hair, her ample body gracefully proportioned.

"How did she die?" asked Savannah holding her breath. She didn't even want to imagine.

"The perpetrator cut her throat," replied Detective Benson. "It was done quickly, if that is any consolation."

"Thank you, not much," answered Savannah letting her breath out in short little gasps. Savannah closed her eyes for a moment trying to get the picture out of her mind of Amelia with her throat slit, this bumbling robot in front of her, and Mr. Drool sitting in the corner. *Please, God, I want a different movie.*

"You okay ma'am?" inquired Detective Stanton.

"Yes, please go on," she ignored Stanton and directed her gaze at Detective Benson.

"We need to know what time she left here last night, if you know of anything bothering her, who her friends were. Anything about her personal life you might be able to fill in for us would be of help?" asked Detective One Note.

"I thought you believed it had something to do with drugs or prostitution?" Savannah leaned forward and looked him square in the eye.

"Yeah, but in an homicide investigation you know we gotta follow any possible leads."

"I understand, but please take it as easy as possible on these women. We all liked Amelia. We were all close. Many of the women here have violent and troubled lives, so please proceed with caution." Savannah pleaded.

"We'll need to talk with the rest of your staff," Benson stood up as he nodded his head at Stanton to get moving. Benson shook hands with Savannah and thanked her for her help. He offered his condolences and nodded again at Stanton. Stanton stood up and held on to Savannah's hand, "If there is anything I can do to help."

Truly you have done more than enough already, Savannah thought as she removed her hand from his sweaty handshake.

Savannah remembered that the questioning had gone *ad nauseam*. For the next few hours they interviewed the rest of the staff coming up with nothing. By the time the detectives had left - Benson with Stanton in tow - they had a mountain of information from her, the staff, any clients unfortunate to have had an appointment that day and a list of clients to contact. Everyone in the office was in turmoil as a result of the investigation and also because of the loss of someone who had been a major success story. For days, everyone discussed the murder, but no one could come up with any evidence or clues that would help connect the Center to her death. If the women knew anything, they weren't talkin'.

Savannah still wondered who could have been capable of murdering this young woman. She had called detective Benson several times requesting information. The best he could do was assure her they were following all leads, and that as soon as they arrested a suspect, he would share more information with her. *When pigs ride on Delta,* Savannah thought, as she hung up the phone after her most recent call feeling defeated once again.

But tonight, even has she sat in her office, listening to Ruby shut the outside door, she agonized over the brutal death of Amelia. She could still see the beautiful young women, with the golden brown skin, coming into her office telling her she had passed her first typing test. She could remember hugging Amelia when she offered her the first receptionist job. She had given her a small gift certificate to spend when Amelia had been promoted to Administrative Assistant. She and Peggy had taken her out for Mexican food to celebrate Amelia's amazingly quick promotion to Office Manager. The staff had collected money and had given her a new pen and pencil set with her initials on it. *No fucking way Amelia was turning tricks again.* Now, probably because of some drug-crazed maniac this lovely, warm woman so full of promise was lying cold and hard in the downtown morgue.

Chapter Three

Might as well finish up for the day, Savannah decided as she finished off a few more e-mails, turned off her computer and thought about this strange Ruby woman. Savannah wondered how Ruby's kids would do in Atlanta. It must be tough for her with her husband trying to find her and the kids and her trying to get settled. She could easily drown under the pressure.

Ruby's daughters' pictures had been compelling, real beauties, not as dark as her, but with the same bright expressions and enigmatic smiles. They were picture perfect she had to admit. Ruby must have made some money in the years before, that beautiful ring and the kid leather shoes and purse. She was precision personified, like a well-oiled machine. So what? An abusive husband, hungry kids, no place to live, what could you expect. *Funny though how little curiosity Ruby had shown about Amelia's death. She's too wrapped up in her own drama, I guess.*

Lately, Savannah's exit from the center would drag on interminably. She would start to head home and then would sit in a fog wishing and dreaming for things that just weren't going to happen. She would replay the events of the last few weeks in her mind.

Savannah wished Peggy were with her tonight. She really needed to talk with her. Savannah remembered that right after the detectives had left, she had felt the same way. Peggy was in Houston and hadn't even heard what had happened yet. Savannah remembered how she had sat alone in her office after having sent everyone home as soon as the cops left and waited for Peggy to return from her trip. She wanted to tell her what happened before it broke on the evening news.

When she heard her come in, she quickly walked past Amelia's old office to her office. She walked in, shut the door and sat down quietly in front of Peggy's desk. Peggy held up her hand while she finished leaving a voice mail on the phone.

At sixty years old, Peggy had put in her time. She had worked in her early years as a professional black woman in a white man's world. She had been a counselor, director, a consultant and was currently a training coordinator trying to share her home-brewed recipe of success, which included a huge dollop of intellect, lots of street smarts, a good smattering of humor doused with a whole gob of common sense.

"Wow, you look like you have just seen a ghost." Peggy put the phone down. She had been through a lot with Savannah and she knew her to be a "pro." They would laugh at how Peggy had greeted Savannah at the Center door over five years ago on Savannah's first day. Peggy said she thought that Savannah was sure a pretty thing, but she was really happy to find she had a big heart, a good-sized brain and knew how to "kick ass and take names." Savannah suspected that Peggy had expected her to be a lightweight and was glad Peggy seemed to be pleasantly surprised after a few months of working together.

Peggy would introduce Savannah as a woman who was a major player in the social service field. She would describe her as a woman with strong instincts and a willingness to work a case anyway she could to get the kind of results that made women want to get off their butts and tackle the most menacing challenges. She would tell anyone willing to listen that Savannah was packed with compassion and all in all was one of the best counselors she had ever worked with. Coming from Peggy that was a great compliment.

"The cops were here. " Savannah let Peggy know the second she hung up the phone.

"Ten years hard labor for shoplifting, right? After all, why catch murderers when…" Peggy stopped when Savannah shook her head up and down at the sound of *murderers*." She tilted her head, "God, what's wrong?"

"It's Amelia. She was murdered. Found her with her throat cut. They found her body in a nasty old back alley in midtown." Savannah sounded like Robot Benson.

"Dear God in heaven, what happened?" Savannah knew Peggy was visibly shaken. Like Savannah, she had put a lot of effort into Amelia. They had tag teamed Amelia's success. Together, they ignored the loudmouth, defensive "in your face" brat and helped her discover a better way to express herself. They knew anyone making that much noise certainly had enough energy to take on the world; just needed a map.

Fortunately, she had come to them at the right stage in her life. They were able to change her environment, help her focus, and give her the education, structure, guidance and opportunities that she was screaming for. She soaked up everything anyone threw her way once she understood the path she needed to take. She replaced the "attitude" with a funny, sly wit that cracked everyone up, giving her the kind of attention she that loved. Typical of funny people, she was very quick and was able to take on a leadership role at the Center.

Savannah remembered that Peggy talked about how Amelia had slipped back recently and on a couple of occasions had sounded like the old, tough Amelia. This was to be expected, since this was what was the most familiar to her. Even on her "slip-back" days, she couldn't hide her vulnerability, desire to be liked and most of all her charming, redeemable self. Rumor had it that she had a new high-powered boyfriend. Savannah had heard Amelia describing him to one of her girlfriends on the phone. Her conversation was peppered with "he's so fine" and "you know that, girl" and lots of sighs and giggles. Savannah knew she couldn't save the world, but this one should have been a "slam dunk." "They don't think it was anyone here, do they?" Peggy asked as she held up her hand heavenward, pleading out loud, " Please, God, don't let it be one of our women."

Peggy was like an Aunt to Savannah or an older sister. She was sophisticated and "hip" and everything Savannah aspired to be. Her life had been dedicated to political activism. As an intellectual, her writings and work were revered both in the US and internationally especially in the humanitarian groups fighting for the future of women.

Savannah loved everything about her. She thought her gray, wiry hair that hadn't been cut in years, but simply wrapped in a bun in the back leaving soft tendrils everywhere, was exquisite. She rarely saw her in anything but deep purple, lavenders, brilliant reds and deep greens that accentuated her hazel eyes. She wore prints from Africa and India long before they were popular and her jewelry decorated her neck and ears in magical combinations of lapis, silver, turquoise and emerald. She wasted little of her precious brainpower and time on silliness like diets, makeup and frivolous worries typically emphasized in women's lives. Her direction was clear. She was a star leading women to a safe place. She started her plight in her twenties and it was apparent she would continue her efforts until she took her last breath.

Savannah had seen how Peggy immediately grabbed her paper and pencil. "I'm going to call Amelia's mother. I've spoken to her before and I know she must be devastated. I'll get some good background on her and we'll get this to the press before they focus on all of the bad. How is the staff doing? The women?"

"The staff already knows. In fact, the detectives have already interviewed them separately. The staff called as many of the women as they could get a hold of and talked with them personally. We met with everyone that was at the Center. John Abbott said he would do some crisis counseling tomorrow with the staff and with the women." Savannah was glad they had Dr. Abbott on the staff now. He would be a godsend to everyone in the next few weeks. He had certainly helped her in the last few weeks after Tommy's death.

Peggy started her list and kept talking. "Can you believe we were able to get John? He's got to be one of the best grief counselors in town. Are we set up to handle tomorrow?" She was quickly shifting into high gear.

Savannah appreciated being with the "Rock of Gibraltar" and felt enormous strength being in the same room with Peggy. "This will be devastating to the women. Amelia gave them hope, you know." She put her hands on the chair arms and pushed herself up. Straightening her skirt and whisking the tears off of her face with her hand, she opened the door and stood out in the lobby. Arms folded across her chest, she prepared herself to spend the evening, along with Peggy, calling clients not reached by the staff to tell them personally about the incident. She hated to have them hear it on the news. *Another sister down.*

Well, that was history and this was now. Time to shake herself out of her reverie and talk with Harold. The day had been way too long, and there was still the long drive home in the Atlanta traffic. She wondered what Peggy would think of Ruby. *Probably wouldn't like her very much,* Savannah thought, as she switched off the lights and walked up to the snoring guard.

"Hey, Harold....get your ass awake here. Do you realize someone walked right past you tonight? This is the third time I've warned you. You're outta here. I'm calling your boss tomorrow. Pack your stuff and get out!" Savannah was furious at his laziness and the breach of security that had put all of them at risk. For all she knew, Ruby could have been a serial killer.

One look at Savannah and he knew he was "toast." He didn't even bother to argue. He just signed off the Internet, cleared his 1500 messages, grabbed his massive thermos, and sauntered out the door. She waited until he left, set the security alarm, and shut the door behind her.

Standing outside the Center, she stopped for a minute and looked at the small, gray painted one-story office building that had been "rehabbed" to death. Although it was pretty old, the offices were more interesting in this building than in the newer versions. Savannah liked the way the office was laid out. Each counselor had an office and there weren't any gray jail-like cubicles. The spacious lobby area had several chairs and even an old sofa for people to sit comfortably while waiting to see someone. She appreciated her big office with windows that opened up, especially when new flowers were in bloom.

She walked by the huge Mimosa tree that along with the row of crepe myrtle trees seemed ready to infiltrate the entire neighborhood. She relished the upcoming season when the trees would burst into bright purples and breath-taking fuchsia. Even this evening, the trees were rich and full, lush green with buds forming for the warmer months. Savannah was struck again at the beauty of the winter night as the full moon peeped back at her through its black lacy cloud cover.

She clicked twice on her remote key and thanked the transportation gods for creating the automatic light and door opener especially for her arrival. Although her car was close, she took every precaution. After all, she was in downtown Atlanta where anything could happen.

As the tail lights from Savannah's car faded into the distance, a shadow moved from behind the Mimosa tree.

*****

You be nice to cut.

Chapter Four

Savannah played bumper cars all the way home, wending her way around the traffic driving up 75 north. She couldn't wait to get home and call her best buddy Irish Sullivan. They still talked several times a week even though they were almost 3,000 miles apart. For all practical purposes, she and Irish were sisters. Actually, by law they had been sister-in-laws; Savannah had married Irish's brother Tommy. Now that he was dead, she guessed that was no longer true. Didn't matter, Irish understood Savannah better than anyone in the world. They had grown up as neighbors and Savannah had spent most of her early years at Irish's house.

Typically, others viewed Savannah as having it all. They were right. She did not want for anything material. She had always been well provided for by her parent's money. Irish understood how money hadn't bought Savannah anything but lots of grief. Although Savannah's parents provided for her financially, that was the full extent of their involvement with her. Their focus was on their own problems, which were drunkenly aired on a regular basis for the neighbors to hear, including Irish's mother. The first few times the fights escalated, Irish's mother Catherine, would call the local police to report the incidents. She feared for Savannah's emotional and physical safety. The police weren't much interested in tackling such a prominent citizen, so Catherine took matters into her own hands.

From the time Savannah was four years old, Catherine made sure her home was open to her. When the fights began, the drunkenness and brawling, Savannah, in her nightgown with her blanket wrapped around her, would run like hell to Irish's house. Catherine would be waiting at the door and take her to Irish's bedroom and tuck her in. The best she could do was harbor a young fugitive who needed safety until the hurricane blew over. When Savannah got older, the door was left unlocked and she let herself in. On many mornings, Irish woke up with Savanna curled up next to her sweaty and hot wrapped up in her blanket that she brought on her quick journey up the hill from her little house of horrors. This was a pattern that continued through most of grade school. By high school, Savannah was perfectly capable of taking care of herself. Her family pretty much left her alone.

Growing up together in North Carolina, Savannah and Irish had for all practical purposes enjoyed "privilege." In other words, good schools cars, clothes, and opportunities that the average person doesn't necessarily enjoy. Nevertheless, Catherine's influence had been strong and both girls were raised with a "no-nonsense" approach that said, "You are no big deal – get out there and learn to do as much as you can and be a decent person in the world." Both had listened. Irish studied Criminal Justice. Savannah earned her Masters in Social Work. They shared a dorm and graduated with honors. Both were modern women with superior education's, excellent careers and Catherine's handiwork shinning through. When Savannah married Tommy, she remained Savannah Hart in name and in everything she did.

Catherine had not been as successful with her son, Tommy. Cute as a bug from the day he was born, he was incorrigible. He could not and would not comply in any reasonable way that could help him get along in the world. He had trouble in school from year one. He was an anomaly. On one hand, he could play chess by the time he was six years old beating many of the adults that challenged him. On the other hand, he wouldn't sit still long enough to learn key elements necessary for him to do well in a structured classroom environment.

He was so restless, agitated, angry and frustrated through most of his school years that by the time he was sixteen, he left home. Tommy headed to the coast to work on a construction crew just to get away from the disappointed look on his dad's face. In his early years Catherine went through the rigmarole of testing for learning disabilities, sending him to a psychologist, helping him capitalize on his interest in working with color and design. He loved working with stained glass and would sit for hours creating designs with such precision that it amazed Catherine that he didn't have the same patience for learning in school. When Tommy loved something he gave it everything. When he didn't, there was no negotiation.

Savannah hit the brakes joining the gridlock of traffic on highway 75. Stuck in traffic, she couldn't help thinking of how little effort her parents put into being decent parents. Thank God they had stopped having kids after they had her. She created her own sibling. Irish was her sister as truly as if they had shared the same genes. Even today as tired as she was after a long day at the Center, she felt Catherine's influence. She knew if Ruby's children were unsafe, she would follow in Catherine's footsteps and do everything in her power to help them to safety. She would never forget the safety and solace the Sullivan's provided her and it was her passion and commitment in life to be there for other children.

She smiled to herself as she drove up to her home. It was such a wonderful place, and she and Tommy had made it perfect. Of course, Tommy had embraced the challenge of turning the simple two-bedroom cottage into a home. Everything Tommy did, Savannah thought, he did well–except trying to figure out how to live to a ripe-old age.

As she drove into the driveway, she caught the muted light behind the stained glass doorway. Tommy had worked for over a year designing two stained-glass windows for their entryway. Meticulously, he drew three large magnolias blooming on a thick multi-green colored vine with rubbery leaves. He had added small pieces of deep red and blue intermittently to bring out the other colors. Then little by little, the paper drawings became something much more. He transformed his drawings onto tiny, hand cut and soldered rich-colored glass recreating the design onto two 10-inch wide pieces, the same height as the front door. He carefully inlaid the glass on both sides of the entrance replacing the cheap plastic that had been originally put into the house. Tommy was generously rewarded for his hard work as a kaleidoscope of greens, reds and blues filtered through their living room. He and Savannah had their own little Eden.

Savannah used her remote to open the garage door and drove in. As the garage door closed behind her, she turned off *La Boheme* on her CD and like Mimi wished she could scream at the top of her lungs at the injustice of it all. Mimi finds the love of her life and then goes off and dies, *"What's wrong with that picture,"* she sighed.

As she entered her home, Lily, her Tabby cat, who as always was glad to see her, greeted her. *It's just you and me, kid.* She picked her up and carried her into the living room, placing her keys and purse on the kitchen table. Grabbing her cell phone from her purse, she headed for her well-worn sofa, her shoes clicking on the wide-planked, hardwood floors that Tommy had so meticulously finished, board by board. Savannah kicked off her shoes and sunk into the corner of the sofa and the thick pillows that had been her refuge since Tommy's death.

As she looked at Tommy's picture on the fireplace mantle, she remembered the first year they were in the house. Tommy, the perfectionist that he was, could not bear to live in a house with a white painted fireplace that clearly needed to be stripped to its natural brick foundation. Patiently, almost every night for several months, Tommy had taken small amounts of muratic acid and a wire brush and labored relentlessly to remove the sloppy, globs of white paint. She remembered how he would drink his bourbon all evening long as he removed the offensive white paint one-inch at a time swearing at the Neanderthal who had ruined it in the first place.

She had been briefly, though precariously, happy, she thought as she waited for Lily to get settled on her lap. Tommy loved his home and he had spent years getting it to perfection. Like everything in his life, it took it toll on him. Instead of luxuriating in his accomplishments, he would focus on one blemish, which would take up months of his time to mend.

Something about the way he worked on the house was part and parcel about how he saw himself. It was never good enough and he was never good enough. His agony was consumed in numerous bottles of hard liquor every week. Savannah still found half-empty bottles hidden in remote places as the weeks after his death unfolded. She knew he was struggling with alcohol - he always had - but she had no idea that it was to this extent. Each time she found another alcohol cache, she was reminded of Tommy's preoccupation with liquor. He had obviously spent his waking hours either trying to get a drink, trying to act sober when he was drunk, trying to hide his liquor and ultimately trying to hide the fact that he was slowly dying inside.

Savannah had to admit he had been more erratic the last few months before his death. She should have seen the signs. He had gone through a severe depression that lasted over a year and then he had seen a psychiatrist who unless he "got clean and sober" would not provide him with any more medication. Unknown to her at the time, Tommy was creative and went to several doctors for prescriptions therefore getting the "high" he needed to keep him going. He was driven. The same intensity that had filled their bed with excitement and passion could and did turn into a monster at the most unforeseen moments creating chaos and havoc in their lives.

Savannah braced herself as she looked around her beautiful, but quiet home, wishing for just one more evening of Tommy quietly working on a piece of wood bringing it to perfection. She loved him in spite of the way he was. There was nothing she could say or do to offset his intense hatred of himself. She wanted to have one more time to touch him, smell him, and taste him. *Stop!*

As she grabbed her cell phone, she hit the programmed number, and waited to hear Irish's voice. Lily, completely comfortable now purred contentedly. Savannah snuggled in ready to talk about her bizarre day. *Be there, come on ...be there.*

"Hi, this is Irish, please leave your name at the sound of the tone ".... beep.

"Oh, fine, don't be home, girlfriend. I've had the day from hell. Fired the guard, still being kept in the dark about Amelia's killer, met a spooky woman and, oh, by the way, hired her – don't even go there. I know what your gonna to say. Suppose you are out with Mr. Wonderful, or stalking some badass fraudulent creep. So call me and let me know if you've run off with Tex yet – ha! Better check your apartment to see if Ms. Ethel has it bugged. It's been an amazingly long day and I'm going to go to bed now. Footnote: I'm finally sleeping in the bed again instead of the sofa. Love ya….talk to you tomorrow."

Chapter Five

Ruby laughed as she remembered Ms. Hart's serious little face all full of concern. *Ugly bitch,* Ruby thought. She'd hit her up for money real soon and make sure she used her daughters anyway she could. After all she needed to keep Tremaine happy and bring in more girls to get their "business" going. *Tremaine a regular P.R. man,* she chuckled to herself. *That Center gonna be a gold mine for whores.*

That guard was so stupid with his big ole gut hangin' over his belt, half-asleep. Reminded her of Big Daddy's friends. Used to come over a lot. Liked Big Daddy's little girl. *Wanna taste a nice big licorice stick?* Big Daddy, one of mama's many men who liked mama's two daughters even better than mama. Big daddy said he liked her better than her sister or her mama. She was his favorite. By the time she left home, the tables had turned. He was terrified of Ruby, and hadn't touched her for years. He was superstitious and knew she had the power to lay a hex on him.

Tremaine my man, Ruby thought as she listened to the soft snoring next to her. She rolled over on her side and curled up behind him feeling the heat from having sex. *I wore him out good,* Ruby smiled to herself. No easy task with Tremaine, 6 feet 2 and built like a truck. Not the best man she'd had ever had but certainly the richest and hottest looking one with lean, rippling muscles, big brown eyes, and cocoa brown skin. His voice was as smooth as his shaved head Ruby mused. Ruby rubbed her long fingers on his back, scraping his back lightly with her long, red nails. She touched her tongue on his shiny body glazed with sweat and rubbed her breasts and stomach along his back. Her hand stroked his ass. Naked except for the thick gold chain he wore around his neck and a diamond earring. Tremaine rolled over with a huge erection ready to go another round.

He'd told Ruby his ex-girlfriend had been kind of big, a little slow. *My baby don't have to worry about her no more.* He liked the way Ruby welcomed him. No matter how tired he was, he wanted her one more time. Sometimes she would sidle up to the front of the dresser while he came up behind her pushing himself up inside of her. She could stay ready for him for hours. Ruby thought, the exhilaration of his sexual power was almost the same high she felt when she cut that whore. Killing was the perfect way to get what she wanted. *Felt so fine, too.*

She heard his big groan as he filled her up and then withdrew. Now he really was tired and went back to bed fully expended. Ruby fell asleep, the most alive she had ever been, wet and filled up from all the excitement of the day.

*****

Tremaine lies naked across the bed snoring softly. Ruby loves watching him as she stands by the bed slowly stroking her own fine body. She croons softly to herself sliding her hands up her slim hips and silently slips out of her skin. Now as she hovers over the bed, she is invisible, crooning and mumbling an ancient chant… binding Tremaine to her evermore.

Chapter Six

Nights like this made Irish Sullivan wish she had opted for living in a new apartment building with indoor parking. The historic buildings didn't come with garages, so she had to house her car several blocks away. Her early 1900's building was one of many that were built in Portland, Oregon after the 1905 Lewis and Clark Exposition.

Walking two blocks in the rain, wind and cold at 11:00 p.m. when she could be tucked in her own bed made her wonder sometimes. Even in this miserable weather, she managed to soak in the ambiance of her turn of the century neighborhood. She loved the mixture of old mansions, refurbished apartments with their wrought iron balconies and even some of the "newcomer" buildings blended together. Although it was trendier to live in the old warehouses that had been converted to lofts, they weren't for her. She loved being part of an area that felt like an actual neighborhood, where there were ancient trees, upscale food marts, lively people milling around, restaurants close by and the sound of traffic throughout the night

Given the weather, she probably would have been better off spending the night with Jack, enjoying some great sex with her favorite hunk. Just like him, she wasn't much interested in a long-term commitment and generally preferred to be in her own space at the end of the day. She had met Jack Pardue at the Portland police department through her own work as a private investigator. Jack had served on the force for thirteen years and was a detective for the Metro Division. Midway through a sticky divorce that followed a very long and unhappy relationship, Jack was "gun-shy" about any kind of permanency in a relationship. This was perfectly fine with Irish. Right now her capacity to feel was limited. She was in such grief and so vulnerable after the death of her brother Tommy that she kept her feelings safely buried and away from public and personal scrutiny.

Picking up the pace, she shuddered off the weariness of her recent loss. She needed to concentrate on staying strong and focused. Her business as an investigator took up most of her time. She was busily building up her clientele and that was a full-time undertaking. As she had found out with her college professor fiasco, relationships tended to muck up everything. She purposely kept an edge to handle whatever was coming up next, which at this very moment looked like trouble.

Irish always alert saw movement near one of the hundred year-old chestnut trees that lined the street in her neighborhood. Even in early March and with no leaves, these trees offered perfect cover with trunks larger than a person. Yes, she was correct there were two of them, scrawny little punks wearing dark clothing. Both also had black "hoodie" sweatshirts hiding their faces. Her guess was car thieves who thought they would have an easy mark. Two could play this game.

Irish heard rustling in the fallen leaves, but they weren't getting any closer. She quickly hid behind a tree of her own, drew her Smith & Wesson 38 special and waited. *Now,* she thought, *we'll see how long the little bastards can hold out.* She could hear them moving, faint whispering reached her as the wind blew toward her.

"Man, let's do it now man."

"You do it man this was your idea, just some old broad, no problem, motherfucker."

"Give it up bitch, you know were gonna stick your ass you make us wait," one of them called out.

Dead silence.

Encouraged by the silence, the two edged out from behind the tree and moved forward. They were puzzled that this bitch had not run or screamed by now, it must be their lucky day. After all there were two of them and one lone broad. The car they had just broken into a block away had not yielded enough money for one drug habit, let alone two. So now this old mama was going to pay.

Irish stepped from behind the tree, gun drawn, her feet spread apart. "You little fuckers know the way back down the hill?" By now they were standing eyes wide and jaw's dropped. They looked to be all of about twelve or so to Irish.

This was not the way they had it figured. Here stood a giant broad, long red hair flying in the wind and a gun pointed right at their sorry asses. The taller one of the two had a little bullshit left in him. "Motherfucker, give us the cash or were gonna cut you bad."

On that note, Irish slowly pulled the hammer back on her 38. The two would be "killers" suddenly broke and ran as fast as their baggy below the crack of their asses pants would allow. Irish laughed in spite herself, given another target other than her the results might have been a disaster. *Probably too bad I gave them a break cause next time around the little assholes might by armed.* She was just too damn tired to call the cops, do all the required paperwork only to have the little scum back on the street before she left the police station. Budget cut backs had the police department pulling their hair out. Child molesters and perverts were among the creeps being let out early due to over crowding. "What a merry go round of frustration," she muttered to herself as she continued to walk quickly up the hill.

Although she was a Private Investigator, Irish seldom carried her gun. She tried to stay away from situations that might require it. Today, however, she had been out to the shooting range, making sure she kept her marksmanship skills finely tuned. It had been a great practice; she had been fast, steady and accurate. As she crossed the street, she barely missed a puddle of water as she jumped on the curb and finally reached the elegant old building she called home.

Her apartment building was five stories high, made of old brick that had aged to a lovely deep rose color. Each apartment was adorned with high ceilings, hardwood floors and built in living room bookcases. Unfortunately, the glass in the transoms was long gone now replaced with wood to meet the fire codes.

Irish walked as quietly as possible up the steps and through the little courtyard to the building entrance. She slipped her key into the entrance lock and held the door as it closed so it would not slam. She was careful to make sure the lock latched. She would definitely forego riding the antique elevator with the accordion door that kept getting stuck. *Fool me once…*

She knew once you got into the elevator and it stalled between floors, the only way you could get the elevator to restart was to have someone else go up to the attic, pound on the upper left hand corner of the door. That would after some effort "jump start" the elevator. This meant, if you were trapped inside the elevator, it was necessary to have one of the tenants hear the bell, which wasn't likely if they were cooped up in their apartments. Most of them wouldn't open the door if you knocked with a battering ram. So, you were stuck waiting until someone came along.

The last time she had been in the elevator, she had just returned from seeing *Tosca* at the Keller auditorium. All dressed up in her opera finery, marveling to herself at Tosca's courage, she trustingly got on the elevator. Irish closed the accordion door and pushed the button. Midway, there was a loud thud, the elevator stopped between floors, and she was staring at four closed-in elevator walls with no exit in sight.

Immediately she rang the alarm bell repeatedly and yelled, "Get me outta here" along with a few other choice words hearing nothing but a mere echo. Finally, an inebriated tenant came home and heard her yells. After several "Ya kiddin' me, ladys" and a slurred diatribe on how helpless women are, he reluctantly agreed to help her. She gave him the instructions. She heard him light his cigarette *–hey, don't let that non-smoking sign get in the way* – and stumble up each floor until he finally reached the attic.

She would have loved to see him when he found the attic. *Probably thought he was hallucinating,* she laughed to herself. She could just see him blindly fumbling in the dark for the knotted string dangling from the ceiling light. He would have to maneuver around the attic filled with slatted, wooden, storage cages and roosting pigeons. By now, he must have found the dilapidated, wooden and glass-over-chicken-wire double elevator doors. Evidently, he wasn't too drunk to follow Irish's instructions, because suddenly she heard him administer two sharp raps on the door – exactly the way she had told him.

The elevator lurched into action and within minutes Irish was released from her gilded cage, but not before he described the entire incident to her, in great detail. "Frigging attic is haunted, heard noises, birds too, I think. Lady, this place ain't for pretty ladies like you. Names, Bill McBain, from Texas, ma'am. My friends call me, Tex. Wanna little nip?" He had generously offered her a sip from his silver flask. Now when she saw him, he thought they were best friends.

After all, he had kind of saved her life, hadn't he? Tex, was quick to explain every time he saw her, had made a killing in Texas and was hanging out in Portland for a spell. He said he was a fixen to return to Texas after he traveled some more up to that Puget Sound area and maybe even Canada. He sure would like to take a feisty little filly like her back home with him and get hitched.

Irish avoided the elevator and decided to forget about her mail. Probably junk mail. She could wait since most of her mail came to her office in Old Town anyway. She prayed to the God of the deserted halls she wouldn't run into Tex. Despite her best efforts, she heard a noise that was seriously bad news, even worse then meeting up with lover boy. She suspected the most aggravating, time consuming, little bundle of narcissism that she had so carefully tried to avoid, was only seconds away from catching up with her.

"Irish is that you? What time is it, dear? How come you're coming in so late? You haven't been with that man again, have you?" She yelled from her doorway in her edgy, manipulative and thinly veiled demanding voice.

Ethel!

Ethel was the classic "landlady" and that was on a good day. At any given moment and with little or no provocation she could and often did turn into a full-fledged bitch. She lived right on the first floor, her door facing the entry, where she could snare unsuspecting residents. What she didn't find out about the tenants from their applications and credit reports she ferreted out with uncanny determination and perseverance, in other words snooping and spying.

Ethel was a tiny, bony woman, who once won a beauty contest. *We're talking way back in the 1930's*, thought Irish as she had seen pictures of Ethel in her prime and she had actually been a beauty. Once asked to double for Janet or Janette somebody. The cigarettes, pills, numerous husbands and lovers had not been able to do her in. She was still able to raise hell.

Now Irish kind of admired Ethel's grit but if you gave her the opportunity, she would have you fetching like a golden retriever in the park. The residents of the building who were not just plain rude to Ethel used Irish's technique of attempting to sneak by her. "Hi Ethel. Just got off a really long case and I need to get some rest. I'll talk to you tomorrow." No need to tell her about the two punks on the way home. They were long gone and she needed to keep moving in order to make an effective an immediate get away.

"Ha. I know you've been with that man again. Mark my words no good will come of it. I ought to know with all the men I've had." To hear Ethel tell it, she was an authority on almost everything. She said she hated to brag, but relationships were her specialty.

Ethel was quite taken with Irish. The fact that Irish came from a wealthy and gentile southern family was a major drawing card to Ethel. Throughout her life, she had married "up" each time, and had done her best to climb the social ladder-with never a chance of making the grade except in her own mind. She knew enough about Irish's background that she considered her in the realm of near royalty. Irish would have been pissed to the max at Ethel's maneuvering her pointed little nose into her private business.

Meanwhile Irish was sprinting for the stairs as fast as she could. Once inside her apartment she drew a deep breath. That was a close one, and she didn't mean the muggers. Irish turned on the shower and took a look in the mirror and laughed. It had been an exhausting day and her hair was tangled, drenched and wind-blown – enough to scare little children.

Her career did not match the high drama of TV, but she still liked her work. She kept in shape, and at five feet-ten inches, and only thirty-two years old, she felt prepared to play a more active role, should the necessity arise. Contrary to the tinsel-town portrayal of private eyes, for the most part, she spent long hours on the web, doing non-physical activities like collecting background date and conducting research for her clients. Even the tailing of a suspect was non-eventful for the most part. Generally, she spent long, boring and usually uncomfortable hours waiting in her car without the benefit of food or a restroom. For right now, Irish's "bread and butter" depended on the overflow cases she received on a freelance basis from the insurance companies. At times it would take days of surveillance to catch an injured person suspected of insurance fraud in the impossible acts of chopping wood, rowing a boat or lifting weights without the benefit of a neck or back brace. She knew that ultimately her patience would pay off. She was also the first to acknowledge that she still had a lot to learn.

Irish brushed her teeth, removed her makeup and put on her satin P.J.s for bed. She didn't like the feeling of flannel against her skin even in the winter and it always seemed difficult to move about when her body was incased in all that cotton. She slid into bed and pulled her down comforter up to her chin. This proved more than sufficient to keep her warm, not that it could take the place of a strong well-built male body. However, a comforter was a lot easier to live with on a daily basis. Wash, dry and use. No ego or bruised feelings to contend with like the male version.

As her body began to warm under the covers she relaxed and reflected on her day. It had been a routine day until she had let Jack into her office just after 7 p.m. Jack had kissed her long and slow, almost convincing her to want to stay and play right there in the office. Sex between Irish and Jack was their main attraction. Put the two of them in a room together and the temperature rose in moments. They wanted their hands all over one another wanted to rip their clothes off and roll on the floor or desk any available flat surface would do. Anyone in the same room with them could not miss the chemistry unless they were totally obtuse

As Irish hugged her pillow, burrowing deeper under her covers, she thought it was amusing that she enjoyed him so much. He wasn't a "10" in the looks department; in fact, he was kind of craggy looking. *Probably that awesome Bruce Springsteen look-alike butt – absolutely obscene in a pair of faded Levi's,* she thought. Thoroughly contented with the memories of a very fine evening, she marveled at his amazing ability to please a woman. He would pleasure her, then pleasure her, and then pleasure her again, not stopping until she was spent. He was the first man who had ever told her that he felt almost as much joy watching her having orgasms as he felt with his own. *That's a first,* Irish sighed. But when they were together, in the thick of it, one look at his face told her he was telling her the truth. There were no sighs of impatience or hurried activity to get to his gratification, just a steady stream of stimulation that kept her aroused. He did admit he thought women "had it made." *Yep, he's truly off the chart when it comes to sex,* Irish thought, *just gotta love it.* Actually, as usual the entire evening with Jack had been exciting.

They had gone to the little out-of-the-way Italian restaurant they often frequented, since Jack was still hammering out the details of his divorce from his ex-wife. They discussed a case of Irish's in a general way without revealing any client confidences. His input was often helpful, that is, when they were not arguing over methodology. Even that tug of war and flying sparks were exhilarating.

After their leisurely dinner of crisp salad, linguine, hot crusty bread and a bottle of Oregon Merlot, they both began to wish they were at Jack's apartment. Jack asked for the check and they made for the door and the car as quickly and as discreetly possible. Their waiter, Louie, knew what they had on their minds. They were regulars, and he had watched them for months now, undressing each other with their eyes. They thought they were invisible as they steamed up the back booth. It was almost cooler in the kitchen standing by the spaghetti pot. *Ah, Bella, Bella,* beamed Louie rubbing his ample tummy, *to be young and have that energy again.*

As Irish drifted off to sleep she sighed remembering Jack's incredible stamina…. m-m-m

Chapter Seven

Watching the rain from her window, Irish sat at her dining room table cleaning her revolver. She was pumped. She had run almost all the way to Waterfront Park, which was a straight shot downhill from her apartment, and back up the hill again in record time. Her neighborhood was a runner's dream offering her a variety of places to get her morning exercise. Some days she would run up Salmon St. heading into Washington Park where she would duck tree branches as she managed to jog on the well-worn path. Other days, she would head out to trendy NW 23rd and jog a couple of miles until she hit Montgomery Park. Then she would do a quick turn around heading back at full speed through NW. Just before she hit Burnside, she would come to a screeching halt at Starbucks where she ordered her favorite caramel latte and raspberry cream cheese croissant. *Savannah can be the purist, I'll run my ass off for sugar* she chuckled. This morning she had made it back just before the downpour. Most of the time, like a true Oregonian, she didn't let the rain stop her from her workout. Occasionally though, she would end up in the cozy gym adding indoor treadmill miles to her daily workout, avoiding the stormy weather altogether.

Her dad had taught her how to take care of weapons. As a substitute son, she had been the one to go hunting with him and ultimately the one who helped take care of his antique collection of both pistols and rifles. So her weapon was her friend, and she gave it the ultimate care that it needed. Although it was a 38, which was a fairly small caliber firearm, it still worked just fine at close range, which would be the most likely scenario. She was glad she had been her dad's hunting partner all of her growing up years, except that she felt it bad been at her brother Tommy's expense. He hated guns and could not bear the thought of killing any living thing. He had not even liked to fish. She and her mother shared the grief of being in the middle of the chasm that existed between Tommy and his dad.

Looks like we are in for rain most of the day, Irish thought as she put her gun away and headed for the bathroom. She put on light makeup, took the time to blow dry her thick mop of hair and slipped into black cashmere, cowl-necked sweater. She rummaged through her closet to find her new dark brown and black tweed wool slacks. *Worth every penny,* she mused as she watched the crease hang perfectly, just meeting the arch of her foot as she slipped on her black, leather pumps. *Lookin' good and can still move like a bandit*! *Croissants and all.*

She checked her messages to see if there was anything new from Savannah before she left for her office. Now the trick would be to get by Ethel. Thank God the stairs were carpeted. Still Ethel had the ears of a cat unless-yes, Irish heard her on the phone with her daughter. *Poor Rosie*, all the tenants called her that, *Poor* being her real first name. Ethel left her door open a crack to further her advantage when catching tenants as they exited and entered. "Rosie, this is your mother, now pay attention." *Big surprise,* thought Irish. *Who wouldn't recognize that shrill and demanding proclamation made several times a day year after year?* This is what I want you to bring me. Toilet paper, Charmin, two-ply. Make sure you read the label. I know you can read but last time you bought a bargain brand and I have to fold and fold to make it work. Now let me see. Hold on. Irish, is that you? Need to see you a minute." By this time Irish was far enough out the front door she could always pretend she had not heard.

Living in uptown Portland and having an office downtown, Irish was able to make it to work in no time. Although her office was small, she had the best view in the building. She had two floor-to-ceiling windows that gave her a perfect view of the Willamette River, which flowed, through the city of Portland. The river served as a divider between east and west Portland. More importantly, it was one of the most beautiful waterways in the NW, especially during special occasions like the Rose Festival. In the evening, when all the bands had played and the food stands and arts and crafts booths had closed, the festival crowd would line up along the riverside, the surrounding parks and even stand on the bridges. Some of the revelers had made a weekend of it parking their boats and in some cases expensive yachts, along the waterway to join the festivities. Hundreds of people surrounded the Willamette right in front of the city to see a magnificent fireworks display burst into a million colors right over the river. Security was tighter on the river during the Rose Festival than it had been before 911. Boats were kept a strict distance from the Navy fleet that lined the docks; however, the restrictions did little to dampen the enthusiasm of the crowds.

Although Irish had a tiny office for now, she had her eye on a larger office in the same building. Rumor had it the new office might become available before the end of the year. If she could find the right partner, she could increase her business and hire office help. For the time being, she only had an answering service and had to use a secretarial service. It was worth it, because she was her own boss. Even though she may have moved to Portland for the wrong reasons, she knew her choice to stay in the area was for all the right reasons.

Initially, although Irish hated to admit it, she had followed Michael Grant, her anthropology professor back to Oregon. He had been on sabbatical for a year in Georgia and then returned the year Irish had graduated to his tenured position at the University of Portland in Portland, Oregon. A recruiter had interviewed her a month before she graduated and offered her a job in Portland in a small private investigation firm. She accepted the position more to be with Michael, but as it turned out the job had been more interesting than he was.

She worked diligently with the Senior PI of the firm, Gus Russo, and gained enough experience that three years later she was ready to launch her own business. Gradually after two years on her own, Irish was establishing an outstanding reputation. Due to her no nonsense approach and diligence on the behalf of her clients, she was beginning to receive a substantial amount of her business through referrals. Granted she was still operating on a shoestring, but she hadn't touched the money in grandmother's trust for some time.

Reaching her office in record time, Irish allowed herself a tiny smile as she plugged in her espresso machine and turned on her new Apple computer. Still loving the graphics part of technology, she just couldn't give up her little jewel colored MAC, with its ultra-modern screen. One of these days, she'd probably have to shift over to a standard PC to accommodate mainstream software, but for now she was interested in creativity and operating in a more contemporary mode. As much as she liked antiques, when it came to her work, she wanted everything streamlined from her Scandinavian armless sofa, to her sleek black leather and metal chair to the contemporary paintings lining her wall. Her office was like her – on the move and ready to go, no dust could land on it or her. Sometimes she had to pinch herself to believe she really had her own business, making her way in a man's profession. In the 21st century you had to be proactive and aggressive at all times and as she poured herself a small espresso, she thought to herself, *and that is what I intend to do best.*

Chapter Eight

Even with all of the events of the past few weeks, Savannah managed to take pleasure from her success as Director. She was good at what she did and for the most part didn't tire of being an advocate for women and their children.

As she walked into her office the next morning, after hiring Ruby, Savannah marveled at how their organization had grown. Starting from three staff to two counselors, two aides, a social worker, a drug counselor, a trainer and herself. She was proud of each and every one of the staff, who worked their butts off trying to help the "hardest of the hardest" clientele. Their clients were typically women who society saw as abysmal failures. They had virtually no education, usually had long histories of substance abuse and in some cases carried a felony record. Many had suffered violence and abuse at the hands of husbands, ex-husbands, or boyfriends. Many of them had little or no parenting skills. For the most part, their personal lives were in shambles and a professional life was non-existent.

Savannah knew she had a better chance of winning the thirty million-to-one lottery in Georgia than she had of getting these women to secure some kind of long-term employment that would eventually help them get out of the poverty trap. She didn't focus on the odds. Savannah smiled to herself as she took off her coat and got herself situated in her office. *Let's see, $500 for a one-time drug deal, or $100 a trick done in one hour, or $10,000 net for a year's worth of traveling by two buses to daycare to work on a minimum wage job guaranteed to create varicose veins by the time you were thirty.* If they were lucky, the women returning to a low-end job would have barely enough money to pay rent on a dump that most of America wouldn't even consider living in. *Let me see, I can't decide. I know I don't want door number three, door number two sounds good. No no, I'll* *take number one. That's the one I want. I'm sure. Yep, door number one.*

Savannah was surprised, yet pleased, when she saw Ruby sitting in the lobby. "Hi, I thought you were going to come in Monday morning" Savannah said.

"Oh, Ms. Hart, ma'am I just stopped by to tell you that I'd be glad to work for you today. The apartment lady said there was the sweetest old woman next door who had been takin' care of kids for years. Miz. Harriet, that's the lady's name, said she could take them this morning. I guess, Ms. Hart, she misses her own grandbabies, that's what she said anyways, so I said, 'well sure, Miz. Harriet, I'd love to have you takin' care of my girls', and my girls took to her right away and all so I know I told you I'd start Monday, but ma'am I can start right away, Miz Harriet can take care of the girls day and night, any time you need me, "*more time for fuck'n ma man what I really means,* she smiled wickedly to herself, almost chuckling out loud.

Jesus Martha, she talks a lot. Didn't come up for air once. Savannah couldn't help noticing. *Not even going to speculate about that stupid smile on her face.*

Savannah had to give her points for organization. Ruby looked ready for work with a crisp white blouse, black skirt, matching nylons and heels. She was impeccable. Nothing like getting two little girls to the sitter, showing up sharp and without a wrinkle or a bead of sweat anywhere.

Anxious to get her to stop talking and grinning and to start getting some work done, Savannah escorted her to the office next to hers. It was decorated in social services shabby chic with an oversized, scratched wooden desk, tall bookcases, and metal filing cabinets. Each wall had pastel pictures underscored with words like *Create, Fly, Live, Believe* and *Trust.*

"Here is the application form and your tax forms, please fill them out. The supply cabinet is in your office, Ruby. You are in charge of the supplies. The key to the supply cabinet, your desk and the file cabinet are in the top desk drawer. Your computer is ready to go, just put in a password. Please write it down and give it to me, so I can get into your computer if you aren't here and I need to access a file."

"After you get the paperwork done, would you look through the Rolodex and find the A-1 Security group? We need a new security guard. Finding him asleep last night was the last straw. Thank God, it was you. Anyone could have been anyone that walked right into the building. When you get them on the phone would you transfer the call to me, I need to talk with them." The picture of blobby Harold sitting slack-jawed and asleep at his desk at 7:00 in the evening with his half-drunk cup of coffee on his desk next to his thermos still made her burn.

"Why, yes ma'am, I couldn't believe he was snoring as I walked out. I'll take care of that right away." *Yes'm, yes'm, you scrawny, white bitch,* thought Ruby, imagining the pictures around her office replaced with her own brand of spirits, roots, herbs and powders to protect her and to harm those who dared to cross her. "Ms. Hart, this is such a nice office. Could I bring in some of my own pictures? I have to paint the girl's new bedroom and I can get a little extra paint. I'd like to touch up that doorway, would that be okay?"

Savannah admired Ruby's initiative and obvious energy. She was in perfect shape and as strong looking as any athlete Savannah had seen in awhile. If she wanted to paint her office, more power to her. "That would be fine, Ruby. This place could use a little sprucing up."

Savannah was unapologetic about the surroundings. It wasn't her priority. The preponderance of funding needed to go to the women who needed it, not for the administration of services. First question Savannah asked when interviewing new staff was "Why are you here?" She expected to hear counselors say something like " I'm dedicated to the mission of helping women get themselves out of poverty." Counselors whose main interest was in the size of their office, their title, or how much time they could get off were not invited for a second interview. The new age social service worker whose mantra was "what's in it for me?" was quickly escorted out the door.

Savannah spent the next hour showing Ruby around, helping her get used to the way the office was run. Ruby was cordial to the other staff and assured them she would be glad to help them along the way. In actuality though, Ruby was hired primarily to assist Savannah and Peggy.

Savannah had a policy of keeping three or four of the toughest clients to herself. As Director, she continued to maintain a caseload for the very reason that a working foreman in a construction crew continues to lay cement, build a foundation and keep up his finishing and framing skills. She wanted to be the best she could be and never lose touch with what she was there to do. She particularly disliked managers who "told" people what to do, never upgrading their skills, and ending up as obsolete as an eight-track tape. She would not let that happen to her or to her staff. Everyone who was qualified had to pitch in and handle a fair share of the caseloads.

By working with the more difficult women, she immediately earned herself respect from her staff for "getting her hands dirty." She forced herself to keep current and most of the time knew the best interventions for the hardest cases. She kept up on the laws which changed on a daily bases and were now changing with the new administration whose focus was really on military warfare, estate taxes and getting those welfare mothers married.

When a woman begged Savannah to help her get more than a handful of food stamps for a family of three for a month, Savannah knew alternative systems and organizations that would help these women find food for their families. She encouraged the other counselors to be diligent in their efforts to help others, and she spent time herself on the website identifying new organizations and resources for people who needed jobs, baby clothes, food, formula, rent money, car repair, and the basics just to subsist. Savannah ran a contest each month – dinner for two at La Madeleine's – for the counselor who found the most innovative solutions to these women's problems. For the welfare women who were the most resourceful on the least and who provided the most creative solutions, they received a $25.00 gift certificate for the local grocery store.

For all the money her parents spent and flouted around town, they had continued to be in the minus column when it came to personal pride and dignity. Savannah knew at an early age that she didn't want to be like them. Her work gave her an opportunity to change a few lives. When women came in, disheveled, tired, and discouraged, she reminded herself and sometimes her staff, not to look at the outside, but realize that inside each person carries a truckload of personal pride and hopefully a measure of self-respect.

Ruby was no exception. She needed help. She was willing to work and she was already busily cleaning up her office. Savannah felt satisfaction in knowing that she had created a win-win situation where everyone would benefit from this rather strange new employee, who at this very moment - thank God - was going lickety-split on her computer. She should be careful. Monday she'd do a background check and ask her for some references. She probably couldn't call her ex-husband. *Okay, whatever.* Today she had her hands full preparing a proposal for next year's funding.

Savannah could physically feel the relief of handing over the overwhelming workload that had been piling up for weeks. She would make sure she contacted her three clients and get them scheduled for their upcoming appointments. If Ruby were good with the clients, she could have her take care of some of their basic paperwork and general services. *This is much better,* Savannah thought, as she listened to the woman next door, talking a mile a minute in her high-pitched voice, "Sir, this is Ruby Ebota. I'm calling from Women at Work in Atlanta. Can you connect me with your supervisor, please?"

*****

My man gonna love me so. I brings him fine girls.

Chapter Nine

"Hello!"

"Hey. It's me. Where you've been? I tried to catch you last night." Savannah could hear the Indigo Girls wailing in the background at Irish's apartment.

"Hey, Savannah," Irish sounded breathless. "Just walked in a few minutes ago from the office. Would you believe some creeps tried to jump me last night – little fuckers?"

"Are you okay?" Savannah already knew the answer before asking. Irish always came out on top. *Pity their sorry asses if they actually got their hands on her.*

"I showed them my credentials, and they took off on a dead run," Irish laughed. "I probably should have reported it, but you know the police. They're up to their asses in alligators already and these were just small time punks." Irish loved the freedom of using her cell phone. She could walk around her apartment, stand out on her balcony, feed her cat, and put dinner on the stove while talking with her best friend. Typically they talked almost every day. The friendship had survived several different life stages and now they were closer than ever after Tommy's death.

"So how are ya?" Irish asked as she perused her closet for something comfortable to put on for the weekend.

Not a casual question, Savannah knew. Irish knew Savannah was hurting, and Savannah knew that Irish was crazy about her brother and missed him as much as she did. A really sore subject altogether.

Even with his drinking, Tommy had been the most exciting person she had ever met in her life except, of course, his sister Irish who had her own special "bag of tricks." *What a family*, she mused as she snuggled deeper into her sofa. If Savannah could have transplanted herself into anyone's family, in a heartbeat, it would have been theirs. Course, then she wouldn't have married the love of her life. *If wishes were horses...*

"Earth to Savannah." Irish tried again. "You there?"

Savannah forced her mind back to her conversation with Irish, "Actually, better,"a slight exaggeration. "You wouldn't believe what happened this week."

"Oh, oh, here comes trouble," Irish laughed. "Is this gonna be about the half-assed scoop you left on my voice mail?"

"Yeah I'm sitting in my office, papers piled all over the place, and this woman shows up, scared the shit out of me. I mean she popped out of nowhere. The guards dead on his butt and she walks right by him. Sure glad we hired security." Savannah groaned.

"You need to get a different guard, Savannah." Irish explained the obvious. "How in the hell did she get in?"

"The no-account guard was sound asleep. You gotta love it." Savannah explained and then continued.

"She said Amelia had set up an interview with her. I didn't even know anything about it. She's worked in an office before and said she could start right away. Poor thing, her husband is trying to get custody of her kids - two girls - and she needs a job right away. She's kind of pretty in her own way. Her name's Ruby."

"Girl, has the cheese slipped right off your cracker? I hope you didn't hire her, because you felt sorry for her. Can she type? I can just see you grabbing the first person with a hard luck story to take Amelia's place." Irish knew Savannah had been experiencing sleepless nights and working long hours trying to catch up. For that reason, Irish had questioned her judgment more lately.

"You'll be happy to know Ruby can actually type." Savannah laughed out loud and then continued. "I don't know what to think about Amelia though. Evidently, she was back to using her body more than her brain. I would never have admitted that to the cops though. Good old Detective Benson and his side kick, the dick with the perpetual hard-on, that I told you about, were convinced that it was just another one of the whores, you know that species that belongs to the sub-human population."

Savannah continued, "You know, Amelia might have gone back to workin' the streets, which I seriously doubt, but she sure as hell didn't deserve to die alone in an alley with her throat cut. Like I told Peggy, we should get used to this, but we never do. I hope they catch the bastard!" Savannah was pissed off all over again. "By the way, I threw that slob Harold's fat ass out the door with his coffee cup, thermos and burrito remains dripping in salsa. Can't believe he would deliberately expose us all to danger, just because he's too tired to stay awake. Thank God, it was only this Ruby woman; could have been Ted Bundy."

"Any new info on Amelia's murder? You know that was kind of hit close to home." Ever suspicious, Irish reminded Savannah. Hoping Savannah was being sufficiently cautious. "You're being careful about locking everything, walking out to your car and stuff, aren't you? You really do need to get a gun. Savannah I hate to harp on this, but…." Irish broached the subject for the umpteenth time.

"I'm more careful than ever, believe me. I haven't heard anything new about the murder for a few days. Thank God, no reporters have been lurking around our office lately. We all need to get back to normal around here," Savannah sidestepped the gun issue.

Irish leaving it alone, changed the subject, "I'm glad you're feeling better. You're starting to sound like your old self." Irish couldn't help remembering that right after Tommy's death, Savannah was close to comatose with grief. On the surface she sounded like she had snapped out of it, but Irish wanted to be sure Savannah wasn't snowing her. She wished she were closer so she could offer more support. The phone was a poor substitute for talking to each other in person. The downside of living on her own in Portland was that she missed spending time with Savannah and also seeing her mom and dad.

Irish thought about her own dad and how different he looked from the wonderfully elegant, lanky powerful man she had known in her growing up years. *Cancer*, Irish thought, *the plague of the modern world devouring my father's last bits of energy and strength.* "Hey, don't forget, I'll be visiting y'all in June for Father's Day. Mom and dad said they couldn't wait to see us. Let's hang out at your place in Atlanta and then drive up to North Carolina. I think I'm one of the few people who can honestly say seeing my folks doesn't feel like an obligation."

"Boy, that's the truth. You know how I feel about your folks." Savannah agreed.

Savannah wished she could wave a magic wand and bring her friend to her right now. She really needed her

"How's your mama?" Even with all her education, Savannah still asked, "How's your mama?" That was what she was raised with and probably would stay on her lips until she died. Good southern folks always started with, "How's your mama, and then worked their way around to the rest of the family. Your dad?"

Irish and her dad were cloned as clearly as if they had been designed in a petri dish. A southern gentleman through and through, he raised his daughter in the true tradition of the South. Having been raised with the tip of the silver spoon, he passed along everything he knew. He taught her to ride horses, train show dogs, hunt quail, dance until dawn at the country club as well as the local barn dance. He loved music and would entertain friends and family with classical piano. He taught her to read music, sing Alto, and become adept at most sports, especially basketball. Next to Catherine, Irish was his biggest challenge on the tennis court. Irish laughed as she thought of her dad when he would take on Catherine or Irish and the two of them would conspire to "clean his clock" on the court. And they could do it. "Sorry I ever started this," he'd grumble to them playfully. Irish appreciated that her parents simply gave her free reign and all the resources she needed to help her succeed. In other words, they would adjust her course from time to time, but mostly would get out of the way, so she could find her own path to fulfillment and success. They had let her know on more than one occasion that she was a delight as a child and that they could not imagine purposely-withholding opportunities out of her reach.

Irish knew that her dad wanted to do the same with Tommy, but just couldn't. It seemed that the harder her dad tried to get close to Tommy, the more obvious it became that they just weren't capable of hardly being in the same room together, let alone building a meaningful relationship. There was no outspoken animosity, just lots of blank spaces, sighs and silences. Neither could feign interest in the other's world. Tommy had told Irish that he didn't feel like he

belonged in their family, and certainly felt like a stranger to his dad. Irish must have heard him say a million and one times, "He just doesn't understand."
.
Irish's voice full of emotion explained, "Dad's about the same. It's really funny, onc minute they say he only has a few months, and then the next minute they are giving him a couple of years. It is such a 'crap shoot', literally. Mom is doing really well. You know mom. She is her usual wise and wonderful self. She still has that great sense of humor. Why don't you go see them or call her and have her come in to shop? She would love to see you."

Savannah responded quickly, "Of course, I just hadn't thought about it." How could she have forgotten Catherine? After having grown up with the most disgustingly weak mother God ever created, the opportunity to share so much of her life with Irish and Catherine had made all the difference in the world to her. Their influence gave her the juice she needed to lead a high-octane life vs. a mediocre, victim-saturated life. Not a year had gone by where she and Catherine hadn't spent time together.

" I'll invite her up to the house soon. I love your mom. Last time I talked with her, she told me that story of your Uncle Louis going to visit your dad and leaning on the tube to his oxygen and the whole time just talking away while your dad is losing his oxygen. He's trying to cheer your dad up and your mom says your dad is feebly pointing to the tube. The way she told it was so funny. I tell you the two of us just howled." Savannah would call her soon and invite her up for the day.

Irish interjected, "I really just called about you. What are your plans for the weekend?"

"Uh, I don't know, uh" Tonight Savannah didn't have the energy to form a complete sentence let alone make plans for the weekend. The toll of having to be a strong leader all day long eventually caught up with her at the end of the day. "I'm sorry, Irish, can we talk later? I really need to go to bed."

"Sure. I know you're tired. We'll catch up Sunday. I'll call you when I wake up." Irish missed her friend tonight and wished she could do more to help.

Savannah appreciated her friend's understanding as she quietly hung up the phone. The pall of her silent house was something she didn't want to experience for long. Her hair at this moment was propped on top of her head with a large plastic barrette. She pulled out the barrette and felt her hair fall down past her shoulders. As she looked in the bathroom mirror, she realized her once healthy hair looked like straw, a perfect complement to the dark shadows under her eyes. She was a mess. She was tired. She was going to crawl into her unmade bed, forego the shower, and remember a time when things were much different; a time when she would fall asleep with Tommy stroking her hair. That is what would get her through the night.

Chapter Ten

She moans as he runs his tongue down her neck to her breast. He slowly circles each nipple, biting oh so gently. She pushes her fingers through his damp hair and then grabs his hair tightly as he begins to circle his tongue down her belly. She raises her hips and guides his head between her legs at the same time. He darts and twists his tongue inside of her until she is so wet he is drinking her juices. She doesn't even try to hold back, coming time after time as he holds her up with his hands under her hips and his head buried between her legs.

Then he slips his hands from beneath her, she spreads her legs out as wide as they will go. He wants to enter her but she stops him, pushes him gently back far enough so she can reach all of him with her tongue. She runs her tongue up and down, around the end, playfully sucking him until he can no longer wait. He pushes her down and enters her. He moves slowly at first, kissing her lips. She tastes herself on his mouth. Then he moves faster as he feels her tighten herself around him.

Savannah sighs and turns on her side reaching her hand out in the dark to caress Tommy's hard muscular body. His body is no longer hard and muscular; once again she is touching his cold stiff corpse. This time his eyes are wide open, no longer that deep seductive blue. Now they are milky white and vacant. His mouth is frozen in a gaping grin. Grabbing her pillow and screaming into it so she will not alert the entire neighborhood, Savannah falls back onto the bed and curls into a fetal position. She curls her fists and beats on the pillow as hard as she can. *Goddamn you, Tommy for dying.* She can barely breathe the pain is so great. She can no longer hurt like this and not do something, but there is nothing she can do. Stand alone and hurt. There is no place to run. No matter how she cries, begs or curses God; He won't send Tommy back - Ever.

Chapter Eleven

Ruby was a quick learner. Soon she was showing promise as a "take charge" person. Occasionally, she was late. Although it was against her policy, Savannah sometimes bent her rules of working from 8:00 to 5:00 especially when Ruby explained to her that she and her daughters had slept in the car to avoid her ex-husband who was snooping around her apartment looking for them. They had moved out in the middle of the night and Savannah had reluctantly given Ruby a small advance on her paycheck, so Ruby could pay the deposit on a new place to live.

Ruby talked so much and so fast that Savannah had a hard time keeping up with her stories. The woman was certainly having her share of bad luck. Nevertheless, Savannah was impressed with how quickly Ruby bounced back. She was a hard worker and barreled through the pile of work in the office in no time. She was an enigma to Savannah. In some ways, although she was eye-catching in an angular, strident way, there was something intensely dark about her. She was polite as most Southern girls are, but there was an underlying hardness that concerned Savannah. This part of Ruby was elusive, so just when Savannah would start to notice the shadow of Ruby's personality, suddenly it would disappear, leaving Savannah wondering if she was just imagining things or maybe projecting her own state of mind on Ruby.

True to her word, Savannah let Ruby paint her office. Ruby had even painted the woodwork around the doors with a strange shade of blue. Ruby seemed happy with her new office. Peggy thought it was a bit over the top, but Savannah had no investment in keeping the rather insipid inspirational message pictures covering every wall in Ruby's office and was actually happy to see more culturally diverse paintings replace them. If the other staff could keep angels, spiritual pictures and calendars, small crosses around their necks, and declare "have a blessed day," certainly Ruby was welcome to create an environment that represented the kinds of things that were important to her.

Looking around Ruby's office, Savannah marveled at how much the décor replicated the art she had seen in Senegal, where years ago she had spent her junior year as part of the International Exchange Program. Ruby's paintings were abstract with what looked like black women spirits in various forms of dance. She had scattered intricate, hand-woven baskets around the room, ones like Savannah had seen in the Charleston area and in Africa. Looking more closely at Ruby, she realized that Ruby's exotic features and her general demeanor reminded her very much of the women she had met in Senegal. She noticed that Ruby pretty much avoided socializing with the other staff and spent her lunch hours in her private space surrounded by the African music rhythms playing on her CD player.

Ruby was good with the women, who came to the Center seeking help. She had a flair for fashion and she would spend a good amount of her time helping the women find appropriate clothes for an interview. Savannah had instituted a clothes closet in collaboration with the local consignment shops. The clothes, in many cases, were unworn, just the castoffs from wealthy matrons, who didn't quite like the color, design or style. The women were less than thrilled with most of the styles that did not match their tastes for stretchier, glitterier styles. So Ruby would hike up a skirt here, tuck in a blouse there, and eventually, she had the flair to make even the dowdiest, old lady outfit, look professional.

She talked to the woman about simplifying their look and would frown when the younger mothers would want to pop their ample breasts into scooped necklines. She pulled and tugged at their clothes like a mother. They could see how sharp she looked and they trusted her to help them look the same way. Savannah appreciated Ruby's help with the closet, but at times she was suspicious of some of the offside conversations and the surreptitious looks she and the women gave each other when one of the staff entered the room.

Savannah had to admit in a calmer time, she would probably not have hired Ruby. The load of problems this woman was carrying around consistently took her back. Just the Monday before, she came in with a broken wrist. She said she had fallen and caught herself at the last minute. Another time, she called and said she had to make an emergency trip to North Carolina to take care of some legal problems with the girls. Although Savannah offered to help her get free legal aid, Ruby refused her help saying that her lawyer was in North Carolina and she had to go there.

Yet another time, she talked about her husband punching her in the stomach, where he had hit her too hard in one of their fights. She had put a restraining order on him, but it hadn't helped. The stories were quickly interwoven with the busy day-to-day routines. Before Savannah could sort it all out, she and Ruby would be propelled into the never-ending business of the day. Savannah was way too busy to focus on Ruby and her problems.

Peggy, on the other hand, cut Ruby no slack. She was not nearly as taken in by Ruby, as Savannah appeared to be. She never missed an opportunity to give Savannah a bad time about the worst hire she ever made. They were stuck with her now, but Peggy knew she was up to no good and had told Savannah she was watching Ruby. She didn't know what made Ruby the way she was, but she knew that she was trouble with a capital "T."

*****

Savannah gal be easy to conjure. I gotta puts da root on dat black bitch tho. I cuts dat hag she mess wid me.

Chapter Twelve

April

Savannah could use a success story about now and looking at Nicole Williams standing in front of her desk, it looked like Nicole might be it. Unlike many of the woman Savannah saw, Nicole dressed reasonably well and looked like most of the "twenty-somethings" she knew. She was about 5 ft. 4 in., maybe 110 pounds. She wore a short sweater set with slacks that fit snuggly a few inches below her waistline. Her shoes were polished and in general she was very presentable. Nicole pulled up her chair next to Savannah's desk and openly and willingly answered Savannah's inquiries. Nicole was still very new to the system and talked with Savannah like she would talk with a friend or aunt.

"Actually, I've always loved to dance and I found a way to make a lot of money and get to dance as well. Honestly, no one was very interested in my ability to create new characters and my routines. I just didn't see people's eyes leave my tits or ass. I'm sorry, ma'am, I don't mean to offend you." Nicole looked down at her lap and seemed at a loss for words. It seemed as though she wanted to make a good impression on Savannah. Savannah wasn't having any of it.

"What did this dancing involve?" Savannah was taking Nicole's moral pulse. On the continuum of truly blighted soul to a saintly presence, where did Nicole fall? Like an insurance adjuster, with so many years experience, Savanna could calculate the extent of the damage and project what degree of recovery to expect. "Was any nudity involved?"

Nicole looked her square in the eye. "Ms. Hart, there was everything. You don't get up in front of a bunch of slobbering men and take off your clothes and wiggle everything you have and head home, fix a cup of cocoa, go to bed, and get up the next day and dance again. It is a life style with lots of players. Some of it is actually kind of fun. The girls can be a riot. I mean we laugh our brains out at some of the characters we meet. For the most part though, it is pretty rough. I avoided the really rough crowd, but even so, there was prostitution, drugs and some pretty wild rides – if you know what I mean." Nicole crossed her legs and leaned in toward Savannah. "The money is unbelievable." Nicole's face lit up and she covered her mouth when she started to laugh. "I'm sorry, but honest to God, Ms. Hart, you can't believe how much money I made. I mean I don't think my folks made as much money in ten years as I could make in one."

"Tell me about your folks." Savannah continued. She hadn't seen much in her file.

"My mom pretty much was responsible for making a living for us after my dad was hurt. They actually were pretty well off when I was young, but my dad was an electrician – he wasn't licensed or nothing – but he knew a lot about it. Anyway, he fell off of a roof while he was fixing someone's antennae and fractured his back. He healed to some degree, but he basically lay around, watched TV, pulled in disability and after while became a real loser." Nicole made a sign of a big L with her hand on her forehead.

"Mom and him used to have fun having a drink, but my dad just got to the point where that is all he did. Mom hadn't had to work, so she picked up a couple of different jobs. First she worked in a restaurant close by where we lived and then she worked in a department store. Like I said, the money I made has been a lifesaver. Mom has never really asked me where I get the money to help them, but she's not stupid. She knows without an education, I probably am not exactly being a neurosurgeon." Nicole laughed loudly.

Nicole continued, "You probably won't believe this, but I was really good in school. I love to read. I mean I read cereal boxes, isn't that funny?" Nicole looked at Savannah waiting for a response.

Savannah wasn't surprised. She had to admit Nicole was much better at articulating her ideas than the average client she worked with. Sometimes the "gift of gab" and "cagey" went hand in hand. Nicole was a cute little thing. She had learned to be quite charming. *If this were an insurance claim and I were the adjuster, I'd be paying top dollar. ...Next?*

"Nicole, I have an opportunity for you to go over to an employer that has worked with us before. He has customer service work two days a week. You can go to the clothes closet and get two sets of clothes. Ruby will help you. She can give you the details on the job." Savannah pressed the speaker key and 348 and Ruby's voice came in loudly over the speaker.

"Yes, ma'am." Ruby responded.

"Ruby, could you come in here a minute." By the time Savannah hung up the phone Ruby had come to the doorway. "Ruby, this is Nicole Williams. Can you help her with the clothes closet and fill her in on the part-time telecom job we discussed yesterday?" Savannah looked at Nicole knowing full well that the odds were against this one coming back.

"Nicole this is Ruby." Savannah noticed Ruby wasted no time in escorting Nicole out of the office. Ruby was like the Alpha dog leading the pack. Nicole followed her – no questions asked. Ruby walked quickly with Nicole barely able to keep up with her brisk pace.

Her next client for the day was Doris Washington. She was waiting in the lobby right outside Savannah's office when

Ruby walked by. Savannah noticed that Ruby did not acknowledge Doris although she was sure they had met before. Ruby walked past her with not so much as a hello or a nod. Savannah stood in the doorway and beckoned to Doris. "Doris, you can come in and sit down." Savannah led the way to her desk and offered Doris the chair next to her desk. "Have a seat."

Savannah had purposely left Doris' appointment until the end of the day. Savannah postponed having to deal with Doris as long as she could. The rest of the counselors were sick of her. Doris weighed over 200 pounds, was pure muscle, and reminded Savannah of a female bouncer, threatening and tough. Savannah imagined that Doris had a cord attached to her. Savannah would simply reach over and pull the cord, which would start Doris talking. "Hi, I'm Doris. I cannot work. I try to work, but I cannot work. My name is Doris. I lie and cheat and have no intention of ever working. I don't have to work, because I can scare anyone into doing whatever I want. If I don't terrorize them into leaving me alone, I simply talk them to death. Hi, I'm Doris, I am a crook and a thief and I don't care about anybody or anything."

Savannah shifted into her real conversation with Doris. "So, Doris, what activities have you completed this week?" Savannah had no idea what transpired in the next 15 minutes of conversation. She simply interjected an "uh-huh" in the appropriate spot and a "and then what happened?" every so often which wasn't really necessary since Doris never took a breath or stopped speaking. Savannah had long ago stopped taking any real interest in Doris' life. She was surprised how easy it was to just write down the same thing week after week

Savannah managed her energy like her savings account. She only had so much and she needed to preserve it. She certainly wasn't going to deplete what was left in her reserve for Doris. Savannah knew that Doris was perfectly capable of killing another human being and had been jailed for serious crimes. Now she was sure that Doris just talked people to death. She rambled on in such a monotone for so long, that they would rather die than have to listen to her any longer.

"Why are you smiling, Ms. Hart?" Doris asked her in the middle of a long diatribe about some bizarre incident that had happened the day before. "Is something funny that I don't know about? Do you think this is funny?" she asked menacingly.

Savannah looked at Doris' hands and imagined Doris wrapping her thick fingers around Savannah's throat. *She could squash me like a bug, before I could get out of my chair.* Before Savannah could answer Doris' question, Ruby appeared at the doorway. "Ms. Hart, do you want me to schedule Nicole for next week?"

Glad for the interruption, Savannah quickly focused her attention on Ruby, "I'd like to see Nicole for the next four weeks." Before Doris could continue her inquiry, Savannah added, "Ruby, why don't you take Doris with you? She should have one good interviewing outfit."

Doris looked defiantly at Savannah, "Why sure, Ms. Hart, I'll go get me some clothes. If that is what y'all want." Savannah stood up behind her desk and stared back at her.

What's your name again," Doris asked Ruby. "What do you do here?" Doris shuffled out of the office deliberately taking her time while Ruby and Savannah waited. She followed Ruby leaving Savannah disgusted and annoyed. *There's always a "Doris".* Savannah sighed. Quickly scribbling the same paragraph in the file, she put it away hoping she wouldn't have to see her for another month.

Chapter Thirteen

Irish's phone was ringing as she opened her eyes to a new day. She rolled over to check the caller ID. It could be her answering service as she was waiting for the results of a DNA test requested by a client who believed she was a potential heir for a large inheritance.

No, it's 6:30 a.m., she groaned.

"Irish this is Ethel are you up? Guess not, call me…this is Ethel."

Irish rolled out of bed and headed for the bathroom thinking she would try to get past Ethel on the way out for her morning run. *She really has no concept of the fact people have to work and have no time for her silly games,* she grumbled to herself. She knew she would be in Ethel's snare before the day was out. She grabbed her Atlanta Braves baseball cap, pulled on her sweats and running shoes grabbed her keys and headed out. Irish made it out the front door unmolested and now she was really suspicious, as Ethel must really want something to let her get away that easily.

Today Irish decided to run up the hill through Washington Park. It was a clear, cool morning and she ran up several streets, past old historic homes, some of which made her slightly homesick for Atlanta. She would make it a short, hard and uphill run this morning as she had considerable work at her office to accomplish. The leaves on the chestnut trees leading up to the park had all filled out making them appear larger than ever. The rhododendrons were preparing to burst into thick splotches of pinks, whites and reds. Irish was becoming increasing acclimated to the Northwest climate and particularly enjoyed the change of seasons. She loved living in the city right down to the "city smell" as she called it.

On her way back down through the park Irish decided she might just as well stop and see what Ethel wanted. Face the dragon so to speak. When she got to her building and entered the lobby Irish headed straight for Ethel's front door A-1, of course. The door was slightly ajar as usual but before Ethel could call out, which was fast, Irish beat her to the punch.

"Ethel are you home? It's Irish. Knock, knock."

"Oh, Irish come in," called Ethel, "I'm so excited."

Kinda hard to tell, thought Irish, *with her hair in all those tight little pink rollers and cold cream at least an half inch thick on her face.* The cold cream had oozed into her wrinkles and shone like glaze on a Krispie Kreme donut.

"I'm having a dinner party tonight, she giggled, and you are invited. Now don't say you have other plans because you can see 'that man' anytime. Besides Colonel Middleton is attending."

"Really, the Colonel?" asked Irish.

"Of course," said Ethel, "he knows a classy lady when he sees one," she winked, using her seersucker housecoat to wipe the cold cream from her eye.

"I'm sure of that." Irish mumbled. "Who else is coming?"

"Colonel Middleton, you, me and… oh, yes, Rosie. I know she has nothing better to do." Dismissing her daughter with a wave of her hand. Irish bet that Rosie, Ethel's daughter, was just about as thrilled as she was by the thought of spending an entire evening with Ethel, less if the truth were known.

"Ethel, I need coffee."

"Right here, dear," Ethel crooned, and the trap was sprung.

"Just a quick cup," Irish said stifling a sigh, "I really have to be at the office early today."

A long hour later Irish was sprinting to the parking garage to pick up her car and headed for her office. She used her key card and entered the garage. Her car was the one luxury she allowed herself to purchase from the trust her grandmother left her. Her three-year-old convertible, basic black, was waiting in its parking stall. Irish had negotiated for a space between two pillars to avoid door dings from her parking neighbors.

*****

Irish gave her appearance one final look in the entry hall mirror of her apartment before she headed down the stairs to Ethel's party. She noticed that the traditional "little black dress" that she had decided to wear failed to cover much of her long legs and actually much her breasts for that matter. *Good thing I ran that extra mile today,* she laughed as she slipped into a pair of black sling pumps. *Girl, you clean up good* she thought as she combed her auburn hair until it hung, slightly curled, and just touching her shoulders. She placed her small diamond studs in her ears to complete the picture. It was just 8:00 p.m. the designated time.

Irish knew everything would be picture perfect. When she had left Ethel's place earlier, Ethel was placing a fine linen tablecloth on her dining table. She had polished all of her antique furniture until each piece glistened with oil. Irish commented on the some of the beautiful wood, which was very similar to the furniture Irish's grandmother had when Irish was a child. Her grandmother had inherited many pieces from her family and even as a young woman she took her time buying one piece at a time ultimately creating a notable collection of very fine furniture. Her mother, Catherine had many of the antiques now, and eventually they would be given to Irish to carry on to the next generation.

Irish had watched Ethel take out her delicate Haviland dishes from her old mahogany china cabinet, which was rounded at the top and had the original, old glass doors that looked distorted when the sun shown on them. The dishes were rare, with hand-painted autumn leaves on a creamy china plate delicately etched in gold. Irish was surprised there was any design left with the way Ethel vigorously rubbed each piece with a soft rag, evidently trying to restore the original patina. Ethel carried on her own personal germ warfare, exterminating and removing every dust particle that attempted to infiltrate her sanitary environment. By the time Irish left Ethel's that morning, she was scurrying around arranging the table. She said she'd talk to Irish later, but that she had to call her daughter Rosie with her instructions for her day.

As Irish knocked on the door Rosie greeted her. Evidently one of the items on Rosie's "to-do" list was to greet the guests. Rosie smiled and welcomed her warmly, but not before she rolled her eyes in her head indicating they were both probably in for quite a night with good old Ethel. Graciously, she took Irish's arm and escorted her into the living room.

"There you are, dear. I am so glad you could make it." Ethel greeted her. Drip, drip! The Colonel as they all called him was on the sofa sitting as straight as if he still had a uniform on. He was a retired Lieutenant Colonel in the Marines and was highly decorated during WWII. He always stood straight and was still way over six feet tall. Irish thought he looked terrific for 87 years old. She had seen pictures of him with his piercing blue eyes, black hair and hawk like nose. He must have made all the women swoon in his day. He rose and greeted Irish with a twinkle in his eye

"A sight for sore eyes, Ms. Irish." The Colonel always spoke as if he were enjoying a little private joke, especially if it had anything to do with their joint nemesis, Ethel.

"Why thank you, kind sir. Your looking very fine yourself", bantered Irish. The Colonel and Irish had spent many an evening together, him reminiscing about the war and Irish sharing certain aspects of her cases with him. His quick wit had caught many a detail and he had provided valuable insight into some of her most difficult cases. A good glass of Covasier never hurt their evenings either. The Colonel had a high regard for Irish and he thought she was by far the most elegant woman he had seen since his Olivia had died.

Irish was seated in an antique wingback chair that was covered with the finest leather. It had been Ethel's latest, late husband's favorite chair. After getting comfortable, Irish took a good look at Ethel who was dressed to kill or capture? Ethel's pantsuit made of raw silk was a sapphire blue. She had on diamond and pearl earrings and a triple row of pearls covered most of the wrinkles around her neck. She was also wearing a ring on her left hand, a cluster of diamonds representing a collection of trophies she had won in her marital conquests. On her right hand was a cultured pearl ring, with two small diamonds that had come from engagements she had broken early on. Ethel mistook marriage for dating. Her hair was still thick for her age and she had it colored a medium brown shade "as needed." Ethel has pulled out all the stops tonight. Watch out, Colonel, land mines ahead.

Ethel said very sweetly to Rosie "Please bring out the hors d'oeuvres, dear. I think we will have a little glass of sherry before we dine. Thank you my dear."

Rosie exited, flashing a backward grin Irish's way, as she prepared to fulfill Ethel's honey-coated request.

This could get interesting. Act I, Scene II – take five, Irish thought, as she gazed around the room.

There was an antique bookcase against the south wall in the living room, centered between two long windows. Several of the shelves had no books only pictures on them. Irish walked over to look at the pictures and saw many pictures of Ethel, Rosie and Ethel's late husband Edward. Funny there were no recent pictures of Rosie but there were plenty of pictures of Ethel in every stage of life: Ethel when she won the beauty contest, Ethel with the high-fashioned hairstyles of the war years, hair rolled artfully at the sides. Ethel and more Ethel. Irish couldn't help comparing Rosie's relationship with her mother to the one she had with Catherine. She was astounded at the way Ethel talked about Rosie to perfect strangers. Irish had heard Ethel comment to any audience she could find that Rosie had such a pretty face if only she would lose a few pounds. Irish thought Rosie was a beauty in her own right with her short, thick blond hair, rosy skin, quick wit and intelligence. As a History professor at the University of Portland, she was like a walking encyclopedia. Obviously, she had the patience of Job.

Rosie returned with the sherry and they made pleasant conversation until dinner. Rosie mentioned to Irish, "Sometime when you are out for a jog in NW Portland, there is a historical marker on 26th and Upshur you might enjoy."

"Hey, tell me about it," Irish responded. She loved to report to Savannah that the NW also had its share of exciting history. She had not given up getting Savannah to visit and eventually move west.

"It's the site where the entrance to the 1905 Lewis & Clark Exposition was located. Across the street is the Hotel Fairmount, it was built to accommodate visitors. You'll see it. It's a two-story building with a waist-high rail around a wide veranda. I think Meier & Frank furnished it. They're small apartments about to become condos."

"I hadn't even realized there was an Expo here," her genuine curiosity trumping her slight embarrassment.

"At the time, it was a really big deal. The Exposition grounds covered more than four hundred acres. There were like two and one-half million visitors, can you believe that? The Historical Society is hosting several interesting exhibits this year commemorating the Lewis and Clark Expedition from St. Louis to Oregon and my favorite "The Expo.""

"I think we should make a point of visiting some of the exhibits together. We could…" Irish began.

"R-o-s-i-e," Ethel interrupted. "Come help your m-o-t-h-e-r."

God does that woman ever stop? Irish looked at Rosie and whispered, "Later."

The meal turned out to be very good, years of practice, Irish suspected. Ethel made quite a production of having the Colonel slice the prime rib, pretending she was quite helpless to do so herself. She had some difficulty refraining from telling him the right way to cut; and at one point Irish fully expected the colonel to recite his favorite mantra, *Lead, follow or get the hell out of the way.* Being the quintessential gentleman, though, he sliced the meat with ease pretending that her gentle nudges were of some help to him. The meat was juicy, rare and tender, the mashed potatoes creamy and yellow with butter, and the sautéed sweet peas and onions were still slightly crisp, cooked exactly right.

Ethel was in her element and fully enjoying herself. She made little side remarks to the Colonel all evening, tittering, flirting and acting quite silly. Midway through the meal, Ethel sang a song she had performed on stage when she was three years old. She sang "I'm as small as I can be, you can't expect much of me" in the same baby voice she must have used as a toddler. The Colonel smiled graciously as she sang. He had dealt with women fawning over him all his life. His staunch military training could help him fight against the very worst of enemies. Deftly, he had shifted his attention to Rosie.

He loved to talk with her; the feeling was mutual. She particularly enjoyed the Colonel's stories of people he met in the course of his travels in WWII. She liked the way the Colonel made the people in all his stories come to life and his memory of events and locations were superior. He began by entertaining everyone with a hilarious story that happened in South Carolina on the Marine base outside of Beaufort.

"It's a true story about a pig and two cooks. This pig did not arrive at our base in the form of a ham." He chuckled. "As I recall, two Southern recruits were trying to decide how to kill the unfortunate pig when the pig escaped their grip scattering pots and pans everywhere in his wake. Just when the kitchen looked like the Three Stooges had taken up the culinary arts, I stepped in to congratulate the cooks. Their meal the night before had made a very favorable impression on the visiting General. The cooks took one look at me and stopped dead in their tracks. They had sweat running down their faces and were breathing heavy from the chase. Without skipping a beat, they snapped to attention and saluted. About this time, I had all I could do to keep a straight face and ask, 'Trying out a new recipe, men? I do believe your main ingredient just ran out the back door.' They looked if they were about to faint but I pretended not to notice. I proceeded to thank the men for their preparation of the dinner the night before and told the men to 'Carry on.' This story circulated the barracks long after the General had departed. I think we all added a touch more drama here and there. It was harmless fun and kept our minds off darker times," finished the Colonel.

"Did you get a chance to travel much around the area while you were there," Irish asked the Colonel.

"I did a lot of traveling and I particularly enjoyed the Sea Islands off the barrier reefs of South Carolina.

Rosie added, "You know I lived in Charleston for about two years." As she spoke, a brief sadness crossed her face, which Irish noticed immediately. "It was a few years ago, but I can remember the area just like it was yesterday." Always the sleuth, Irish wondered what that was all about.

Rosie continued, "The Sea Islands and the people were fascinating. The area is rich with history dating back several hundred years before the Civil War. Unfortunately, much of it is tragic, I mean thousands of slaves were imported to the area before slavery was abolished in…"

Ethel, taking back center stage, interrupted Rosie, "Rosie, you do go on so. We don't need to worry about those slaves no more now, do we? What an utterly depressing subject. Dessert time! Colonel, a little apple, dumpling?" Ethel asked demurely, successfully destroying any attempts to carry on an intelligent conversation.

Irish executed her exit plan once she felt a decent interval had passed since dinner. "This has been very nice, Ethel. I really enjoyed the dinner. I've got an early morning." Not too much to her surprise, Ethel didn't argue. She assumed the Colonel would not be getting away so easily.

"You must be tired, too, Rosie. You both need your rest. Don't worry about the dishes. The housekeeper will take care of everything tomorrow." Ethel moved them both quickly to the door.

 As Irish and Rosie prepared to leave, Ethel put a record on the old record player the colonel had admired earlier. Saying their good-byes, Rosie and Irish slipped out the door while Ethel and the Colonel started dancing to *I'll be seeing you in all the old familiar places,* each lost in their thoughts of days gone by and partners not forgotten.

Chapter Fourteen

I've made a pretty good living for myself, Nicole thought as she drove her little Civic Honda up to her stucco two-bedroom apartment in Midtown. She had enjoyed the good life with lots of sexy clothes, boyfriends and just about anything she needed. Her place was furnished with a "Rooms to Go" quick and easy design that she had paid cash for and purchased in less than two hours. Although her lifestyle wasn't one she was particularly proud of, she didn't really mind dancing in front of men and having them look at her with longing.

Although it was after 9:00 in the evening, she found a parking place right in front of her building. *Maybe my luck's changin',* Nicole mused. What had that black whore at the Center promised her? *What's that chick's name?* Nicole tried to think. Sometimes her brain was a little fuzzy from a few too many nights of various pleasures that she smoked or injected. At any rate, maybe she would just curl up and what? She hadn't spent a night alone for so long, she couldn't imagine what a woman did to occupy her time.

Usually her apartment was a hangout for her crowd from the club who sometimes wouldn't make it home until the next day. Frequently she would entertain overnight guests. The dancing was only a drop in the bucket compared to her overnight clientele.

Nicole frowned as she let herself in the front door of her apartment house that was supposed to be a security entrance. Rarely did she go in that someone else didn't slide in when the door was open. Some security. She unlocked the door to her own place and let herself in. Her apartment was dead quiet, as she knew it would be. She had hung out at the mall and wasted as much time as she could before coming home. Usually, she would be going to the club about now. This was her routine. She liked the nightlife, lots of noise and activity. Suddenly this was all supposed to end, and she was expected to change over night. *Yeah, right!*

Nicole tried to imagine spending the rest of her life coming home to an empty apartment. For the life of her she couldn't fathom the allure of working a day job with a bunch of women. I mean what would they talk about? Nicole knew her tit was in a wringer. If she started up with the old crowd again and got picked up one more time – her ass would go to jail. She'd done the rehab thing just to get out of jail and here she was staring at a life sentence of no drugs, no booze, no friends, and no fun. After all, she was only 23, not some old lady ready to hang it up. She couldn't believe how easy it was to make up the story about her folks. She was right about one thing, her mother was stupid and her dad was a drunk.

She flung the ugly sack of clothes across the room that some trash chick at the Women's Center had sent home with her. Nicole had about gagged when she handed the second-hand clothes to her as though it were some big deal. *I got it, her name was Ruby something.* Nicole thought she had seen her around before. Probably at the club or one of the local bars, she couldn't remember.

Nicole replayed the conversation she had with Ruby. It had been brief, but the woman was drummin' up some business. Ruby told her she looked "mighty fine" when Nicole stripped to try on some baggy, outdated piece of shit outfit. She had even asked Nicole if she was a model – *yeah, right!*. Nicole had sneered. Nicole told her she couldn't cuz her tits were too big. Ruby sort of half smiled at her and said somethin' like "Girl, I know men who would give anything to take care of that problem." Nicole hadn't skipped a beat, "I know, I've met quite a few of them." They were fairly quiet as they spoke, but the meaning was clear. Nicole figured she could hook her up with a pimp that could get her some big bucks. She'd call this Ruby chick and they sure as hell wouldn't be talkin' part-time job at $10.00 an hour. Nicole rummaged around for the card Ruby had slipped her.

Nicole could hear the clock ticking in her apartment but was too bummed to even turn on the stereo. She was down to two cigarettes and the day had been a bust. She couldn't go to the club. She needed to keep a low profile for a while. Maybe this Ruby chick knew some people. Maybe she could find her some way to make money away from the scene. She'd heard of women who made a thousand a night just for a private party. They didn't have to pay the taxman, but they did have to split the money with their pimp. Nicole had to go get some more cigarettes. She wasn't going to sit around this mausoleum. She couldn't run out of cigarettes. Maybe she'd just go out for a while, or she could give this Ruby a call. All she really needed was a pack of cigarettes. Hell, the woman said to call. She dialed the number.

The phone rang at least ten times while Nicole paced around her living room. Finally, a man answered. "Hullo," His voice sounded like he'd just woke up.

Nicole waited.

"Hullo, Who's this?" The man was awake.

"Hi, uh this is Nicole. Is Ruby there?" Nicole curled up in the corner of the sofa and put her ashtray on her lap. "She told me to call."

"Who?" The man asked again but with much more interest. "You say Nicole?"

Nicole sat up. She could tell he recognized her name. "I talked with Ruby today. She thought we might get together.

Is she around?" Nicole lit her last cigarette with the one she was just finishing. She let out a big sigh.

"She's ain't here. What's up, whatcha doin?"

"Hangin', nothing goin' on."

What do they call ya? Nicky?"

"Why, honey, you can call me Nicky."

"Hey Nicky girl, I'm Tremaine. I bet ah can help ya. Whatcha need, girl?" Tremaine's voice was definitely much more awake and quite warm and friendly.

Nicole loved the sound of a man's voice, especially when it was deep and lusty. "I was just hoping maybe Ruby could go get a drink or something. You wanna get together?" Nicole stood up and put her cigarette in the ashtray and decided to pare off her clothes while she was talking.

She needed to lose the clothes she had on and wear something a little more interesting even if it was only for a quick trip to the store. She unzipped her slacks and slid them off of her with her free hand. Her dancing had paid off; she could gracefully step out of her slacks, keep her balance and keep talking. She unbuttoned her top, letting it slide over her arms onto the floor. Holding the phone against her shoulder, she undid her bra.

"When do ya expect her back?" Nicole grabbed her cigarette; drop kicked her clothes into the corner and walked to her with only the tiniest lace thongs on to her bedroom to find something to wear. Finally some action, *kinda like old times*, she thought as she stood in front of her dresser putting a face to the voice on the other end. She knew without even meeting him that he would love looking at the petite, voluptuous body staring back at her from her dresser mirror. She imagined this man with the silky voice wanting to toy with the tiny lace panties one of her 'overnighters" had given her. Suddenly Nicole became aware of her cigarette. "Shit! Sorry, just burnt my finger."

"Careful, girl that smokin' will kill ya." Tremaine laughed, "You okay, want me to kiss it better?"

Nicole giggled, "I'm okay, just standin' here almost bare ass naked. Got to get some clothes on. Going to the store for more cigs. Nicole softened her voice when she asked, "So, do ya think Ruby'll want to go out? You could come too, Tremaine. We could go out later tonight." She hoped Ruby wouldn't even bother to show up.

"Tonight's just fine. I'll have Ruby call ya soon as she gets back." Tremaine used his super sexy drumming up business voice.

"Later." Nicole hung up. She quickly put on her favorite red-lace bra and a great little red knit top with a very short, matching skirt that snuggled tight against her body. Bare legged, she slipped into her and her favorite, pricey, red, kid-leather stilettos. Nicole loved the feeling of high-thin heeled shoes with just a tiny strap over the toe and behind the heel holding them onto her feet. She grabbed her purse and key.

Just as she was heading out the door, the phone rang again. Nicole grabbed the phone and answered on the first ring, "Nicole."

"Hey, it's Ruby. Tremaine said you called, girl. How are ya?" Ruby sounded a lot different than when she had talked to her earlier that day. She sounded like they'd known each other for years.

Nicole, still standing with her purse in her hand, was happy to hear a friendly voice. "Hey, I'm just heading out for cigarettes. I thought maybe, uh, uh, well, you had mentioned that," Nicole was at a loss for words. She slowed down and tried to sound more relaxed, "Hey, I was just chillin' and thought maybe you'd like to pop a few Buds or share a buzz."

"Tremaine, you wanna meet Nicole for a drink?" Ruby held her hand over the phone and Nicole could hear her muffled voice checking with Tremaine about meeting somewhere. They talked for a few seconds and then she came back on the phone. "How about Starks, you know it?" Ruby asked.

Nicole was thankful that Starks was a pretty remote bar that few had heard of. She wouldn't have to worry about bumping into her parole officer. Fortunately, it was close by, kind of a neighborhood hangout place, quiet and a good place to talk. "Yeah, I know where it's at." Nicole was surprised that Ruby knew a place so close to her. "Is it close to y'all?" Nicole asked.

"Sure is, we'll meet ya there in 'bout an hour." Ruby replied and hung up. She had already planned the location when she talked to Nicole this afternoon.

"It's all about me." Nicole said out loud to herself. Tonight she would only drink a coke or something. Maybe she'd walk to the store, get her cigarettes and go to the bar a few minutes early for one drink just to take the edge off. As she opened the door to leave she suddenly felt cold as ice. Something had changed in her apartment. She could feel it. *What was wrong with her tonight? Like that old saying- someone just walked over my grave,* she shivered. She closed the door and was glad to be back outside where the street sounds broke the dead silence that she called her life.

Midtown mid-evening was always busy. The corner store was packed with people picking up beer and cigarettes for the evening, or picking up milk and bread. Nicole quickly purchased four packs of cigarettes and a couple of rolls of breath mints. Her long nails tore open the package of cigarettes and she lit one as she headed two blocks down the street toward Starks. The bar itself, although it was situated down a dark alley and it was really old. She had a little trouble maneuvering her heels as they tried to lodge themselves in between the brick path to the bar. The place was empty.

"Come on in, good looking," the bartender looked up from the bar and waved her on in. He was probably in his 50's and looked like someone who had been his own best customer. His bulbous nose made him look like an ex-prize fighter. The veins on his face stuck out and his hair was thinning on top with lots of gray sprigs of hair around his ears and a few wiry long hairs in his nose. He walked around the battered bar and patted a thick, leather stool for her to sit on. "What brings you to this neck of the woods?" he asked congenially.

"Meeting some friends," Nicole mumbled. "If you don't mind, I'll grab a booth." No way would Nicole sit up at a bar like some old broad that had spent her lifetime picking up men at bars. She slid into a booth and looked at the bartender. "How about a club soda for now?" She felt a little embarrassed ordering a club soda at a bar, especially one that didn't seem to be doing much of a business. "Actually, make that a CC and water. Light on water" Nicole clicked her ashes into the ashtray, took a large drag on her cigarette and waited.

Chapter Fifteen

Ruby pulled out her list of names from her purse. Third name on her list read:

Nicole Williams, hooker, big midtown club, lap dancer, young, pretty, white girl, needs money fast, she's gotta hang low or goes to jail. Can probably meet at Starks.

This little white bitch'll be just fine for us, she realized as she shoved the list back in her purse. *Lots a old fools with big money gonna wanta piece of her ass.*

Tremaine's stable of women was filling up with plenty of action these days. Doris was no threat. *Uglier than shit.* She was a good business manager though, and she helped Tremaine with the steady stream of girls. At first he was all sugar and honey with them, but within no time he and Doris made it clear that "no one messes with Doris or Tremaine." One look from either of them and the girls stepped right back in line. Business was just fine.

Tonight me and Tremaine would get pretty, little Nicole makin' them real money, Ruby thought as she prepared to go to the bar. Usually, she didn't meet the girls, but since Nicole was hot to trot, they'd play it Nicole's way. At least at first.

She looked at her face in the mirror and applied a deep purple lip liner and then filled in with a matted deep purple lipstick. Pressing the tip of her red nail into a small pot of bronzy mauve blush, she highlighted her cheekbones. Expertly, she lined her eyes in black, dabbed on lavender eye shadow, and then finished up by applying a substantial amount of black mascara on her lashes.

If auntie were here, she would have grabbed a tissue and wiped the excess makeup off of her face, but auntie wasn't here and she never would be again. A surprising change came over her face when she thought of her aunt Ada. She felt like a young child again worried about what her auntie would say. It had been a long time ago, but when Ruby looked in the mirror, it seemed like only yesterday when she would stay with her auntie during those hot summers in South Carolina. Sunday mornings were spent in the praise house learning old-time way of religion.

Her summers with auntie were short breathers that allowed her time to recover from nine months of sexual abuse from Big Daddy. He had her first tender years, then as time went on he sold her to his friends. All with mama lurking in the shadows, a beating ready should she dare to defy her. Ruby never told auntie Ada of the abuse for even as a child she had learned all too cruelly never to expect anyone to save her.

The first time he had pushed his nasty part into her, Ruby fought and tore at him for all she was worth. Big Daddy laughed and held her down. When he was done he grunted, exhaled his whiskey breath in her face, rolled over and went to sleep.

"Mama, mama," Ruby screamed running into the other room and finding mama sitting in the chair in the dark, smoking a cigarette. Ruby stood before her mother, blood trickling down between her legs, and tugged at her mother's skirt, which was hiked up above her thighs. "He hurts me mama, I tries ta stop him but he kept..." Mama had grabbed her by the hair and slapped her face so hard she became dizzy. "You dos jus like Big Daddy wants, ya here girl? It won' hurt no mo. Ya treats him fine or ah beats you till you can't walk no mo. Think ya gits sumpen ta eat fo free girl?" As a minor sample of the kind of punishment she could expect if she made any attempt to revolt, mama had taken the belt to Ruby until she was too worn out to complain again. So for a few years Ruby was cornered with her growing hatred for everyone except auntie. She was expert at disguising her true feelings.

Big Daddy brought Ruby small treats and trinkets cause she pleased him best. One time he gave her a big diamond ring he'd stolen. She hid it from mama. Turned out to be a CZ. For a few years, she learned every method of pleasing him and his friends. Mama would get too drunk for Big Daddy and his friends to use and before long Tanya started drinking too. Whenever that happened they got a beating and Ruby took center stage, one of her favorite places to be. She lowered her eyes and hid her vicious hatred for them all.

Ada, typically a believer in the Gullah ways and also a Christian - a faith taught to her by the good folks in St. Helena - suspected much of what had taken place, but, thank God, she did not know the extent of the evil the children endured. She prayed to the Lord for Big Daddy, and for Ruby's sister and mother, that they would mend their "wicket" ways. It pained her until her death the way their girls suffered at their hands. A younger sister had escaped the torture, as she died very young. The doctors said she had a flu or virus and should have survived, but she just didn't seem to have the will to live. Then there was just Ruby and her sister, Tanya who in Ruby's mind deserved what she got.

Ruby remembered her baby sister's funeral. It had been an emotional time, lots of stompin', chanting and a mixture of spirituals, hymns and Gullah songs. Ruby had to be protected once she looked into the coffin. To satisfy any lingering spirits, she was passed back and forth over the coffin as their Gullah custom dictated. Ruby had nightmares for years to come, waking up inside her sisters coffin. Even auntie Ada's reassurance that she had been saved never banished her fear of the evil spirits.

It was plain to see why Ruby was always different from the other children. She had needs, wants, dreams and hatreds far beyond that of anyone in her family. Her auntie Ada had recognized how complicated and gifted Ruby was and she feared for her. Ruby wasn't satisfied with learning to use the old Gullah ways to benefit her people as Ada had always taught her. She had consistently missed the opportunity to capture the beauty and wisdom of the Gullah culture. Instead she kept every cruel injustice she had experienced, close as a possession, and vowed revenge for each one. She'd take what she wanted at any cost.

On a summer day a few years after Big Daddy had moved in with them Ruby was sitting in the old swing in the front yard of auntie's farmhouse. A neighbor man, Sam Johnson, whose wife was about to have her baby, had come for Ada. He had driven up the drive in his old pickup so fast the dirt had blown all over her. The dirt got in her eyes, mouth, up her nose and all over her clean dress. She glared at him from her seat on the swing, but Sam strode right past her without a glance. Sam stopped at the foot of the steps and waited, hat in hand, for Ada to appear. He was a large man, hair cut short to his head, black skin shining from the heat. Sam wore overalls with a blue shirt had been mended in many places. He had been out back in his barn caring for the livestock when Ella called him from the back porch to fetch Ada. This was to be his fourth child and you'd think by now Sam would have taken it in his stride, but no, he still panicked each time.

"Sam, jus you calm down now, you gotta gets me there in one piece. Ruby you be a good girl while I'm gone bringing dat baby. Mis Johnson be hav'n her babies as nice as you please. Ah be home to fix your supper."

"Yes, ma'am." *I hopes dat nasty baby don turn green an dies.*

Soon as Sam's old truck disappeared in the dust Ruby hopped off the swing and started walking down the drive. The air was so humid it felt like you were breathing in water, but that didn't bother Ruby. When auntie got back she would prepare their supper and later they would sit on the porch and wait for a sea breeze to drift across the marsh. For now it was Ruby's chance to do as she pleased.

When Ruby came to the end of the drive she didn't hesitate she turned left and followed the main road for about a half-mile then turned left again on a tiny trail into the woods. She followed the trail through the moss hung oak trees until she came to the edge of the marsh. Her movement startled a snowy egret into flight, but Ruby hardly paid any attention. There was a purpose to her trek and it didn't include bird watching.

Ruby had skirted the edge of the marsh until she came to an almost invisible trail back into the old oaks. Walking slowly and watching for snakes kept her full attention. She would have missed the old woman if not for the tobacco juice the woman spit out in her path. "What's you wants wid ole Lizzy girl? ef i's don knows", Chuckled the old woman. "You com'n back down learns abouts dat root magic, ain't dat true?" She appeared ancient and ugly to Ruby, who could care less what she looked like. Most children would have run from her looks alone let alone all the fearful stories of witches, hags and hexes from adults. The tiny, bent over creature played her part to the fullest.

And so through her growing years Ruby went to visit the old woman and learn her evil ways whenever she could sneak away from her auntie. When she heard the grownups speak of the old hag Lizzy with dread and fear she simply smiled to herself. By the time she was in her early teens, she had terrified her family and all those nasty little girls in her school. No child ever had the courage to tell on Ruby. The threat of her conjure magic stilled their tongues. Ruby returned home long before Ada came home. Ada had spent most of the night, with no success, trying to save Sam's baby.

Ada was getting older and didn't have much longer to live. She knew she had to teach Ruby "the ways." She taught Ruby the gift of the Gullahs that she had inherited from her own mother. Her mother had been a healer learning through the ages from her ancestors from Africa and Ada had carried on the tradition. She had learned from the best healers on the islands and had grown to know the most potent and powerful ways to survive.

Ada knew Ruby had the eyes of a spiritualist. She could feel the heat radiate from Ruby's body, the vibrant, almost-overpowering energy flow necessary to heal others. What she didn't know was that the power had turned inside out in Ruby and Ruby used it only to elicit bad spirits and to charm, intimidate and terrify others into getting what she wanted. For a woman as revered as Ada for her infinite wisdom, unfortunately Ada had a major blind spot when it came to Ruby.

Ada died leaving her small cabin and what was left of her land to Ruby. There were several others that thought they should have been in line first for that land. It was pretty safe to say everyone hated everyone in this family. Ruby's sister, Tanya hated her auntie Ada and Ruby. Ruby's mother, who sided with Tanya, loathed Ruby and Ada. Ruby despised them all and almost everyone she met.

Yes, she had the eyes of a woman who could conjure anything she wanted any time she wanted it. Ruby looked in the mirror at her piercingly deep brown eyes, dabbed a speck of white on each bone just below her perfectly shaded eyebrows and smiled at the hard, angular, perfectly groomed face looking back at her with deep satisfaction. Tonight Tremaine and Nicole would be hers.

As Ruby looked into the mirror, she whispered, *he ma mans now,* and then calls out to Tremaine. "Hey, baby, ready?" her face radiant.

"You go ahead. I'm gonna drive my own car there. I'll meet ya."

Determined, she smiled at the anxious woman staring back at her in the mirror. Although Ruby knew there was usually no use arguing with Tremaine, she tried again. "I don't mind waitin," but as she looked back at her frozen face, she knew she would be driving alone. It was Tremaine's way or the highway. Although this didn't set well with Ruby, she knew she could hang on to him no matter what. Sure he had his ways and that had bothered Ruby. She couldn't help wondering what he had in mind that he couldn't go somewhere with her and come home with her at the same time. She wasn't anyone's fool and if he decided to mess around, she would change his mind real fast.

Tremaine didn't even bother to answer, so she grabbed her car keys, took one last look at herself on the way out and closed the door. She was glad they lived close in Atlanta, because her drive to meet Nicole was short. As she pulled up, she noticed only a few people were starting to file in. *Dead here tonight. Just as well, we'll hook this little bitch then I'll show Tremaine a fine night of real sex,* Ruby thought. She parked close by and walked down the alley to the entrance of the remote bar, feeling hot from the humidity that was setting in and moist from her thoughts about Tremaine.

"Hey, girl," Ruby spotted Nicole right away in a booth toward the back of the room. She slid in the seat across from her. "Tremaine's comin'. He'll be here in a minute." Ruby was proud of her find. Nicole looked damn sexy. *She'd bring in some bucks*, Ruby thought. "Glad ya called, I was…." she didn't get a chance to finish her sentence, because a middle-aged blond with tits falling out of her skimpy top interrupted her.

"Wadda ya want to drink?" The woman asked, as she stood right next to the table looking more than semi-annoyed at having to ask the question. The woman had definitely seen some miles and the only really attractive thing she had going for her was her tall, tan legs which were more than visible under her very short, tight skirt. She was about five feet eight inches with the high-heeled sandals she was wearing. Her tone packed an attitude as she stared at Ruby waiting for her to order.

Ruby had seen her here before and was pissed off at how she sweetened up when Tremaine was around. Ruby even remembered that her name was Estelle, and she also knew that Estelle recognized her. Whenever Ruby came in though, she would act like she'd never seen her before in her life. Ruby could play that game, "Bourbon and water, not much ice." *Bitch.* She kept her eyes on Nicole without even looking up at Estelle. As Estelle walked away, Ruby leaned toward Nicole and whispered viscously, "Stinkin' cunt." She leaned back and Nicole laughed nervously at Ruby's remark.

"Tremaine'll be here any minute. We've got lots" …Ruby stopped mid-sentence when she heard Tremaine's voice messing with Estelle who had turned into quite the hostess.

"Hey good lookin'. Your mama's been waiting for you to come back. Where ya'll been." Estelle's voice had become wind chimes on a summer's eve.

Tremaine, smelling expensive, and looking good slid his hand around Estelle's curvy bottom and squeezed it. He pulled her just close enough to whisper something in her ear, which made her nod her head and smile. "The usual," Tremaine said as she patted his ass and headed toward the bar.

He strutted toward the booth where Ruby and Nicole were sitting. "Nicky Williams, What it is, girl?" Tremaine reached over and took her hand and kissed it. "Now you're a fine piece of woman, ain't that the truth, Ruby" Ruby knew the drill and took the cue without skipping a beat. The episode with Estelle wasn't lost on her, but for now Ruby needed to reel in their new little moneymaker.

"Told ya you'd like her." Ruby smiled and patted the seat next to her for Tremaine to sit down. Tremaine ignored the invitation and scooted in next to Nicole leaving no space between his thigh and hers. Ruby sat up straighter in the booth and wished Estelle would get her whoring fat ass over there with their drinks. Her makeup felt heavy on her face, and she could taste the bile in her throat as Tremaine leaned into Nicole taking a quick inventory of her attributes.

"Honey, we can make ya some money. Tha's what I'm talk'n about,' as his eyes caressed her body. "We gonna sweeten your little money pot right away. Big bucks, Nicky. Know some folks in town that'll pay just for a dance. Course it has to be the right dance, if you get my drift, and with the right payin' customer." Tremaine talked fast as he ignored Ruby. He looked up to get the drinks from Estelle who had just arrived with a Jack Daniels neat for Tremaine and the bourbon and water for Ruby.

"Hey, Estelle, baby, get Ms. Nicky here another one. Thanks, sugar." Tremaine reached over and wrapped his long fingers around Estelle's leg – close to the top. His eyes caught hers as he leaned over and bit her playfully on a small rose tattoo she had placed carefully just inside her inner thigh. "Wha's this?" His hands rubbed the tiny rose she had painted on her leg.

"Ya'll come over to ma place and I'll show you the whole garden," she laughed pretending to push him away.

"Ruby, call Doris. I just talked to her on the way over. Told her about Nicky. She says she has somethin' right away. Friday night, Nicky right?" Tremaine explained to Nicky that she would be working with Doris mostly and that Doris would set up the contacts. He inhaled his Jack Daniels, caught Estelle's eye and held up a finger for one more.

Nicole was warming up to him, but one glare from Ruby had cooled her down quickly. While Tremaine was in the bathroom, Ruby leaned in close to Nicole, drink in hand, "You keep your trashy little slit away from Tremaine, understand?" Ruby's raspy voice and cold eyes left no room for negotiation.

"Hey, I ain't messin' with your man. It's cool." Nicole said quickly and convincingly. She had met enough people in her line of business to know when to back off. "Girl, it's cool." Nicole looked straight at Ruby until Ruby sat back in her chair.

Once the deal was a "go", Tremaine lost interest real fast. Not one much for small talk, he left the conversation part up to Ruby, who went over a few details and then sat still without saying a word.

Nicole quickly finished her drink when it was clear they weren't interested in being friends. After all, it was a business deal and the good news was she'd be workin' tomorrow night. It felt great to be back in business, Nicole thought as she excused herself, thanked them and headed down the street toward her apartment.

"She gonna be a fine ride, Ruby." Tremaine said as he fidgeted in the booth apparently at loose ends. "Hey, baby, I got business going on tonight, I'll meet ya at home, okay?" Tremaine looked at Ruby and leaned over the table and cupped his hand under her chin. "You look mighty pretty tonight, girl. You ma girl, right?" Tremaine leaned over the table and kissed her, his mouth soft and wet with his tongue tasting her lips. "You go home and get ready and your daddy will be home in a while with a big surprise for his little girl." Tremaine caressed her hair and guided her out of the booth. "Be a good girl, now." he spanked her playfully and walked her to the door. "Night, Estelle."

*****

Five-thirty a.m. and no Tremaine. The bedroom was in disarray. Ruby lay eyes wide open flat on her back, staring at the ceiling alone in her big bed. She had left an early morning voice mail for Savannah letting her know she had to go to South Carolina – her mama was sick and her sister had called her to come home.

Mama and sister that a big laugh, smiled Ruby as coherence came and went. She lay in her bed alone reminiscent of many nights she had experienced just before Big Daddy came in her bedroom. *Mama sick all right. She full dat debbel. He taken her most a year gone by now. Sister gonna rots in hell soon too. I gotta cuts her. Bitch. A fight'n for dat little bit of land left, taxes done got most. Auntie Ada wanted only Ruby have dat farm. Bitch not walk on dat land. Ada still belong onlys to Ruby. Ada knows dat Ruby got the spirits like she done.* On and on evil thoughts coursed through Ruby's sick mind.

*****

The tears had been planted on Ruby's face for hours. She felt the loneliness she had felt when she had been at Auntie's funeral. Everyone knew Ada was the hardest workin', most respected healer and midwife in town. Ada's carried her "medical kit" in a canning jar, consisting mostly of cotton balls and silver nitrate to tend the newborns. Along with her kit, she had carried healing roots and herbs. Many had their lives to thank her for. The funeral had been packed with all her neighbors on the island. Every friend from the Penn School still alive had also attended. All the people she had healed over the years were there, and of course the uppity white folks who had been kind enough to give her enough work to keep her petite body taut from scrubbing their floors and runnin' after their kids.

"Ruby, remember me, girl? I'm Mrs. Wilkerson. Your aunt worked for me for years. I hear y'all just finished that typing school and that you might be able to do some work."

Ruby remembered that plastic looking white bitch with the too blond hair plastered in place and her scrawny rooster neck that she would have cheerfully loved to slit. "Why yes, Mis Wilkerson," Ruby mustered a quiet response.

"Ruby why don't y'all come over to the house tomorrow? We could use an extra hand around the house now that Ada is gone."

Now that Ada is gone. Ruby sobbed in her bed. Now my auntie gone I can get down on hand and knee and scrub white bitches floor. Ruby's face contorted into a rage. Auntie I knows you is a watch'n from your coffin all dem folks round look'n at Mis Wilkerson and me. Only respect for Ada keep Ruby from slapping Mrs. Wilkerson's face that very day and now thoughts of going back and killing the old bitch took root in her.

Ruby had to clean up the mess. There were torn tissues full of purple makeup everywhere. She hadn't remembered what happened to the room. Everything had been thrown all over and she had put out her powders and roots. In her frenzy she had somehow resisted cutting the bedposts down. *I don' let ma Tremaine sees me puts da root on dat gal, not till he a real conjure man fo sure.* She had hexed that bitch Estelle. She knew when Tremaine came home, she would smell that Channel #5 on him – Estelle's signature perfume she had smelled at the bar. Who could miss it? While she lay in bed alone, her man was with that whore.

She remembered how he had loved her own sweet little ass when she went to the party, a girl she knew from the old days, Clarissa, had invited her to. It was on a Saturday night at her place in Buckhead. Clarissa had made good, expensive clothes, lots of paying customers, and a great looking apartment. Her friends were the kind of friends Ruby wanted, so she worked the room starting with that hunk Tremaine. Amelia was easy to get rid of. Ruby lay in bed and laughed to herself. *I's done sum'p' right. auntie sees how smart your Ruby baby done been?* She slid into that party, into the nightlife, into Amelia's old job, into Tremaine's bed and now she would keep everything she deserved.

The night had not been her friend. She hated nights alone and this one had been full of the devil himself. Ruby went into the bathroom and looked into the mirror surprised at the ragged face staring back at her. She pulled herself up, turned on the shower full blast, let it run while she picked up the mess she had made, walked into the shower and washed off the misery of her night.

As she came out of the shower, she was hit with the smell of Channel #5 and sex. "Why, hey there, Tremaine, where ya been hiding your sexy ass?" Ruby walked out of the shower into the bedroom thinking, W*here you been sticking that dick, asshole?* As she stood in front of Tremaine with her towel draped around her wet body. She walked over to the bed, put one leg on the bed and leaned over drying herself slowly and seductively.

Tremaine was surprised Ruby was up and lookin' mighty fine. The place looked good. She even had candles lit all over the room. He thought he was spent, but watching her in the candlelight, all dried off now and her hand messaging his favorite warm, juicy spot between her legs, he laughed to himself. He'd fuck this bitch no matter that the last one's smell was still on him. Too bad he didn't see the look of madness in her lowered eyes.

*****

Dat bitch gonna pay fo pu'nt her sex on ma mans.

Chapter Sixteen

May

Savannah veered off highway 75, caught 285 and treated herself to an evening at the Perimeter Mall. She might even catch a great winter coat buy. She'd been watching an Ann Klein beauty that she hoped was still there at just the right price. Turning into the mall, she vied for a coveted parking place nearby and headed toward Macy's coat department.

Her instincts were right on. There was her coat, almost 70% off, screaming "buy me, buy me." She grabbed the coat and headed for the dressing room. *Perfect fit,* she thought as she wrapped the black cashmere coat around her and looked at her reflection in the fitting room mirror. She had always been thin. She had danced when she was young and had been athletic so her body was pliant and worked well for her. Although she loved to eat, she could go days without giving it much thought. In fact, sometimes – especially lately – she had to remind herself to remember to eat.

 Savannah was surprised how much weight she had lost since Tommy's death. She was back into her college day's size 4-6 and although she looked a little "McBealish", she did kind of like being able to feel a few bones here and there. Tommy used to tease her. He said she looked like Sharon Stone. She could hear him, "Come on, Savannah, do that Basic Instincts routine for me again.

Now just a fond memory. Not devastating, just really extraordinarily sad. Savannah looked straight into the mirror at the same determined look she had plastered on her face as a little squirt barely out of diapers trotting down the hill toward Irish's house. *It's spring, and I'm surrounded by the new growth of dogwoods, magnolias, azaleas so breathtaking that I have to stop to figure out if it is the salmon and lavender combination I like best or the brilliant purple and red combos that knock me out. Spring fever...I definitely have it.* She laughed as she slowly turned in front of the mirror admiring her new purchase.

The Hair, she almost gasped aloud as she took a close look at it. It had grown well past her shoulders, was stringy and needed highlights in a big way. On the quick chance that Marla would have an opening, she pulled her cell phone out of her purse and "speed dialed" her hairdresser.

"Marla's Way" Marla answered on the first ring. Marla was a peaches and cream kind of gal with a musical sound in her voice. She loved people and they loved her right back.

"Marla, it's Savannah."

"Hey, girl, I thought you croaked." She paused, "I mean, well damn, girl, where ya been? I've been worried about you. I wanted to call, but I thought you'd think I was checkin' on your business – and didn't want to fuss." Marla scurried on.

"You're not going to believe how bad my hair is. I know this is so weird, but I just had to call to see if by any chance you'd take me in – sort of like an emergency case – know what I mean?" Savannah stumbled and half-heartedly laughed at herself.

Marla messed with her bangs as she looked at her auburn hair with deep purple highlights in the mirror while she talked on her mobile phone. "I was so pissed off. This lady asked me to stay open tonight. I'm not taking her on any more as a customer. Anyway at the very last minute, she canceled. Here I sit with an open space this evening, when I could have been out parting with the girls. Can you come in about an hour?" Marla pulled her smock around her to cover her middle-aged spread, which she had noticed was spreading even farther as of late. *Maybe I'll try that ice cream diet.*

"Hey, I'll be there in an hour or less." Savannah couldn't believe her good luck.

"I'll put the 'closed' sign up on the shop. Come in the back. I'll have some wine for us. Do you need the works?" Marla sounded happy to hear from her.

"The works and then some." Savannah laughed. "See ya soon. I'll stop and get us some sandwiches." Unlike Savannah who could go forever not thinking about food, Marla loved to eat. She looked like it, too. She was a roly-poly, fair-skinned, over- forty, confident and opinionated, lively woman who would happily consume any morsels Savannah brought to her door.

Savannah folded up her phone, threw it in her purse, slid the coat off and headed to the cashier's desk. Within minutes, she was the proud owner of a drop-dead gorgeous, Ann Klein cashmere coat with a "just a touch of fur" on it. Quickly, she headed for the food mall to pick up sandwiches.

Maybe I'll pick up some hummus, babaganoush, and a sack full of delicacies from the food court. Savannah felt her energy start to rise as she planned for an evening of lively conversation, a brand new hairdo, and an array of delicious food guaranteed to move her out of her 4-6 to an 6-8 level. *Who cares,* she thought as she grazed her way from food stand to food stand picking delicacies from each food group – especially the chocolate one.

As she headed back to Macy's to find her parking spot, she noticed an upscale, children's shop. *Look at the tights. Oh, my God, those matching hats, striped leggings and hats. It would have been fun...* Savannah sighed as she walked inside. She and Tommy had always been careful, but she loved children and knew that eventually the time would have been right, *after he stopped drinking. Un Huh.* She decided to just stop in for a minute.

She found at least eighteen items that were guaranteed to match and drain any reasonable pocketbook. There were skirts, tights, jeans, coats, dresses, socks, shoes, pillows, comforters, towels, small pierced earrings, necklaces, bows, elastic head bands with flowers and gizmos attached to them, lace trimmed denim vests, blouses, tee shirts, undershirts, panties, and on it went. Savannah was fairly overwhelmed with the many choices in front of her.

Her mind drifted to Ruby. Here Savannah stood with shopping bags loaded up with her expensive coat and enough food to feed half the people in China. *What would it hurt,* she thought of Ruby's girls. *I won't make a deal about it.* Savannah proceeded to pick out two "Clothing Groups" – one for each of the girls. The sales girl was delirious over her selection and just kept piling up the "Mixed and Matched." Savannah went to the teal and rose striped with flowered pieces to match and a colored tee with a big heart in the middle that said, "I luv my mama." She topped off her purchases with a splashy-colored beach bag covered with farm animals. This little detour had cost more than her coat. *Rightly so,* thought Savannah.

Savannah hurried to the parking lot, threw her packages in the trunk and quickly clicked her remote to open her car door. She started up the car as a line of new parking hopefuls waited impatiently behind her parking place. With barely enough room to back up, Savannah headed out of the mall, to the 285 West exit. With her car smelling like a Greek delicatessen she sped toward the Galleria area where

Marla was hopefully popping the cork on the wine, letting it catch its breath for Savannah's arrival.

Savannah hadn't had such a relaxed day in months and she felt like she had reached a turning point. She'd found something really fine for herself, and she had a great time following Catherine's old adage – be just as generous with others as you are with yourself. She had so much that certainly she could afford to share her wealth with someone who needed it like Ruby's kids. Savannah would tell her that this was not something she normally did, but that Ruby had her hands full and Savannah had the resources to help. She hoped Ruby would take it in the spirit it was meant. It was spring and her kids needed clothes. Savannah would downplay the value of the clothes and package them to look like no big deal. She would, of course, ask Ruby to be aware that this was an exception to the rule – and should not be discussed with anyone else. *Peggy would just croak and Irish ...well, I won't even go there,* Savannah thought as she pulled up into the parking lot in front of Marla's Way.

Savannah had found Marla when she first moved to Atlanta. Marla had come from up her way, a little south of where Savannah grew up. Marla's dad had been a mortician and Marla had started by fixing hair for corpses and had worked her way up from dead people to live people in her own independent shop.

She had been a hairdresser for years and knew half the people in Atlanta and lots of the small town folks in the Carolinas. Her mom had worked for the transportation department somewhere over on the coast. Between Marla, her folks, a half-dozen siblings, they had a better gossip line going than the worldwide web. She had sisters in Kentucky, Virginia and Tennessee. One brother lived in South Carolina and the other in North Carolina. They pretty much had the whole southeast area covered.

Savannah clicked her remote and her car honked back at her letting her know it was locked. *Noisy, but effective,* Savannah mused. When she was in a crowded area and everyone looked around when her horn noisily announced that her car was now locked, she would walk away looking as though the noise were connected to something unrelated to her doing. Today, though, Marla heard her and waved her around the back.

"Did you buy out the store? Marla asked as she helped her carry the boxes of food into the small kitchen area just inside the back door. "M-m-m—m, this looks good. Greek olives, feta cheese. I love this hard-crusted bread. Let me get the wine and some sweet butter."

Within minutes, they were spread out sitting comfortably in the front of the shop with their plates piled with food and their wineglasses full. "Thanks for bringing the food. This is wonderful," Marla wasted no time digging into the pungent feast.

"Hey, thanks for seeing me on such short notice." Savannah replied.

"How are you girl? I've been asking half the people in the county about ya. No one has heard much from you." Marla asked casually.

Savannah noticed that Marla's hair was a different color today. Normally, she had heavily bleached, blond hair with silver highlights, but she had changed her hair to the "messed up" short look changing the color from blond to red with purple streaks. She looked terrific, especially with her huge blue eyes. *My grandma, what big eyes you have – and they don't miss a thing,* Savannah thought.

Savannah knew that when Marla said she asked around that meant that she talked to her brother's wife who knew Irish's aunt or Savannah's cousin or someone from the area. Or she had talked to her dad who had been friends with the mortician who had handled Tommy's funeral, or talked to her sister-in-law that worked at the hospital where Irish's dad had been in for emergency surgery or she had gone to a hair show with the hairdresser that did Catherine's hair.

Savannah dipped her pita bread into the hummus as Marla continued, "If your hair is any indication of how you are doing, I'd say you aren't doin' worth shit!" Not one for brevity, she continued, "When was the last time you used a conditioner? God, girl, this is damn scary." She stood up from the large swivel chair, put her plate down on one of the girl's counters and walked over to test Savannah's hair. "Uck, look at these split ends. Don't you tell anyone I took care of your hair. Girl, this is a disgrace!"

Savannah just kept eating. It was heavenly having Marla fuss over her.

"We'll do a heavy conditioner first. Then we'll get the color right and then we'll cut. You sure let this go, honey. Someone with your kind of hair shouldn't look like this." Marla fussed.

"M-m-m h-h-h –m," Savannah licked the hummus off of her fingers and started in on the tabouli – snarfing up the pieces of parsley happy as a little pig in shit. The hair was no longer under her domain. She had successfully transferred all of the hair responsibility and the resulting mess to Marla who at this moment looked like she had just been handed a turd.

Marla ran her hands through Savannah's hair as she studied it and came up with a series of solutions necessary to make

Savannah an acceptable candidate for the human race. She went over to the stereo and slipped in Bonnie Raitt's new CD and took Savannah's plate of food away from her temporarily while she guided her to the shampoo bowls.

It was a toss up. What feels better? The food or the wonderful head massage she was getting right now. Her head tingled as Marla massaged away the months of sorrow she had held tightly in her head. She massaged the pores sore and abused from day upon day of stress and exhaustion. *Unlike Marla's dad, Marla could actually bring back the dead,* Savannah thought. The tears trickled down her face and with no fanfare Marla quietly took a soft towel and wiped them away.

"So, how are the women doin'?" Marla, as a donor and volunteer, had worked with Savannah on last year's fundraiser and was responsible for increasing the local donor base. She had even enlisted several family members to contribute and was genuinely interested.

"Well, let's see, since you were there, we added a drug counselor. You know how we needed someone to handle that part. I have good counselors, but there are lots of problems with drugs. Oh, and Peggy is still there. I don't know what I'd do without her. One of the women there was murdered, my office manager, in fact. Course, I'm sure you heard that already." *Of course she knew. Did Raggedy Ann have a cloth clitoris?* Marla knew everything. She probably knew more about the case then the cops.

"Thought you'd never get to it, girl. I saw you all on TV. Don't leave out anything. Your hairs look'n like shit I might add. Too bad you didn't come to me sooner. So what is the scoop?"

*****

When Savannah finished giving Marla all the tidbits the papers had left out, Marla's eyes were as big as her ass. "I had to find a new office manager. Believe me, it would have taken less time to go to the Vatican and kiss the pope's ring." Savannah sighed as Marla rinsed off the remnants of her hair mess. "I finally found someone. Actually, you might even know her. She's from your area. Ruby Ebota?"

Marla left Savannah dripping with her head propped on the washbowl in a really uncomfortable position, "Ebota. I know the Ebota family. Let's see, what was her name, Sarita, maybe. She was married to this no good son-of-a-bitch. What did they call him – Hot Daddy – Big Daddy! Some absurd name – boy she was a piece of trash. Been married a few times, had some daughters, last time I heard the kids were really screwed up. My grandma knew Sarita's older sister Ada Ebota, one of the nicest women you could ever meet. She was a simple woman, petite but just as tough as nails. Never married. Good lady with a huge heart. She was a healer – I mean she really was – she knew herbs and roots. No kidding, she actually saved people when the doctors gave up. She learned midwifery from her mother. I think she went to the Penn School on St. Helena a long time ago."

"Have you ever been over there?" Marla was oblivious to Savannah trying to find a comfortable place on the ceramic bowl to rest her neck. "It's really something. Anyway, she's actually kind of a legend, but that sister of hers and those no good kids are worthless. Ada died sometime back. She had a little place in St. Helena's. My brother wanted to try to buy up some of that property, but he said he couldn't track down the owner. I think he was over that way this summer checking it out again. He said it was a mess. No one was taking care of it. He was surprised, because Ada was pretty tidy although it was a really old place with an outhouse – no indoor plumbing. I mean, it would have to be torn down –

but the property is worth a fortune. I think they sold most of the land. Someone said thr one girl got all the money. That one's sister she carried somethin' awful. It was nasty."

"Oh, I'm sorry, here, Savannah, let's get you over to the comfortable chair." She wrapped a towel around Savannah's head and guided her to her station.

Once she got Savannah comfortable, Marla handed Savannah her plate of food and poured both of them more wine. She sat in the chair opposite Savannah with her own plate of food and took a sip of her wine. "The last person in the world I would want working with me is anyone in that Ebota family except Ada."

"That bad huh," Savannah moaned.

"Worse," Marla looked at Savannah, eyebrows raised, clearly surprised that Savannah could have even considered hiring someone like one of the Ebota girls. "How can I say this? Any Ebota is trouble with a capital "T." They lie, cheat, whore around, and create a ruckus you can't even believe. They are pure trash. There isn't one of them worth a plug nickel." Marla took another sip of wine and watched as Savannah put her plate aside and reached for her wine. "Half of the local jail is filled up with their kinfolk. The girls marry creeps and most of them have been in jail and their husbands have done time one time or another."

Savannah felt protective of Ruby, even though she didn't like her. Maybe she was different than the rest of her family. Perhaps she had she had broken the mold. After all, she had two happy-looking daughters, worked hard and seemed to have brought herself up from this dismal heritage.

Savannah had heard Ruby talking to herself once when she was in the restroom and Ruby didn't know she was in the stall in the end. She was looking in the mirror and talking about a aunt Ada, carrying on a conversation kind of spooky like, when Savannah flushed the toilet and came out to let her know she was there. When she opened the stall door, Ruby was gone.

Marla interrupted her thought. "Ada was the exception. The rest just didn't turn out good. My grandma told me that Ada kind of adopted one of the girls, and it turned out she was the worst."

Savannah appreciated the new look. Her hair was now shiny, clean and styled, blond and silky. That was good. She always took Marla's advice with a grain of salt. She liked Marla, but she was a major gossip and wasn't always entirely credible.

In some ways Savannah was a little defensive. After all, the whole town talked about her own folks in a derogatory way behind their backs, but sucked up to them when they wanted something. She could only make a judgment on what she had in front of her. What she saw was a hard working, somewhat eccentric, semi-desperate woman, trying to make a living in a new area and maybe trying to escape a disreputable past. Who was she to judge?

Chapter Seventeen

Savannah had certainly had her ups and downs with Ruby Ebota, but she had to marvel at how her office had changed for the better. She still missed a lot of work usually with a good excuse, and she had been tardy on several occasions. Nevertheless, the place was definitely shaping up.

After her shopping and hair cut breakthrough, Savannah brought in the package of clothes she had purchased for Ruby's daughters. Ruby came into her office to plan her day and was sitting in front of her desk with a card her youngest had scribbled for her. "Look at the mother's day card, I got." She held up construction paper with some scribbling on it, folded in quarters. Ruby teared up. "Isn't it cute?"

Ruby's demeanor, as usual, touched Savannah, when she talked about her kids. She genuinely found pleasure in their achievements.

"Ruby," Savannah began, " I was at the mall the other day and found these outrageous bargains on kids clothes. I mean, they were just giving them away. I don't have any kids, but I just love to pick out clothes. I bought a little something for your kids." Savannah pulled out the sack and in it was two small boxes – not wrapped. "It's no big deal. I mean they aren't gifts or anything." I just thought you could..." She was at a loss for words.

Ruby opened the packages and looked at Savannah. "Why, Ms. Hart, I can't accept all of this. I..."

Savannah interrupted, "Please, it will make me feel bad it you don't take it. I had a little extra money. I know you are having a hard time. I thought this would help." Savannah said matter-of-factly. "Of course, this is confidential."

Ruby took each outfit out and touched it and held it up. "Why, Ms. Hart, thank you very much, said Ruby in her best talk'n to the white folks grammar. No one ever done nothing like this for me before – except my Aunt Ada. She died a long time ago, but she would have loved my girls to death. She would have sewed dresses for them. . I don't know what to say." Ruby looked down at put the clothes back into the boxes. With tears in her eyes, she looked at Savannah, "My girls will be so happy."

Savannah prayed she wouldn't hug her with those cold, clammy hands. She felt ashamed for thinking that, but she did not like this woman. In some ways, Savannah felt like she had made a breach in the relationship. She had overstepped or did something that wasn't quite right. She couldn't put her finger on it. Although Ruby seemed pleased and was polite, Savannah sensed that Ruby was less than thrilled with these new gifts.

"I'll be sure and have the girls wear these. Thank you, Ms. Hart." Ruby smiled. "I won't tell a soul."

*****

Ruby don' want nothin' from any uppity white bitches.

Chapter Eighteen

"I thought Marla was going to have a stroke when she saw my hair," Savannah laughed as she held the phone up to her ear with her shoulder and zipped up the bag with her new coat in it. She talked while she hung up her coat in the second closet where she stored her winter clothes. She filled Irish in on her week. "You should see the coat I bought. Remember that Ann Klein number I was telling you about. Bought it. Got it for a song. I'll show it to you when you get here."

Savannah was sounding more like herself. The old piss and vinegar Savannah she knew and loved. "What does your hair look like?" Irish asked while she found a comfortable spot on her patio. *Geraniums would be the best this year,* she thought as she stared at the empty flower boxes. *God, it's almost summer, and I haven't even planted my flowers. Better late than never, I guess.*

"It's just a few inches past my shoulders, Champagne highlights or what did Marla say – *platinum."* Savannah imitated Marla's overly dramatic description of her new hair color. "Anyway, there aren't any birds nesting in it any more and I have to say, I feel different."

Irish, not one to waste an opportune moment, asked, "In what way?"

"Just feeling better. You know what I mean?" Savannah retorted sounding vague, but knowing Irish would recognize this as a significant turning point.

Irish's throat caught. The silence between them resembled the nights when Irish was just a little girl and Savannah would come tumbling in her bed, not saying a word, putting her thumb in her mouth and curling up on the pillow next to her. Nothing had to be said, it was just understood.

Red geraniums and bright purple petunias with white border flowers, Irish took a twig and churned the soil – her grandmother would have done this with her hands. She never saw her grandmother or her mother walk by plants that they didn't work the soil, pull off a dead twig, "dead head" the flower or just talk to it. *Course, they would have done it two months ago,* Irish winced.

"Marla knows the Ebota family." Irish's ears perked up as Savannah broke the spell. "She says they are 'a piece of work'." Savannah hedged.

Irish wanted to put Savannah under a swinging light bulb and give her the third degree. *By a piece of work do you mean challenging, Ms. Hart or are we talking about them being a load of pure crap?* Irish had been listening to the Ruby stories for a while and wasn't buying. This Ruby woman sounded half nuts. Irish kept quiet waiting for more.

"I guess their family really had some problems although Ruby has an aunt Ada that was really great. She was a midwife years ago and I guess she died a few years ago." Savannah ventured into uncharted territory. "I guess there was kind of a 'bad seed' sister, lots of trouble."

"So how does Ruby fit into all of this?" Irish brushed the dead leaves off of her potted plant and vowed to water it that very day.

"I don't know. I'll keep you posted," Savannah shut the gate on the conversation, locked it tight and stored the key away for another day. "How are Rosie and the Colonel?" Savannah headed for safer ground. "Any new Ethel stories?"

"Did I tell you about her performance at her infamous dinner party? She sang some little children's song, and I tell you I couldn't look at the Colonel or Rosie for a full five minutes after she sang it. She is the weirdest thing." Irish laughed and sang the song to Savannah who cracked up in spite of herself.

"You and Ethel should take that one on the road."

"Funny. Rosie is completely different. She is amazing. I can't believe she is Ethel's daughter. I'm going to spend more time with her. I'll tell you, when she and the Colonel get together, they are like walking encyclopedias."

Making one more stab, Irish said, "Anything I can research on the Ebota family for you? Rosie lived in Charleston for a time and did some research in the Beaufort area." Irish asked.

"No, I don't think so. Is the Colonel still helping you with the cases?" Savannah countered.

Irish sighed, "Yep, he is. I'm working on an insurance fraud. This dumb jerk is trying to cheat his employer. The old back injury scam. I just want to be there when the fool slips up. Gets a little boring waiting sometimes though. Running things by The Colonel is a big help. He's one of the most interesting men I've ever met."

"You'll get your man, so to speak," Savannah yawned. "It's late; I'm headed to bed. Let's talk tomorrow. We should discuss your plans for your trip home. Oh, and you can fill me in on Jack. Okay?"

"Sure, talk to ya tomorrow." Irish replied.

"Ciao!" Savannah hung up surprised how she had sidestepped the issue of Ruby.

Chapter Nineteen

Ruby struck a match and lit the candle on the dresser and the flame fluttered and came to life. She held the match before her face, gazing into the depths of the fire until her finger betrayed her by giving into the pain. She blew out the match and transferred her gaze to the candle. Staring into the flame she felt the call of primitive times, times across the water and way back before the Christian influence of her Auntie. Gone were the nights and stories of the old times her family had shared before the crackling fireplace at Auntie's farm. Her blood beat to the rhythm of the drums and she could feel her feet move through the dirt as she danced around the fire. Others performed a frenzied dance with her and she caught a glimpse of their faces in the firelight. Her skin was now as black as the others were and her nearly naked body had the smell of untamed musk. The sound of the drums increased and sweat ran off their bodies as they danced until the light began to show itself in the horizon.

The candle was almost completely burned down when Ruby's eyes flickered and she slowly drifted back through the ages and returned from her roots in another continent. She opened a drawer and took out an ancient stone bowl with a smooth elongated rock showing centuries of use. Hidden under her lingerie there was a round tin container filled with white powder and a plastic bag with various ground roots and bark. Ruby chanted, clapped and swayed to music heard only by her as she added the ingredients to the bowl and ground the mixture into a fine powder.

*****

Ma man follow me, follow me, onlys me. Ma man follow me home.

Chapter Twenty

Estelle and Dixie walked together out of Starks bar and stopped at the curb to chat. It was still hot and humid even at 2:30 a.m. Thunder rumbled closer as a summer storm rolled across the city. "Ronnie's on his way, sure you don't want us to see you get to your car, Estelle?" Ronnie was Dixie's husband of three months and they were both working hard to save up for a little house of their own, but not in Atlanta. Ronnie had family in Alabama and could hardly wait to show off his new bride to the folk's back home. It was going to be the small town life for them. Dixie was a little blond cutie and way too good for the bar life. Just ask Ronnie. He couldn't believe his good fortune.

"Nah, thanks anyway, my old clunker's just up the block. I got me a little after hour's gig then I'm home free until Monday." Estelle knew Dixie didn't approve of Estelle taking chances like she did. What Dixie didn't understand was there weren't a lot of opportunities for a soon to be middle-aged gal like herself. She didn't have a man to care for her, and if she had to make a few extra dollars on her back, well she just had to that's all there was to it. Not that Dixie was a snob, just a worrier. *She'll be a great mom.*

"See ya'll next week, hon." Estelle flipped her cigarette in the gutter and headed down the street for her car swinging her ample ass. Her red leather mini skirt showed off her legs to their greatest advantage. She needed to move along if she was going to be on time. The guy waiting for her at his motel had to be on an early flight out, so she didn't want to keep him waiting. She'd make an extra hundred tonight and for an hour or maybe less of her time. *Depends how long he can keep his business up.*

Estelle turned back at the sound of a car toot. *There's Ronnie right on time for Dixie. Lucky little gal. Those two will have a house full of babies before long,* she thought wistfully. Estelle reflected how different her life might have been if...*well I still have some fine long legs, round bouncy ass and some great tits. That big hunk of a man, Tremaine, sure does like my legs wrapped up around his neck and his nose in paradise. He must be about sick of that mean bitch, Ruby. Who knows maybe he'll dump her and we can have ourselves some real fun. Don't know what a guy like him sees in her anyway.*

As she approached her car, Estelle looked up toward the sky and saw the lightning quickly moving in closer with every flash. The wind was accelerating as the storm drew nearer. The breezes felt so good on her hot skin. The sounds of the rapidly moving storm blocked out any noise around her. A dark shadow detached itself from the side of the building in the alley she had just walked by. The shadow moved along behind her, but Estelle was concentrating on getting to her car before the rain began. When she reached her car she bent down slightly to insert her key in the lock.

*****

Raindrops splatters into her sightless eyes, but she no longer blinks. The rain runs down her face and into the long gash across her neck, washing her blood into a pool around her head. Lightning streaks across the Atlanta skyline and loud claps of thunder follow but Estelle no longer sees.

*****

Evil bad girl goes to cold grave for touchin' ma man.

Chapter Twenty-One

The apartment building was sizzling today. Ethel had been on a building inspection as she called it. She had stringent requirements for the superintendent whatever the latest one's name was. *They don't last long around here* thought Irish. Ethel told her this one had a bottle hidden in the basement workshop and she would ferret it out sooner or later. It was bad news for him when she found his cache. The good news was Ethel ran a tight ship. The building was always clean and well maintained. Irish suspected the recent upgrades to the building must have set her back considerably; however, her rents were a little steep even for this historic neighborhood. Irish was certain Ethel was running the building in the black. *More power to her, spunky old gal.* .

Ethel timed these inspections of hers so she would end up in the lobby just about the time residents were leaving for work. She was dressed in dark gray slacks, matching belt, a long sleeved white blouse and pale pink sweater around her shoulders. Every hair was in place, held down with enough hairspray to give any self-respecting environmentalist a coronary. Surprisingly, Ethel did an okay job with her makeup. She had the savvy not to overdo it. She didn't try to enlarge her mean looking little lips or make the round apple cheeks so many older women went in for. Still, by late afternoon she would have lipstick oozing in the lines around her mouth and no amount of makeup could hide her wrinkles at any time of the day.

Ethel would have a "to do" list all made out for the super when he arrived for work and perhaps wrangle a compliment from that nice Dr. Drake on the 4th floor. He had figured Ethel out from the first day he'd come to view the unit. It was "you oughta be in pictures, my your hair looks extra nice today, what classic taste you have in clothes." *Oh yeah,* thought Irish, *this guy is smooth.* He had Ethel eating out of his hand. She perked up at the mere mention of Dr. Drake or as Irish had noticed anyone who fed her a line of flattery. If the adulator was a man, and they always were, Ethel zeroed in on them and planted land mines to trap them at every opportunity. Irish didn't think she had gotten lucky yet!

The Doctor was young, average looking except for his boyish grin. He was clearly practicing his bedside manner on Ethel and Irish figured he would move from being a resident at a nearby hospital to his own practice before long. He had confided in her that he was looking for a partner already. She didn't doubt that he was a reputable doctor but his gift for gab wouldn't hurt either.

"Perverts, I mean it, perverts," Ethel's husky smoker's voice surprised her from behind as this time she was lurking by the mailboxes "You were out running at dawn today. You need to watch out for perverts. They're everywhere. Where are you off to so fast? Come by for a drink tonight and we can have a nice little visit." Yeah, her daughter Rosie must have wrangled a way to ditch her tonight. *Not a chance Ethel.*

"Gotta run, Ethel. Insurance case, *don't give any more info than you need to,* thought Irish. I don't know when I'll be back, it might be late." *Who needs a security guard when we have Ethel?* Between the locked entry, the phone entry system and Ethel, the building was safer than a bank vault. *God help the unsuspecting burglar or pervert that ran afoul of Ethel. Savannah should have an Ethel at her security desk. Old Ethel would have Ruby going down the road in record time* Irish laughed to herself.

*****

Hours later as Irish sat cramped and cold in her car she questioned her instincts. It had been a dismal, wet day with no results. Springtime in Oregon could be a long, damp season and today was a good example. Irish had parked almost a block up the street from the suspect's house. She had to pee, big time, and there was not even a gas station in this small residential neighborhood of NE. Her long legs were beginning to cramp from sitting in one position so long. Irish longed to get out and stretch but didn't want to draw attention to her presence. She wore old sweats, little makeup and had pinned her hair up and into an oversized baseball cap. *Damn, I'm sure this guy is going to slip up and I want to be there to catch him in the act.*

Ever since she had opened her own P. I. agency, Sullivan Investigative Services, she had maintained an excellent relationship with her former employer Gus Russo the founder of Russo & Sons Private Investigators. He was an old softie, who took her under his wing and taught her the "ins" and "outs" of the business. Gus funneled her work when he had an overflow as he put it. She knew he was slipping her a few extra cases to help her along. Irish respected his trust and always gave 150% to everything she did. A positive result from this case Gus had recommended her for could help establish her reputation with a major moving and storage account.

The guy under surveillance, Joe Bradley, was suspected of perpetrating an alleged back injury following a recent disciplinary action due to his driving record. Bradley was on thin ice with the company and one more blemish on his driving record would mean his termination. There were no witnesses to the injury and the company suspected the Worker's Comp. claim was fraudulent. Bradley had fooled the doctors up until now and Irish was here to obtain a record, on film, of him performing an act inconsistent with his alleged injury. Irish had established that he was divorced and his two children lived with his ex-wife. The guy was a loner and suspected of also having a drinking problem.

Coupled with a short fuse toward his co-workers this made for a fun kinda guy.

A few minutes after 4 p.m. the sun came out and so at last did Bradley. He came out of his little two-bedroom bungalow and headed for the one-car, detached garage. Irish slid down in her seat and had her Nikon N80 camera up and snapping shots of him the minute he had come out of the door. She had an 80-400-zoom lens on the camera and could get the pictures she needed at this distance. *It's a miracle,* thought Irish. *He's able to get around without his back-brace, and what about the painful limp I read about in his file? A few more minutes, Bradley, and I would have been gone for the day. Now I've gotcha.*

He looked around and seeing the street was quiet he raised the garage door and attempted to roll out the large green trash container. One wheel appeared to be sticking and Irish got a good shot of him wrestling with the container. At one point it looked as if he had lifted the container up off the cement. *These photos will expose him for the scammer he is, big time.* Irish had invested in excess of two grand in this camera equipment. It was a necessary tool of the trade. It didn't take a zoom lens for her to get a good look at him. Joe Bradley was close to six feet tall, red faced, balding and a nasty beer gut hanging over his baggy pants. His dirty well-worn tee shirt didn't quite cover his gut and the waist of his pants was located somewhere under the expanse of his stomach. When he bent over to inspect the wheel Irish got a revealing shot. In full view was his "Dan Aykroyd repairman's crack" exposed for all to see with his pants headed into the danger zone. He had to yank his pants up often to prevent losing them completely. The wheel on the trash container refused to co-operate so Bradley had to half carry it down to the pick-up area. *Perfect timing,* thought Irish.

Having completed this chore, Bradley went back to the garage bent over without even wincing from the painful action and pulled the concrete blocks from behind the back wheels of an old Pontiac Firebird. He set the blocks aside, climbed into the car and backed out onto the driveway. After putting the blocks back behind the back wheels, he opened the trunk and took out a jack. He jacked up the Firebird and began to change a tire. *The tires are definitely oversized, too, not stock, that's for sure.* She had a perfect view of him changing the front passenger-side tire, which was in plain view from her vantage point. After what appeared to take some concerted effort on his part, Bradley pried off the old tire, rolled a replacement tire out of the garage and installed it on the car.

When he finished with the car he pulled back into the garage, took another look up and down the street, appeared satisfied and returned to the house. Irish watched the house for a couple more minutes and then turned her attention to packing-up her camera and heading for her office. By the time she had written her report it would be time to call it a day. She had a date for drinks with The Colonel tonight at 7 p.m. and she was looking forward to spending an enjoyable evening with him. She preferred his company to that of most men half his age. The Colonel not only told exciting stories of his days in the Marine Corps, but he kept up with current world events better than anyone in her circle of friends.

Irish reached to turn the key in the ignition when a huge, red and angry face appeared at the driver's side window. It was Joe Bradley and he was furious. He attempted to open the car door, but thank God she had locked it. As he pounded on the glass with his ham-bone sized fists, Irish searched for the car keys she had dropped to the floorboard when this maniac had startled her. *There, I've got the keys.* She jammed the key into the ignition, but the steering wheel was locked. After jerking it loose, she started the car and jammed the shift into reverse instead of going forward. She backed the car up about a half a block laying mega rubber on the street before taking off around the corner. This had been the edge she needed to throw Bradley off balance and give her a few seconds to get away. Irish suspected that in a fight she could hold her own with "old beer gut," but at what cost to her camera and the damaging evidence? She wasn't sure how he had sneaked out of the house and come up behind her, but he had spotted her somehow and made his move. That took quicker thinking than she would have given him credit for. Well, she was on her way now and no harm done except to her ego. She had some nice results, too, for Bradley's employer. This might be the "in" she needed.

*****

Irish leaned back against the large plush sofa and sipped the glass of brandy just handed to her by The Colonel. "Thank you sir. This is a far more pleasant way to spend time than the case I was on today." His apartment was decorated in comfortable warm and manly tones and furnishings. He had expensive taste and memorabilia from his long and eventful career, which filled the apartment. Bookcases filled with leather-bound books lined the walls and a Civil War Southern officer's sword hung above the brick fireplace. Only the top floor penthouses had fireplaces and on a cold wet evening such as tonight, it was a welcome reminder of Irish's roots.

"Please tell me all about it, my dear, I am longing to hear the details," as he leaned forward in his large well-worn leather armchair. He eyed Irish from under his bushy eyebrows appreciating her loveliness, as a younger, more inexperienced man might not. Oh, they wouldn't miss her beauty and sex appeal, but this woman had style and character, a total combination of womanhood that was unsurpassed. The Colonel stretched out his long legs and felt a longing he had not felt in years. If he were a few years younger, wouldn't she be surprised to know where his thoughts had gone?

"It began as a routine surveillance but nearly turned into a disability claim – for me!" Irish gave an entirely factual accounting of the day, up to and including what she felt was her failure of underestimating the suspect. The Colonel gave no quarter in his subsequent remarks even where she was concerned. She deserved his gentle criticism and some of his pointers might save her from repeating the same type of incident in the future. Irish got a brief glimpse of what his troops must have received the full brunt of. The difference was she welcomed his comments and advice. Her mind drifted and she wished he were not almost triple her age! If she could find a man like this her own age, she might consider a commitment. *Once I do, the evening will not be ending with a quiet glass of brandy,* Irish promised herself.

Chapter Twenty-Two

"Vivian, hold all my calls and remember no information to the press," said Savannah.

"Yes, ma'am."

Savannah and Peggy had just come from an emergency staff meeting. They had no sooner closed the door and sat down when Savannah's mobile rang.

"Hey, it's me," said Irish. "I just turned on the morning news and saw that there was another woman murdered. Looks like the media is all over you guys again."

"Yeah, big time. Peg and I just came from briefing the staff again on the importance of 'no comment.' The reporters and cameras are coming out of the woodwork again. I feel so sorry for Amelia's mother having to relive all the pain of seeing her daughter's death on the news once more. It's disgusting the way they give a sick killer a title. 'Call Girl Killer' strikes again. To say nothing of what it does to our operation here. Bastards. The cops are coming back again to question us. Another visit from Benson and his lecherous companion no doubt."

"The cops have to keep digging until they get a lead. Sounds like they don't have much to go on. Dead women lying on the ground with their throats cut. They're after some guy who doesn't rape them so, no semen left behind, no DNA. The only links so far, at least that they are releasing, are that the women were prostitutes and had their throats cut. They'll beat the bushes until they get a break. It could be a lot of leg work before that happens."

"I know but it doesn't make our job any easier. But what the heck, who said it would be easy."

"Listen I won't keep ya. Just wanted to check in. Hang in their kid and say Hey to Peg for me."

"Will do, love ya."

Chapter Twenty-Three

I'm definitely rakin' in the bucks, Nicole thought as she tucked another five hundred dollars in her purse. This was the easiest money she'd ever made, all for a few lap dances, some kinky sex, short sprints with the older Johns who usually went off quickly and then, of course, the basic blowjobs.

Nicole pirouetted in front of the mirror in her apartment. *It's all about me,* she giggled at her reflection. Frowning she wondered why Tremaine had called. She hoped she wasn't in trouble with him. She knew enough about people to know that you never crossed a Tremaine, a Doris or a Ruby unless you wanted to end up dead in some alley, like those other women. *God, I knew Estelle and she's dead just like that black chick who was killed. I could use a big man like that hunk, Tremaine. Damn, I hope he's ain't mad or nothing.*

She called Tremaine on his cell phone. He had said he was out and she could call him as soon as she got home. He had flat out told her not to bother Ruby. "Hey, Tremaine, it's Nicky, what's up?" Nicole tried to sound casual but in her heart she was afraid someone had complained to him. She had pleased numerous men in the last few weeks and no one seemed unhappy. In this business, you never know. Someone could get ticked.

"Nicky," Tremaine yelled into the receiver. "Nicky, how are ya baby?" Tremaine's voice was husky.

"Had a good night. I have your share all ready to go." Nicole wondered if he was checking on her. She had never kept an extra cent. She was real interested in living to be twenty-four.

"Oh, Nicky, I know ya do, honey. Ya always pay up right away. We been hearin' good things about little Nicky." Tremaine laughed loudly. "That Nicky, she somethin'. That's what everyone says. That true, baby?" Tremaine asked.

Nicole was flattered. She wasn't in trouble. "Hey, keep em happy, right Tremaine?" Nicky laughed then sobered and said, "Guess I'm a little scared about the murders. You know, we sorta knew Estelle."

"Now, baby, don't you worry your pretty little body none. You gotta big Daddy to take care ya," said Tremaine like the slick con man he was. *Good thing this whore don' know about Amelia being one o' my old gals or she really would piss herself. Gotta keep a moneymaker like this one away from all my trash whores, so she don' get jumpy,* he thought proud of his business sense.

"So what cha doin' now, baby. Maybe daddy would like to try out the merchandise, too." Tremaine asked.

Nicole could hear traffic sounds on the phone. He must be in the car driving around. She wouldn't mind some time with the big guy. Never hurt to please your boss. In her haze, she had forgotten one critical point of "hands off" driven home by Ruby the first night they met. "When?" Nicole looked at herself in the mirror as she waited for his reply.

"About 10 minutes." Tremaine, hung up the phone, made a u-turn and headed for Nicole's.

Chapter Twenty-Four

Irish waited for Savannah to answer the phone. Feeling feisty, she couldn't resist teasing Savannah, "Just calling to find out the latest Ruby story and/or crisis? Has she been beaten, raped or tortured yet this week?"

"Very funny, you don't have to hear, or try not to hear her wild tales, every day." groaned Savannah.

"Neither do you missy, fire her ass like I've been saying from the beginning. I know, I know, she has a hard luck story for every scenario. How is she getting along with the rest of the staff? Don't tell me they hang at the water cooler with her or share their PB & J sandwiches? Bet she uses witchcraft to keep them in line." Irish says this good-naturedly but with a slightly serious undertone. The sooner Ruby is out of Savannah's life the better.

"Funny, that makes me think of an incident with Vivian the other day. She's our receptionist."

"I remember her, so what happened?"

"Oh, nothing much but I need to remember to ask her what she wanted to talk to me about. She was standing in the doorway to my office and asked if I had a minute to talk to her when Ruby came up behind her. Ruby moves as silently as a snake. You never know when she'll pop up," Savannah shivered. "Vivian's a nice girl, she's doing real well – course we said that about Amelia."

Irish cuts in. "Get on with the story and leave out the social injustice spiel, I'm not making a donation."

"Vivian already appeared nervous as it was, but about that time Ruby walked up behind her and spoke, 'Ms Hart, may I interrupt for a second?' was all she said, but Vivian jumped like she was scared to death, made an excuse that it was nothing important and fled. Ruby didn't want a damn thing. At the time I thought she was just being nosey, but now I wonder," says Savannah.

"Like I've been telling you she sounds like bad news, Savannah"

"Thanks for the diagnosis Dr. Freud. I guess we are all a little jumpy since there is a real serial killer on the prowl. The hair stood up on my neck a couple of times on the way to my car lately." Savannah hated admitting her skittishness. She had "taken back the night" many years ago and usually wasn't scared of anything.

"I know you are trying to side track me, but I'm not falling. You can do something about Ruby, she is right under your nose. The killer is probably some impotent, middle-aged mother hater - that's what the police always say - who just kills pitiful prostitutes not do-goodie, social workers. Hey, not to change the subject, but I caught old beer gut in the act. The guy…"

Chapter Twenty-Five

Hmm, that feels so good, Irish thought to herself referring to the afternoon breeze as it gently caressed her face. *No more sun for this face or I'll be able to play "connect the dots" with the freckles on my nose.* Like most redheads Irish had numerous freckles on her arms and legs but in her case very few on her face. She wore sunglasses and a billed cap pulled down as far as possible with her hair in a ponytail hanging out over the small strap on the back of the cap. She wore her usual summer garb of white shorts, a tee and sneakers.

Having zipped through her Saturday morning errands and apartment cleaning chores, she was relaxing on her balcony with a cold bottle of beer and her big orange cat Beau. Her tiny balcony was no more than a 4 ½ X 10 feet opening off the living room. Irish was lying on a folding chaise lounge, which meant she had to shove the tiny round ice cream parlor table and two chairs to one side to make room. The balcony was microscopic compared to the veranda on her parent's home in North Carolina. *Funny how your priorities change when you're on your own.* Her little apartment suited her just fine. She had added her own special touches to make it unique. Irish had developed a fondness for the "shabby chic" look and would often spend her leisure time in the eclectic Sellwood antique malls searching for just the right piece of wrought iron or an architectural molding, formerly known as junk, to decorate her nest.

Irish's thoughts were drifting here and there touching down like a dragonfly on the lake where she and her Father used to fish on Saturdays. She frowned as she thought of the conversation she had with Savannah last night. *That girl just worries me. Oh boy, now I am beginning to sound like Martha,* the old housekeeper from her childhood. Irish was always "worrying" Martha that's for sure with her tomboy ways. Irish did not believe Savannah was being totally honest about her concerns regarding Ruby, her somewhat mysterious office manager. *That's not exactly right either,* thought Irish, *maybe she isn't taking a good look at the problem,* but Irish smelled a rat. *After all she was a hotshot private eye, right? Okay, so Savannah is still busted up over losing Tommy and not thinking clearly as usual. I saw that the last time I was home.* The pain was razor sharp when it hit her that she also would never see Tommy again. It caught her off guard, nearly took her breath away for a minute. When she was back home for Tommy's funeral, she and her mother had a damn good cry alone together. They stayed strong for Irish's father and sometimes even for Savannah. Although Savannah had made great strides, she still definitely had her moments.

Irish glanced down toward the street and saw Rosie, Ethel's daughter, pull her car up into the loading zone. Rosie climbed out, took a deep breath, straightened her shoulders and began to unload packages for Ethel. "Rosie, hang on I'll come down and give you a hand." Irish called and waved. Rosie gave a wave back and Irish stood up wrecking Beau's resting-place. "Sorry baby," she murmured. She ran down the stairs two at a time and reached Rosie's car just as she was unloading the last bag.

"Bought the store out?" She asked jokingly.

"I tried to," answered Rosie, "It beats taking Ethel with me for two or three items."

"I'll bet, I mean," stammered Irish. Visions of Ethel behind a shopping cart issuing commands flashed before her eyes. It must have been funny when the no smoking law went into effect at the market. The clerk that first told her to snuff out her cig. must now be wearing cement overshoes.

"Never mind, I know what you mean," laughed Rosie.

As they carried Ethel's groceries up the walk and through the courtyard Irish asked, "Would you have a few minutes to come up, when your are finished with your mom?"

"I'm never finished with Ethel," as she called her when not in her presence, "but I would love to. What's up?"

"It sounds a little silly when I say it out loud. I'm concerned about some of the things happening at my friend Savannah's office, there's a little voodoo or something going on, and I thought you might give me a take on the history."

"Let me put Ethel's groceries away and I'll be up in a few," replied Rosie as if it were no big deal to get away from Ethel.

Irish had made a surprisingly fast break from Ethel, who was zeroed in on checking to see if Rosie had purchased all the correct brands. Fortunately for her, Ethel had trouble concentrating on two things at the same time.

By the time Rosie tapped at Irish's door, Irish had folded up the chaise lounge and rearranged the table and chairs so they could enjoy sitting on the balcony. Irish opened the door, invited Rosie in and asked her if she would like a cold drink.

"What do you have?" Irish went through the list of juices, iced tea, and beer. Rosie stopped her at the beer. "Beer, in the bottle, would be perfect. I could use a little boost. I'm taking Ethel for an early dinner in a while. Either she's in a bigger snit than usual or I'm on a short string today. Enough about that, tell me about Savannah." They were both mindful of the fact Ethel would be hot on Rosie's trail before long. No way would Ethel appreciate Irish cutting into *her* time.

Irish pulled two bottles of beer from the refrigerator, popped the caps and handed one to Rosie. They made themselves comfortable on the balcony and then Irish was at a loss for a moment.

"Okay, when Savannah and I were on the phone recently, she casually mentioned she found a funny little bag about the size of an almond in her desk drawer. It had a smelly white powder in it and she just threw it away. Just like that. Didn't check it out. Just dumped it and it could have been poison for all she knew," exclaimed Irish coming up for air. "She was always too trusting. You'd think working with some of the most desperate of people she would have wised up by now, but no - she still gets burned. She hired this woman named Ruby Ebota to replace the office manager that was murdered. Some of the things I'm hearing about her creeps me out. Not to mention she has some of the staff in Savannah's office jumpy." Irish stopped to catch her breath and organize her thoughts.

Rosie could tell that Irish was really worried about her friend because she was generally so clear and matter of fact. "What do you think I might be able to tell you about the situation?"

"The best I can put together from the little tidbits I got from Savannah over the past few months is that this Ruby is from South Carolina, one of the islands off the coast, St Helena I think. She's African-American and had some family there or something at one time. She's got two little girls and running from some "no good" that beat her, blah, blah, blah."

Rosie interrupts, "Even though Savannah is an experienced professional I'm sure it's difficult for her not give way to compassion especially to someone with children in dire need as it sounds like Ruby was."

"You're right but Ruby's done some other weird things. Every time Savannah gives her an inch she takes a mile. Savannah told me was that this Ruby painted her own office and doorway with some dark blue paint. She decorated her office with African artifacts and played African drum music full blast during lunch. Things like that. It just made her seem a little eccentric until the bag thing, which I think Ruby is responsible for. I remember learning a little about the African-American people of the Sea Islands but history was never my strong suit. You would think coming from the South I would have paid more attention to…"

Rosie cut in "It's like living three miles from Disneyland and never going until you get guests from the mid-west. You always know it's there but you don't take the time."

"Yes, I guess it's like that, but I wanted to see if you could fill me in on some background and beliefs of the African-Americans from that area." Irish picked up a spiral notebook and pen from the balcony table. She had quickly placed them on the table when setting up for Rosie's visit. She would treat this the same as a case and begin a file at the office on Monday since her business didn't warrant a laptop yet.

Rosie took a sip of her beer and got comfortable, "I'll give you a condensed version of the area and its people. Keep in mind that African-Americans did not come to this country of their own free will." Irish listened intently, eager to hear what Rosie had to offer to demystify Ruby. "I'll tell you about what I think makes the Sea Islands off the coast of Georgia and South Carolina so interesting."

"Talk at your usual speed and I'll keep up," said Irish

Rosie nodded, "The slaves brought to that area lived in an isolated condition. Before bridges linked the islands to the mainland, boats were the only form of access. Life on the islands kept them virtually cut off from the rest of the world and for many generations most slaves scarcely saw a white person. For that reason, they were less mixed with other races and retained more of their beliefs, practices and language than any other population in the United States. Their farming skills made them highly coveted by plantation overseers."

Irish raised her eyes from her note taking and took a deep breath. Many white Southerners had a deep sense of guilt over the treatment of the African-Americans at the hands of their ancestors. She continued her note taking without a word; however, the moment did not go unnoticed by Rosie.

"Eventually, they came to be called Gullahs and that also referred to the dialect they spoke, the word most likely born out of a word for Angola. All these conditions and more have made them one of the most studied populations, in our history."

"Where can I get more info about their beliefs and customs?"

"I'll make a list of resources for you. Topping the list is The Penn Center, one of the first schools for freed slaves is located on St Helena Island about six miles from Beaufort. Amazing people that founded that school. Compared to other cultures there are few artifacts or historical sites to preserve their history, but the people survived, produced a language and their own religion right under the noses of their captors. Being from the South, you know most of the hardships the slaves had to endure, but did you know they were not even allowed to bury their dead during the daytime?"

"You're kidding? Why not?"

"A funeral would take away from the endless plantation chores and so the slaves had to bury their dead at night by lantern light. It's no wonder they gravitated to the occult." Rosie paused and took a minute to form her next thoughts.

Irish asked if she would like another beer and Rosie replied, "No thanks, I need a clear head to keep up with Ethel; however, I'll most likely have a stiff shot of brandy after I get home tonight!" She chuckled.

From her eyes you could tell Rosie was quickly making the transition again from thoughts of being Ethel's personal assistant to self-accomplished historian. "Getting back on track, we now come to the part that should interest you and has always fascinated me. As you know I lived in Charleston for several years and in my profession, like yours, we are always curious about people and what they did. Knowing that others believe in certain practices is one thing. Being allowed to see it first hand is another. As you can imagine, any dealings remotely connected with the supernatural are generally kept secret from outsiders. So, it is hard to grasp what practices are really taking place. I know I tried when I lived there. Hit a wall every time I thought I was about to get a glimpse inside."

Rosie stood up and turned her chair away from the sun. She sat back down and began where she had left off, "They have kept their religious customs and over the centuries their beliefs were joined with that of Christianity." Rosie continued, "I'll say we would do well to study more of their herbs and old 'cures.' Their 'witch doctor' or spiritualist is called a 'root doctor,' their charm or 'gris-gris' is called 'the root.' The root doctor could execute or remove 'spells' and 'hexes' for good or evil, administer cures and soothe restless spirits. After the cultivation of indigo died out, Gullah slaves continued to use the blue dye to paint window frames, shutters and porch supports as protection against evil sprits."

Irish's interest is immense about now. "That blue you are talking about on Ruby's door – ten to one – is probably indigo blue. The practice is now thought to be merely a tradition, but she may carry some of the old beliefs. There are all kinds of other things they did."

"Like what?"

"Well for instance, cutting down bedposts so a hag can't perch on them and slip into your man's bed at night and sex'm up," Rosie explained playfully. "A slip skin hag has been believed to slide out of her skin at night and rove around. Believers also decorated graves broken belongings of the dead proclaiming the end of this life. Of course, similar practices are common in many cultures. We all know about King Tut's treasures, however they were to be used in an after life. It's kind of funny, some of the Gullah graves would have telephones or toasters along with dishes-basic everyday items." Rosie grinned. "The thought that some of these practices may still be going on in the area doesn't surprise me."

"It is easy to get caught up in the historical aspect of it. Sorry, if I'm going too much into detail, but the culture is complex and can't be described in simple terms."

"This is great, please don't stop, I'll need all the details I can get if I'm going to convince Savannah to get rid of this woman. She's hell bent on helping her." Irish was quickly taking down everything that Rosie had to relate.

"Ruby may very well believe she is a witch or conjurer and those who believe can be affected by her actions."

"Does it make any difference whether you believe in these root doctors or conjurers?"

"This is a gray area and who of us can really say what works and what doesn't? Reported cases of success with supernatural practices go on through out recorded time and before." Rosie replied thoughtfully. This is a powerful practice and not to be taken too lightly.

"Rosie, I'm so glad we've talked. I really appreciate your time."

"My pleasure, and you can call me anytime, I'll attempt to help analyze Ruby's conduct within the context of the Gullah culture. It certainly wouldn't hurt for Savannah to keep a careful eye on Ruby, just in case. She may have it in for her for any number of reasons but I wouldn't be overly alarmed at this point if I were you. It's possible that she is dabbling in "the root" for silly love potions and would-be hexes. She may hate authority figures. Not to mention young white authority figures. It does seem blatant but…

As if a timer went off, Irish's phone rang. Both women looked at one another, "Ethel" they exclaimed. Sure enough, "Irish would you please send Rosie home? She is supposed to take me out to dinner and I'm still w-a-i-t-i-n-g." The queen had spoken and therefore demanded attention from the court.

"Thanks so much, you've given me a lot to think about." Irish stood up and walked Rosie to the door.

"Like I said call me anytime, in fact, let me write my number down for you."

After Rosie left, Irish went back onto the balcony to reflect on the information Rosie had given her and the possible implications. Irish still trusted her gut feeling that something wasn't right with Ruby. *Duh, if this "root" business doesn't sound like crazy behavior for a 21st century office, I don't* *know what does. Think about it- it's over the top. At the very least she's a con artist.* She also felt Rosie was trying to soft pedal things so as not to worry her. She was determined to get to the bottom of it. She would keep closer track of Savannah and this Ruby person's activities. Now if she could get Savannah to promise to be alert and, more importantly, to make her keep Irish informed as to what was going on. Although getting Savannah to keep her fully informed would be the most difficult part, Irish knew Savannah could match wills with her on any given day.

*****

"Savannah it's me, listen I had a long talk with Ethel's daughter, Rosie. Remember I told you about her? She's a history teacher at University of Portland. Anyway, I asked her about Ruby and she gave me an ear full about the "voodoo-root magic", whatever practices that Ruby is up to. Rosie even seems to think it would be worth keeping an eye on her, her words, not mine. Call me when you get in so I can fill you in. With any luck Ruby will mix up her 'powders' and make herself disappear. Did I say you need to dump her? Okay. Love ya."

Chapter Twenty-Six

June

"Morning Glory," Savannah laughed as she heard Irish answer the phone in her sleepy voice.

"Must have had an *all nighter* with Jack, huh?"

"You certainly sound chipper." Irish groaned as she put the coffee pot on. "No, actually, no such luck with Jack. If you could see me now, you'd know why. What a mess. I'm glad you called. I need to get myself pulled together. I'm starting to get some things ready for my trip back home. Did you buy that gun we talked about?" Irish pursued a subject that she knew Savannah would just as soon not discuss.

"No way. I'm waiting until you get here." Savannah couldn't even imagine purchasing a gun, let alone shooting one, but Irish had been adamant about her at least learning the basics.

Irish had learned how to handle a gun practically from the day she could hold one. "I'm going to get you started when I'm back home. They have some great trainers in the Atlanta area. I don't expect you to become a sharp shooter, but I do think you should at least know how to protect yourself. Have you had an opportunity to go over that info I e-mailed you about Ruby? All that stuff I got from Rosie?"

"I did."

"And?"

"Thank you."

Irish didn't say out loud that the more she added up all the conditions surrounding Savannah right now the more concerned she was. A serial killer running loose in the city and the fact that Savannah had mentioned on two occasions she felt like she was being followed. Savannah's office was in a really bad area.

Irish continued, "Remember in March when I was coming back from parking my car. We need to be able to take care of ourselves." Both Irish and Catherine were strong women who not only could physically take care of themselves in a pinch, but who were perfectly capable of defending themselves with a gun if they needed to. Irish poured herself a cup of coffee while the pot was still perking.

Irish found a leftover "mini-moo" and poured it into her coffee. "I talked to Mom. She said Dad has had a really rough week, and she has been up almost every night with him. She's really looking forward to us coming over. She loved the idea that we would all have dinner in Atlanta at the end of the week and that Peggy was going to join us at the Georgian Terrace. Did I tell you Mom got a new Saab convertible?"

"What color?"

"Black. We always end up with black cars, but you can bet it is a beauty." Irish could just see her mother sailing along on the highway with hair flying in the breeze – no scarf for Catherine – just the freedom of the wind blowing through her hair. Irish laughed to herself thinking of the scene in *Terms of Endearment* when, unlike Catherine, Shirley McLaine's head was covered with a scarf while she was riding along the beach in Nicholson's convertible. "So, I'm traveling light and I'm sitting in the front of the plane. I'll be the first one off and in the terminal 5:30 sharp."

"Can't wait to see ya. We have a lot of catching up to do." Savannah petted Lily who was curled up next to her. " Lily said she wanted to see ya, too. She wants to know if you could bring that good-looking dude cat, Beau, along with ya." Savannah laughed as Lily's purr kept getting louder. "I have to work a little bit while you are here, but I'll be ready to head over to your folks on Wednesday. I had thought about seeing Mom and Dad, but they are staying at their place at the Isle of Hope. I'll just hang out with your family." *What else is new?* thought Savannah.

"I've gotta get going, too. Won't it be great when I get there? Let's plan on doing breakfast at La Madeleine's like usual okay? Maybe pick up a Krispie Kreme to tide us over until we get to the strawberries with all that French cream over them." Irish wished she was there right now and was getting ready to polish off the perfect French breakfast of strong coffee with hard-crunchy rolls and thick butter topped off with fresh fruit and the light, creamy, spinach quiche just enough for one.

Irish opened up her refrigerator and looked at the empty shelves. "I'm starving. You should see my refrigerator. One wilted head of lettuce, twenty bottles of water and some really scary leftovers. Something here looks like a lab experiment - green, fuzzy – yuk."

Savannah laughed knowing that Irish, for all her wonderful traits, was not exactly Martha Stewart around the house. "So is Ethel watching Beau while you're gone?"

"Ha. That would be the day. I could imagine her snooping through everything. She probably does anyway when I'm gone." Irish suspected Ethel went into the apartments when the tenants were gone and she was sure she wasn't an exception. "God, I'll have to parachute out my window to avoid her."

"Good luck." Savannah laughed. "You have your very own private eye-security guard right in the building."

"Lucky me." Irish groaned. "Gotta go. Call me."

*****

Savannah was happier than she had been in a long time knowing that she would be seeing Irish soon. She really missed her. It was great to just lie on the sofa with Lily, Savannah thought as she fluffed her favorite pillow and stretched out. Evidently, Lily thought so, too because by now she was on her back, stretched out with all fours up in the air purring her little brains out. "What a life, Lily. To be a cat with nothing to do all day but take care of my creature comforts." *This is definitely moving into a morning nap.*

Usually, she and Tommy would be heading out for breakfast and then some errands together, but all she had today were her memories of him. Going back home to the place where Tommy was born and spending time with his family would feel good in some ways. Unfortunately, thinking about Tommy brought with it some really sad memories, including the most painful one of all. How could she have felt so upbeat minutes before and then be hit with this? She could almost smell the pine wreath as it hung on her front door. It was two weeks before Christmas and they had fashioned their decorations after an *Architectural Digest Perfect Christmas* picture Tommy had saved from the year before.

They had decorated the tree the night before and the house was chilled from just using the fireplace and not turning the heat on. The day Tommy died was permanently etched in her brain. Savannah knew there was something wrong the moment she awoke. That brief second before she was fully awake filled her with icy dread. As she turned over, she realized that Tommy was not moving, not breathing.

Savannah called his name "Tommy" once in a normal tone of voice. She called his name once again. No answer. She began to scream his name over and over. Silence. "Tommy, Tommy, Tommy...." She knew but would not, could not, believe. She grabbed the phone and dialed 911. When the emergency operator asked the nature of her call she told her that her husband was not breathing and she thought he was dead. Her heart was racing so hard she could barely breathe. Savannah gave her name and address. As soon as she hung up she tried mouth to mouth. It was like two people were talking in her head at the same time. One was the observer, who knew it was too late. She felt from touching his body that *rigor mortise* had set in. Nothing she had ever touched before in her life could prepare her for the way it felt when she moved her hands over his bare skin. Then there was the real Savannah, the woman, wife of six years; lover and friend to the man, she had found cold and stiff by her side and the Savannah, who was trying desperately to hold onto him. This could not be true. Tommy was not dead.

Savannah hardly had time to grab a robe and get to the front door before the paramedics arrived. "Hurry, hurry," she screamed, "this way," as she led the way to the bedroom still trying to believe they would bring back precious life to Tommy. Tears streamed down her face and her eyes were pleading them to find a spark of life. After the paramedics, came the fire truck and ambulance. The observer in her had always wondered why they sent a fire truck. One of the paramedics named John had led her away from the bedroom and into the kitchen. In a few minutes one of his partners came out of the bedroom and spoke quietly to John. Savannah never did know, or if she did, she couldn't remember any of the other paramedic's names. She had been sitting at the dining room table, feeling as exhausted as if she had run miles. As John walked back over to the table, Savannah rose from her chair eyes searching his face for an answer that would offer some hope.

"Please," she begged, "please." It was not to be. Just like that Tommy was gone and he was never coming back. From that day forward she would learn that the most difficult thing in the world was to stand and hurt and not be able to stop the pain or change the way things really are. She had never had to face anything like she would now.

Savannah took a deep breath, went to the kitchen and put on water for coffee. John offered to make coffee; however, she knew that if she did not do something she was going to scream. As John and Savannah were sitting in the dining room having a cup of strong black coffee two police officers arrived and went directly to the bedroom. John excused himself in an apologetic voice and joined them.

A few minutes passed and he returned with the two policemen. Savannah remembered John was tall, clean-shaven and had a crew cut. To this day she could not remember what the police officers, paramedics or anyone else in her home that day looked like. They asked all the usual questions about names, occupations, next of kin and almost all of the rest is a blur. They asked if Tommy always slept in the nude and if they had had sexual relations the night before. "No we did not," she replied. How Savannah would wish later on in the months to come that they had made love one last time. Their questions seemed to be none of their business; however, she knew they must be relevant, so she tried to concentrate and provide them with clear answers.

The coroner arrived and John suggested she stay in the kitchen so that she would not see them take Tommy away. Savannah asked John if they could put one of her own blankets around him so he would not be so cold. He said he would ask. Of course she realized later that would never happen. A sound made her look out the kitchen window and she saw the gurney with the black plastic bag that held

Tommy's body being wheeled out and loaded into the coroner's van. The pain came so swiftly it almost knocked her to her knees. Savannah turned quickly around and squared her shoulders. Her southern upbringing took over and she realized it was time to begin making calls to family and friends. Savannah called Irish first, of course, however she could not speak for several seconds.

When she did Irish hardly recognized her voice. "Savannah is that you?" asked Irish, puzzled.

"Yes, oh Irish how can I tell you?"

Irish exhaled "Just say whatever it is and we'll deal with it."

Savannah and Irish had been so close for so long that even the distance of a continent didn't matter. "Is it Tommy?"

"Yes."

"How bad?" whispered Irish.

Silence.

She knows.

"Dead?"

"Yes." cried Savannah holding her breath. Knowing how Irish felt about her brother made her pain even worse.

Irish asked the cause and Savannah said it must have been his heart. She had never heard anything during the night. "He did not move or cry out or anything. I'm a light sleeper."

Irish understood the full implication of her statement immediately. "Stop, don't go there right now. We will face that together tomorrow. I'll be there on the next possible flight out of Portland. Why don't you call Peggy to come stay with you till I get there? I'll call Mom right now. Are you going to be okay? "

Savannah assured her she would be fine. She was, of course, in shock and did not know it. She also did not perceive that adrenaline would carry her through the next few days and then she would collapse. She would hold her head high until after the funeral and perform all the duties expected of her. Irish would make the dreaded call to Tommy's parents. God, how she cringed when she thought of the pain this news would cause Catherine and John. Irish would help her make the necessary arrangements as soon as she arrived in Atlanta. She wouldn't think of that today, she would concentrate only on calls that duty demanded.

They were to discover that along with Tommy's usual fifth of bourbon, he had ingested five or six sleeping pills. How, when or why he had taken them Savannah would never know. There was no note left behind and in the coroner's report the cause of death was listed as "accidental".

Chapter Twenty-Seven

Ruby lies on her back, hands protecting her face, as Tremaine beats her. Oh, her man do love her so. *He give a better beat'n than Ole Big Daddy ever do. Big Daddy can't poke me no mo. Not where he be. Tremaine be mad cuz he come home and find his Ruby done cut dem bedposts down. Can't let dem hags gits on da posts an wait to climb ma man. They gonna sex him all night they gits in, that fo sure. He a northern black, don know Ruby needs to save him from all dem other spirits, except'n me o'course.*

He's careful not to hit her where it shows, even as angry as Tremaine is he won't mark her for her fine job. He has a good thing going with the bitches Ruby brings him and he's not about to give it up. *Bitch can crawl to work on her knees she messes with me.*

Tremaine lowers the leather belt and asks Ruby " is you had enough girl?"

Tremaine has a hard-on from the good feeling it gives him to see her put in her place. He just wants to ram it into her mouth.

"Not enough of your fine body that fo sure," she answers running her hard, long fingers up his moist legs. Tremaine's naked body glistens in the moonlight streaming in the window. He's worked up a sweat from the effort he's spent beating her.

You ma fine conjure-man, you jess don know it yet but you will baby, you will.

"No more of that stupid old way or I'll beat you till you can't crawl out of here, and then I'll throw you away like the trash you is."

No, baby you never gonna be free o your Ruby.

Tremaine is a little high right now as he does enjoy his Cocaine. He isn't aware of the madness that grows daily in Ruby. If he were, he would never threaten to be rid of her.

Like a cobra ready to strike, Ruby flicks her tongue at the tip of Tremaine's erection and tickles his balls with her tongue. No sweet talk from Tremaine; he jus wants his licken and sticken. When she feels he is about to come in her mouth, she quickly stops and sits over his face rubbing her wet pussy in his mouth. Tremaine pulls hard on her ass and sucks none too gently. Ruby screams as she comes and quickly turns again to slide her pussy on him. She rides him until he gives one last shudder and fills her with his magic juice. Then he throws her aside and reaches for a cigarette. She's not to think he is anything but her master.

*****

From the end of the rumpled bed where she landed, Ruby peers out under her long lashes at Tremaine. She is crazy and crazy about him. *Tremaine mine, someday he gonna crawl to me a beggin me-someday soon. No one takes anything from me no mo.*

Chapter Twenty-Eight

Irish's feet fairly flew down the Yamhill Street hill as she headed toward her destination, Pioneer Square. She needed to catch the Max, Portland's mass transit. Totally out of character, she had over packed. With her dad's gift, workout clothes and other summer wear, she had managed to stuff her "carry on", and her extra large tote. Irish covered several blocks in a few minutes. In her haste, she had not taken time to secure her hair, so the June breezes were having fun with her, sending her hair flying every which way.

Her emerald green, spaghetti-strapped knit top came to her waist, leaving a strip of tan skin between the top and her slim, almost-to-the-waist white slacks. Her grandmother's sapphire ring shone in the sunlight along with her red toenails peeking out of her summer sandals. She had dressed lightly, because she knew that in a few hours she would be standing bone-deep in the Southern summer furnace heat she had grown up with. Atlanta would greet her with a blast of heat, but she was a southern girl, and she was prepared.

Just a half block from her destination, Irish crossed the narrow street with the tracks and picked up her pace when she saw "the Max" pulling up to the square. Almost tripping on an itinerant musician's violin case, she scurried around two "slow-as-molasses", blue-haired women and raced across the street to Pioneer Square.

Pioneer Square served as the city's central meeting place where students, shoppers and the general working lunch crowd could sit outside and enjoy the street vendor's hot dogs, burritos and elephant ears. Today the crowd was enjoying the Latin rhythms of a local Marimba band.

At Christmas, hundreds of Portlanders gathered to light the tree and to listen to the local groups sing carols. All year long, musicians set up their drums and amplifiers and strummed out blues, jazz and rock as the appreciative audience stopped to listen. Predictably, a loud-mouthed, attention-seeking group of teenagers, usually those not in school, showed off their tattoos, and various body piercing. Their public display of affection included, but was not limited to, grinding against each other and standing in the middle of the square in shabby clothes crudely fondling each other's body.

Irish ignored the slew of adolescents hanging close to the kiosk. Purchasing her all zone ticket, she jumped on the train and found her spot, she marveled at the fact that she would be at Portland International within a half an hour and in Atlanta in less than six hours.

The glass and beams surrounding the airport terminal were specially designed to impress travelers. Irish caught her reflection in the glass, stood a little straighter and walked with a sense of confidence to the ticket area.

Irish secured her boarding pass and ID and headed for her gate." She smiled through her tears, thinking of her dad as she boarded the plane, throwing her luggage effortlessly in the top bin. *One for the tall girls* she laughed to herself. She nestled into the window seat and was soon joined by two rather drunk, gawking college boys who smelled like they had been dipped in a beer keg. After two unsuccessful attempts to get her attention, the boys settled down when Irish gave them a choice: clean it up or have a "come to Jesus meeting" with the flight attendant.

The rest of the trip was as non-eventful as the book she read. When she tired of reading she stared out the window into the dark and drifted to nighttime thoughts: *I've lost my only brother and Dad doesn't have long, but on the plus side I have the best women friends in the world, including my own mother Catherine. Then there's Jack, my friend and lover.*

She shook herself and switched gears remembering how happy Rosie was to hear Irish was headed to Atlanta. She had even briefed her on a few points to investigate regarding Ruby's behavior. Although Rosie didn't make a big deal about it, she did express some concern about Ruby having the potential to use her hexes to hurt other people.

I'll get the scoop from little Miss Savannah one way or the other. Depend on it. She's covering for Ruby because of the kids, that's a given. I'm wise to her M. O.

As the plane descended, Irish watched the city lights come into full view. She couldn't wait to see her buddy of so many years. She knew they would be up half the night talking about their families, friends, jobs, Jack, Ethel, the Colonel, Peggy, wild Ruby, their cats, the state of the world, their hopes and dreams along with the usual discussion about Savannah and Peggy coming to Portland to visit. If Irish had her way, she would Shanghai her little buddy and haul her west permanently.

Irish knew Savannah had set up a dinner at the Georgian Terrace with Peggy and Catherine and she looked forward to that evening. She didn't look forward to visiting her dad. She knew he was deteriorating fast; her mom had been pretty blunt about that. Not one for drama, Catherine, nevertheless was a realist and let Irish know how much her dad had changed. Irish suspected nothing would prepare her for seeing her once formidable father looking like people look when they are battling cancer, gaunt and pale. Irish's mom had insisted that she "Candy stripe" one summer at the local hospital. Irish's assignment had been the cancer ward. Little did she know, that this would be a precursor to her own experience with her beloved father.

As the plane skidded to a stop, bumping and bouncing the passengers like a bunch of rag dolls, Irish scoped out her exit. Fortunately, she had the foresight to reserve a front row seat, so it would only be minutes before she would be out the door. Her college boys were fast asleep now in a drunken haze. Irish gave them a quick nudge and suggested they be ready to go. Smelly, half asleep, and semi-conscious, they both listened up and sat ready to spring out the door at the first opportunity

Within minutes, she was standing in the middle of Hartsfield airport terminal headed for the Atlanta Bread Company, she and Savannah's meeting place. There she was, her friend of many years, unabashedly grinning from ear-to-ear, sprinting toward her. Irish put her luggage down and waited for Savannah to give her a huge bear hug. Tears fell on each other's shoulders as the two young women rejoiced in the fact that once again they were like two little peas in a pod providing sustenance for each other.

"Wow, you look gorgeous, Irish. It's great to see you."

"You too, Ms. Savannah!"

It was 3:00 a.m. before they could begin to think about going to sleep. They gave up trying to sleep and talked until dawn. Irish was the first one to wake up. She got up and walked to the door in Savannah's bedroom.

"Okay girl, hit the deck. It's time to go shopping." Irish flipped on the light in Savannah's bedroom.

"Are you nuts? We talked all night. It's still dark out," grumbled Savannah.

"My stomach is screaming for good old southern biscuits and grits. Did I mention I was going to take you to breakfast first?"

"First before what?" Savannah pulled the covers over her head.

"Don't play dumb missy, we're getting you a gun today and signing you up for a class at the shooting range."

Savannah peeked out from under the covers. "Yeah, Yeah, Yeah, where's my coffee?"

"At your service. Here's your coffee in bed, your majesty." Irish set a steaming mug of strong black coffee on the nightstand. "Made from fresh ground Starbucks beans that I found in the refrigerator."

"My God, you're chipper and all ready to go. How long have you been up anyway?"

"Long enough and if I don't get food soon things are gonna get real ugly."

"I hope you get fat." Savannah rolled out of bed and headed for the bathroom thinking, *Just like when we were kids.*

*****

"So show me where you are going to keep your gun." Irish pushed.

"Well, my desk in the spare bedroom has a lock on it and I think that's the safest place, don't you?" Savannah headed down the hall and opened the door to the bedroom Tommy had used for his office. She had only been in the room when absolutely necessary since his death. She even paid bills at the dining room table to avoid seeing his belongings. Straightening her shoulders she walked over to the desk, opened the top drawer, found the key and unlocked a lower drawer.

Irish had noticed Savannah's reaction but did not comment since things were going too well today. She observed that her lifelong friend was much stronger. *The squirt is a survivor* she thought to herself. *She looks like a million too with the new do.*

That morning Irish had finally prodded her best friend out the door and off for a big southern breakfast at the OK Café. While Savannah had been in the shower Irish went through the yellow pages and found "The Gun Merchant" listed close by in Marietta. She also found a shooting range within a reasonable distance. They offered a Basic Handgun Skill Development course and had weekend classes. She made note of all this for Savannah, so she couldn't plead her inability to locate a class.

At the gun store Irish had helped Savannah choose a 38 special Lady Smith & Wesson with rosewood grips. It just sounded a little less deadly when in fact it was the same as the gun Irish used. The only real difference was hers was no Lady and she had rubber grips. No need to bother Savannah with those details. She was squeamish enough.

Savannah slipped the gun and box of cartridges into the drawer, locked it and made a face at Irish. "Happy?"

*****

 The drive back to Irish's folks in North Carolina was a trip down memory lane. They had made this trip so many times together. Savannah, of course, was greeted as one of the family. Before the engine was turned off, John and

Catherine were out in the driveway. The house across the way where Savannah grew up was dead quiet. She hugged both of them, noticing how incredibly thin John was except for his face that seemed bloated from all the medications he was taking.

He put his arms around both of them. "What a sight for sore eyes, you two." John laughed with a glint of tears in his eyes. "We've been waiting. Catherine was even more excited than I was – and that's saying a lot."

"That's absolutely true, girls." Catherine walked behind appreciating having her family together.

"Wouldn't miss it for the world, Dad." Irish smiled at her dad and held back her tears. "Father's day is a day I always remember, because you were the best dad a girl could ever have."

"Me too." Savannah chimed in, relishing John's arm around her shoulder. She knew a year from now that probably would not be happening. She felt as if John were her true father and she loved him as much – if not more – than Tommy had.

"Come sit down on the patio. Catherine, get them a drink, honey. Sweet tea okay?" John barely made it to the back of the house before he had to sit down to catch his breath. Savannah and Irish pretended not to notice when he shakily grabbed the chair and got himself settled.

Savannah listened to Catherine humming as she fixed the sweet tea. As she stood in the Sullivan's back yard, she remembered the night of her graduation party. She could recall it like it was yesterday. Tree toads were yakking away as the Southern night offered a warm breeze lightly dusted with the pungent smell of sub-tropical flowers and trees.

Looking back, she pictured the guests arriving. John and Catherine Sullivan, the hosts for the evening, greeted each guest. Savannah adored everything about Catherine and John. They could have been the Kennedy's as far as she was concerned. They were equally as poised and charming. Savannah loved the way they looked. Catherine, thin and athletic, with little makeup or pretense to cover obvious laugh lines around her eyes and mouth. John typical Irish, burly but not fat, sturdy and still sexy. The sexiness came with the twinkling blue eyes and all of it was saved for the obvious object of his affection, his wife Catherine. He was still enchanted with her after all these years. He was the first to tell anyone willing to listen that he couldn't believe his good fortune in getting someone like Catherine.

Savannah experienced a bittersweet experience when she was with the Sullivan's. Although they had practically raised her and for all practical purposes she was like a daughter to them, the truth was she wasn't their daughter. She was the couple's daughter sitting across the patio from her. Her dad, a successful developer and a political influence in town, would usually take any opportunity to grab the public eye whenever two or more gathered in a public place. Tonight he seemed a little more subdued. Her mother Laurel was speaking in a soft tone earnestly to her father. He, in turn, was whispering back to her. They both had tumblers full of their usual bourbon and water without much water. She was curious about what they were talking about, so she finally walked over to where they were sitting.

Immediately, Savannah knew she had made a mistake, "Well, here comes our little *prima donna* now. I suppose you think the high and mighty Sullivan's did this just for you." Savannah's dad lifted his glass as though to toast her and took a big swig. "Well, I got news for you, little darlin'; they don't even know you are here. Watcha get your Ph.D.

in – what are you now a psychiatrist?" Her father started talking louder.

"MSW, dad, Masters in Social Work," Savannah corrected him. Savannah sat on the edge of her chair trying to think how to make an exit without exciting them. She knew if she angered her dad, there would be a scene. "A psychiatrist is a doctor. That would take years." She knew she had said the wrong thing.

"Well, you are still a shrink, aren't you? I suppose you won't even talk to us now. Saw you sitting over there by yourself. Didn't even have the decency to come over here with us. So, what's the matter? Aren't we good enough for you? I think I did all right, wouldn't you say, dear." He looked at his wife who was non-committal in her response. He put his hand on his wife's arm and pressed it, "Look at me when I'm talking, Laurel. How much did you spend for that dress you are wearing tonight? I bet it didn't come off the rack, now did it? Look at you two. You're pathetic. You'd think the rich and famous Sullivan's could figure out a way to get a guy another drink, wouldn't you?" Her dad held up his empty glass.

Given the perfect opportunity for an exit, Savannah stood up and took the glass, "I'll go get you some more, Dad. I'll be right back. Do you want anything, Mom?" She looked at her mother whose eyes were flat with fear.

"Please, Savannah dear, another Bourbon and water." Her mother handed her over her glass.

Savannah could feel her dad's eyes boring a hole in her back as she walked away. She reached the patio bar to find, in great contrast with her abusive parents, Catherine graciously waiting with a look of concern and compassion in her eyes. "You doing all right, Savannah honey?" Catherine filled the bourbon glasses with more water than bourbon. "Everything okay? Hey, you remember our Tommy, don't you?" And that was it. Savannah looked up to see one of the sexiest men she had ever known looking at her with such obvious joy that all she could do was smile right back at him.

"Well, look at you, Ms. Savannah," Tommy stepped in next to Catherine and took Savannah's hand in his continuing to hold it even after the introduction. "Last time I saw you, you and Irish were raising hell in high school." Tommy laughed quietly and stared at her with the most seductive blue eyes she'd ever seen. Tommy was taller than her by just a few inches. She could feel the heat from his body and she knew he could wrap himself around her just fine. His face was so close to hers that she could smell his cologne and see the light perspiration over his face. Savannah wanted that mouth all over her. His hair was golden from the sun, not pretty boy golden, just a nice medium blond thick and curly from the summer night. His body, muscular and tan was the body of someone who had been working outdoors.

"Hey, Tommy." Savannah tried to sound casual as her heart crawled up into her throat and she thought she would just dispense with all the formalities and tear his clothes off right there and then and jump his bones before he had a chance to say one more word. Catherine took the drinks from Savannah, "I'll take these down to your folks, Savannah. You and Tommy catch up."

"Catch up" was an apt term, thought Savannah as she laid in bed laughing to herself at the way the two of them took off for the weekend, "catching up" for three solid days.

Chapter Twenty-Nine

The trip back home to North Carolina was bittersweet for Irish. Seeing her dad in such dreadful health had fully unnerved her. Savannah had to leave early and Irish could see her tear up as she said goodbye to John. As Irish and Catherine drove back together to Atlanta, Irish could tell her mom was trying to come up with just the right words. She would take a deep breath, start to say something and then be quiet. It seemed as though her thoughts were not quite formed the way she wanted them to be when she said them out loud.

After the second long breath, Catherine finally was ready to discuss what was on her mind. "Your dad is very sick, Irish. Honey, I don't think he will be with us even this Christmas."

The closest conversations they had ever had usually took place in the car as they rode along together. Something about the coziness and safety of the car engendered intimate conversations.

"I know, Mom. I can see it. He's been the best father any daughter could have ever hoped for." Irish faltered as she tried to convey the depth of her love for her father. Although his death was impossible to comprehend, Irish was grateful that her mother could talk openly with her. She appreciated her trusting her with the responsibility of knowing the truth.

Irish knew her mother would miss her dad immensely and would have given anything to be able to take away the pain. "Mom, I promise to come back as often as possible. I'm sorry I'm so far away." Even her beloved Portland couldn't erase the distance that lay between her dad and herself.

Catherine, typically assuring, said, "Don't you worry for a minute about the distance. It's five or six hours by plane, and I wouldn't have you miss your adventure for anything in the world." She parked the car in the Fox theatre parking lot and gave her daughter a nod, letting her know that they would work this out together.

Before they walked from the Fox Theatre parking lot to the Georgian Terrace, they both took deep breaths and Irish on a whim, grabbed Catherine's hand and swung it as they walked down the street. This had always been a little joke between them. It made them both feel light and joyful in each other's company. By the time they arrived at the Georgian Hotel, they were laughing and talking in anticipation of spending a great evening with two of their favorite people, Savannah and Peggy.

The evening was truly textbook Southern, sultry and warm. Onlookers turned their heads as Irish and Catherine joined Savannah and Peggy. The four women, full of life and each one stunning in her own right, were privy to the city scene. As they ordered their drinks for the evening, they watched perfectly coifed older couples, arm in arm, walking toward the Fox Theatre, which was showing a contemporary Carmen. The crowd was mixed: some students learning about opera probably getting a much needed credit for attending; single men and women casually dressed staying downtown after work and showing up for the evening performance; women dragging bored-out-of–their mind husbands; and usually a significant amount of sequined and expensively dressed patrons who were spending the eighth or ninth decade of their lives – perhaps even the last decade – at the opera.

"When I was in Paris," Peggy offered, "one of the most memorable evenings of my life was spent at the opera house just down the street from where we were staying. It was a spine-tingling time, I had just turned 22 and decided to go back to live there for the summer after I graduated from

Columbia. At any rate, at that time, I actually thought I could be another Billy Holiday. I'd always sung, actually my whole family was musical. My mother was a concert pianist and she insisted all of us play piano and sing." Peggy looked up as the waiter brought her Manhattan. "Thank you." She took her drink and continued waiting for everyone to receive their drink, so they could toast the evening.

"I needed some money, so I would just set up shop on the Champs-Elysees. It was really fun. I just found a small space, put down a little box for tips and sang right on the street. It wasn't long before I was offered a little gig in one of the small clubs. Instead of staying three months, I ended up staying a year." She picked up her glass and each one in turn clinked glasses.

"Cheers, to friendship, to Paris, to the Opera, to …" They all started laughing as each one sang out a personal toast and warm thoughts into the evening air.

"You sang in Paris?" Catherine asked curious about Peggy's adventure.

"I did. It was easy then. Although Parisians weren't wild about Americans, in many ways I was treated better there than in America." Peggy continued. "Black men were certainly better received and they were able to move about much more freely in Paris than in the country they had actually defended. I met a lot of men in Paris who had served their country, returned to the cold shoulders of Americans, and came back to Paris where they were much more welcomed."

"Oh, oh, here it comes," kidded Savannah, "Which gorgeous lover did you spend your year in Paris with?" Savannah sipped her Martini and felt the warmth from her drink, the summer night, but most of all from the friendship of the women she loved most.

Peggy laughed into the warm air, filling the night with her rich voice. She was one of those rare people, who when she laughed it started at her toes and worked its way up through her entire body ending in a lustrous rich sound that made everyone around her want to be part of her party. People sitting around them smiled and looked at the table with obvious enjoyment. "He was mighty fine, let me say that, but that is a story for another time." Peggy moved on to her opera story.

"I had been singing at this club for some time and showed up one evening to find it closed down. It just went out of business and no one even bothered to tell me. I mean we aren't talking the Ritz Carlton here." She laughed.

By now the women are enjoying their drinks and are especially enjoying the opportunity to share an evening together entertaining each other with their life stories.

"See that blue sequin dress over there," Peggy nodded toward a blond, who looked like a news anchor who had recently made good. " I found a dress that was almost like that in a second-hand boutique in Paris." The women knew Peggy would get them to the connection to the story and they enjoyed the journey. "Anyway, I was at the club, there was nothing that was going to happen. It was completely shut down. I'd saved every cent that I earned, because I wanted to be able to live out the year there, so I went home and put on this dress that I had bought the week before. It fit me like a glove. I was skinny as a rail then." Peggy patted her stomach laughing at the obvious change.

"I put on the dress, a pair of high-heeled sandals, and I walked into the opera like I owned the place. It was the most exciting evening. Here I was twenty-three years old, all by myself in Paris, feeling quite chic." She smiled. "I had already made up my mind that by the time I was an old lady, I would not regret what I hadn't done. I would make sure I took advantage of every opportunity."

"Isn't that the truth," Catherine chimed in. "I've always used that as my motto. I didn't want to have any regrets later on. I think that's why I took some real chances along the way."

"Mom, what was the biggest risk you ever took?" Irish picked up the conversation.

"Well, let's see. I have lots of stories to tell, but uh." Catherine thought for a minute. "Oh, you gals will love this one. When I was about the same age as you were," she looked at Peggy, "twenty-three, I had just gotten married coming right out of college. I was used to being on my own and getting to do pretty much what I wanted. Boy, was marriage a shock. John had other ideas. He was expecting this nice stay-at-home wife, who followed along doing whatever he wanted. That lasted about six months, and I just met him at the door one day and laid out some ground rules. I would work. I would be a great partner to him, but I would have time to write and to use my journalism degree."

"The most important demand I made was that every year – and I kept this one every year now for almost forty years – I would have a New York City week to myself – catching all the Broadway shows, taking in the sites and most importantly spending one night at The Met. It really set the tone for our whole marriage and actually paved the way for me to have an interesting life. Probably doesn't sound like a big deal now, but believe me women during those years – especially in The South – didn't spend time in NYC by themselves." As the women nodded and obviously enjoyed

Catherine, she also remembered that not many women spent a week with a perfect blond haired, blue eyed-artist, came home pregnant, produced a perfect replica of their relationship, called the little boy Tommy and proceeded to not ever tell a soul.

Catherine quickly moved off a memory that would stay with her until her last breath and continued, "The Metropolitan Opera was my first opera. I was never a debutante type and avoided anything to do with the cotillions and silly stuff like that. I mean all of my girlfriends belonged to Junior League, but I was just never interested." She paused.

"But going to New York City, walking down Fifth Avenue in four inch heels and a sleek, little black number at twenty-three, jostling for space to walk along with a thousand other New Yorkers – even if it was only once a year – was important to me. Still is. I love to go off by myself and John has never interfered in that part of my life. He knows he has my full attention the rest of the time, but that one week – is mine." Catherine exuded the kind of confidence that comes from maturity and wisdom and everyone at the table was mesmerized by her tale. Not one to focus on herself, she quickly added, "Enough about me. Irish, we want to hear more about Portland"

Everyone shifted her attention to the other half of the mother-daughter team. She was as stunning as Catherine, only in a more untamed way. She had done many of the things her mother had only dreamed of. Irish had been less constrained with the Southern ways and although she had loved her mother immensely, she didn't even know how little she really knew her. "I am having a ball living in Portland." Irish smiled. "Course, you've all heard my Ethel stories. My God, that woman is so funny. Love her daughter, Rosie. If Ethel, alias Curella Devile of 101

Dalmatians, could pull it off, she'd have Rosie wrapped around her every whim."

"Didn't you tell me Rosie lived here once?" Savannah asked. "In Charleston or something?"

Irish nodded, "Yeah, she did. She sneaks over to my place to get away from Ethel. She teaches history and knows more about the South than we do. She lived in Charleston for two years. I suspect she had a lover here at one time. I'm working on getting the story, not that it's any of my business. Every time she talks about Charleston she gets all melancholy. You know what The South does to you." Irish laughed, "Course, we all are like that when we find the love of our life." As soon as she said it, she saw the smile freeze on Savannah's face, and Irish wished she could ask the table of friends to *disregard that last dumb remark.*

Peggy interjected, "You know Ruby's family came from down Beaufort way, I think. You all must have heard about Ruby Ebota by now. That woman's got some evil twisted roots I say." She looked at Savannah who seemed distracted.

In fact, all three women were looking at Savannah who had become completely quiet.

"Ruby?" Savannah in her efforts to thwart off the memories of Tommy suddenly left herself wide open for a sucker punch from her nemeses, Ruby. "Oh, yes, dear, creepy Ruby," Savannah recovered. "She's something from another culture all right. I think she's from another planet." Savannah smiled weakly and knew this was not a topic she wanted to entertain for long.

"She painted her doorway indigo blue, which is a part of the Gullah tradition. It's supposed to ward off evil spirits. Has it worked?" Peggy looked over at Savannah and laughed.

Savannah had to admit, "Hardly."

"I hate everything about the way she looks, acts, behaves with the other women. I can barely tolerate her lying. She must think we are so stupid. I know she has children, but this woman is malicious. I know this kind of woman. She is pure evil. She takes anything good and turns it into something that none of us wants to see. She reminds me of the darker, possessed voodoo queens in Louisiana. We don't need her in our office." She shook her head. "I tell you, she gives me the creeps. Savannah knows how I feel about her." Peggy wasn't pulling any punches.

"I told Savannah, she should have dumped her." Irish chimed in. "I checked out some of the info Rosie told me about the weird stuff Ruby's into. It's powerful stuff. Peggy we are countin' on you to get rid of her. Savannah, you listening?"

"I know how much you care about kids, Savannah, but you need to be careful." Catherine advised, "This doesn't sound right. Irish has told me some pretty strange stuff about her. Maybe those girls shouldn't be living with her." Catherine felt her protective forces kicking in. No question about it, Catherine wouldn't blink an eye at tearing into anyone who would ever harm Savannah.

"I got it. I got it, y'all – it's not that bad. She's just a little different, and I'm takin' care of it soon." Savannah's mind rewound to remember all of the weird things Ruby had done. There had been several incidents including the tiny conjure-type bag found in her own desk dismissed and thrown away at the time; the drum beats and chants coming from Ruby's office and the peculiar inch-long indigo blue root she found under the mat underneath her desk chair. *God knows I rolled over it enough times before I had to pull up the mat under my chair to find out what in the hell it was.*

After they sat for a few more minutes, catching up on the latest, they watched the street empty in front of the Fox theatre. The first act of the opera was starting as the women looked around for the waiter. Catherine gathered her purse, left a tip and stood up at the table.

"I'm sorry I have to leave so early, but John is too sick to stay by himself. I have someone staying with him for the day, but I need to head home." She hugged everyone, giving Irish an especially long good-by hug. "You have fun in Portland, honey, ya hear?" Another quick hug, "You girls have a good evening. Next time I'm in Atlanta, we'll get together. Love ya all." Catherine smiled. "And you, missy, you take care of yourself" she kissed Savannah on top of the head. "You call me now, okay? It's great seeing you again, Peggy."

The Terrace was still packed as Catherine made her way around the waiter, who had just arrived to take their order. Catherine still turned a few heads as she moved with grace and poise through the crowded room. She still had it.

*****

Being married to someone like John was a lot harder then it looked, Catherine thought as she drove down the highway with *The Phantom* at full-blast. She smiled as she remembered a story she had heard about Ghandi. Evidently, people were waxing eloquently about how Ghandi had changed the world and as they were going on about his courage and impact, one follower mused, "Do you know how many people it took to make Ghandi look that relaxed in his pursuit of peace making?" *Do you know how many people it takes to make John Sullivan look like a successful host, father, husband?* Catherine was mildly ashamed of herself for such thoughts, especially with John being so sick.

His cancer was cantankerous and simply would not go away. This was a change for John to not control his destiny.

The very thing Catherine loved about John was the thing that nagged at her as well. His power. He was a man who could make anything happen. She could count on one hand the times she had seen him powerless. He was completely devastated when Tommy died, and she suspected that is what triggered the reoccurrence of his cancer. He was truly knocked down for the count with the disease, which these days was the center of influence in his life. Nevertheless, this weekend there would be a dinner party, as though nothing were going on. The food would be delicious, the company lively and stimulating, the garden in full bloom, and she and John in perfect form. That is what they did best. What went on behind the scenes was a bit different.

The focus in Catherine's life had been Irish and Tommy. Actually, as she thought about it, she would have to include Savannah – *somebody had to get busy and raise that child.* In retrospect, Catherine thought, what better way to spend your life than to help others flourish. She could honestly say that she felt great pride in her ability to raise the three of them. Even though Tommy was a mystery in some ways, in her heart and especially in her mind, she knew Tommy was only a visitor – a guest – on earth. He had never really become part of their family or the world at large. It was part of his beauty and yet, she knew it was part of the psychic agony he felt. She was glad she had never told John the truth about Tommy. She had spent her life harboring a secret that she knew was probably a key to Tommy not fitting in. She was glad now that she had never shared her secret with anyone.

John was a smart man, but not particularly complex. He was kind and generous with Irish and with Catherine. The generosity came with a price, which was that the focus remain on him and he would simply take center stage and in return adore her. Adoring to John meant providing and being proud of how she looked. In many ways, this was plenty for Catherine.

In her private moments, she grieved deeply the loss of her cherished son and the imminent death of her husband. Catherine sighed at the weak responses the doctors had given John to his question of "How long?" She hated telling Irish her beloved Father would not even be with them to enjoy Christmas this year.

Catherine cherished the evening with her daughter. Although it was nearly a perfect evening, Catherine experienced a slight foreboding of something wrong. It seemed to have something to do with Savannah. Savannah still seemed troubled. Of course, Savannah was still sad from Tommy's death, but to Catherine, this felt like something more. She had the sense someone was watching them during dinner. *Oh, Good Lord, Catherine, get a grip! Next thing you know you will be seeing killers behind every Magnolia tree.* As Catherine pulled into her driveway, she joined the legion of women, who when they ventured away from home leaving their desperately sick husbands, never knew what they would find upon their return.

Chapter Thirty

At the end of another packed day, Peggy pulled the bottle of brandy from her bottom drawer and found two clean Styrofoam cups. As she was pouring a drink for her and Savannah, she asked "So where was Ruby today?"

Savannah sighed and started to tell her at a minimum the fifth goofy story that Ruby had told her to explain away her absenteeism. The list went on and on, stalker husband, eviction out of her apartment, sleeping in the car with the girls, car crashes, and this time: "She had a court date today to get custody of her daughters."

Peggy laughed, "That's a "Slam Dunk, I wouldn't give Ruby custody of my pet parakeet." Peggy held up the cup for a toast. As their cups touched, she said, "To no more Rubies on the payroll," she held her cup up in the air as though she was appealing to the gods, "Dear God, please." And then she looked at Savannah. "That girl is nothin' but trouble Savannah. The women here almost act scared of her. I know she acts nice when she's around you, but she's evil, Savannah. She is mean and ugly to the core."

"I know. I know." Savannah agreed. This was a sore subject between them. She was still embarrassed that she had given Ruby the clothes and in one of their many talks had told Peggy about it. Peggy could hardly hide her surprise at Savannah being "suckered" in. Unfortunately, lately Savannah realized that Peggy was absolutely right, but Savannah had to admit that she felt like Ruby was trying to control her. She sure as hell wouldn't say that out loud to Peggy. "I'm talkin' to her tomorrow. She has had so many absences that I'm putting her on warning." Savannah didn't relish that task. She didn't want to take the security away from Ruby's daughter and put them back on the street again. If she were perfectly honest with herself, she'd have to admit that she down right didn't trust Ruby. She knew Ruby well enough to know that she would fight and claw all the way. Savannah's instincts told her she didn't want to be in the way of those claws.

Peggy segued into the news of the day. "I heard that detective what's his name called again today. At least he's persistent. Any leads?" Peggy inquired.

The police were looking for a potential serial killer at this point, someone local who was preying on women prostitutes. Nothing new about that." *They are the perfect prey for the beasts out there,* thought Savannah. "Detective Benson called to ask me some more questions about Amelia, but honestly it was just about the same conversation as we had the last time we met. I think he's trying to come up with some clues that tie in the other murder." Savannah had wished she could have helped him more this time, but she couldn't come up with anything.

"What are the women here saying?" Savannah asked Peggy. Peggy was always in the "thick" of things and could take the pulse of the office at any given time.

"They are scared and spooked. I will give Ruby credit; she really pitched in this week and helped the women organize a plan of safety. I asked her to contact the police and see if there is a Public Safety Officer available for safety training. She said they couldn't schedule us for a few weeks, as they are inundated with requests, as you can imagine. Ruby got the girls to give each other their phone numbers, and she is looking into getting some donated phones and maybe some money for emergency calls, so the girls can have a cell phone on them and be better prepared. Ruby has worked hard with every single woman to make sure they had a buddy to call in case they got into trouble. She has the women's phone numbers and is going to check with them in the next few weeks to make sure they are okay. Course, knowing Ruby, she will have created a major crisis in her own life by that time." Peggy sighed. "Hey, how is Irish doing?"

"She's great. She said to tell you thanks for the books. She's reading the last one now. She has a new mystery series she's sending you. She said to tell you what a great time she had seeing you. She said she hadn't laughed that hard for a long time. Well, except maybe at the infamous Ethel." The three of them had closed down the Terrace and then hit two more blues bars staying out until 3:00 a.m. "She and Catherine have a lot more to face with John as sick as he is. I wish this weren't happening to them."

Peggy continued, "Vivian said Irish called here the other day. I think she was looking for you. You know she's a little concerned about how you're doing." Peggy poured Savannah some more brandy as she pursued this "off-limits" topic. "How are you doing?" Peggy asked pointedly.

Savannah knew she was lucky to have strong friends who really gave a rip about her. "I'm fine. You know, I can understand what you don't like about Ruby, but she has two daughters, Peggy, and those girls need to have a mother that is earning a living. I'm don't want to be the one to put her out on the street."

Peggy was amazed at how quickly Savannah had slid away from the spotlight. "We are talking about you now, Savannah. Believe me Ruby can take care of herself." Peggy toyed with the silver bangles on her wrist and waited.

Savannah had the feeling that Peggy would just sit there and stare at her until September if she didn't respond. She tried to think of a way to talk about it all out loud. She'd kept it inside for so long that she just couldn't think of the way to open the emotional gate without flooding the entire room with her tears.

Savannah spoke quietly, "First Tommy dies, then Amelia's murdered in such a gruesome way. These were real people, Peggy. They are gone, I mean forever. Sometimes, they are interchangeable in my dreams. I'll be dreaming of Tommy and suddenly his warm body turns ice cold, and I can feel it next to mine. Then as though that isn't the worst thought that I've ever had in my whole life, the dream becomes a true nightmare when I see that his throat has been cut, but it isn't him any more it is Amelia.

Savannah continued, "I woke up screaming the other night when my cat Lily curled up around my neck. I thought I was being strangled or someone was going to cut my throat. Savannah started to laugh, " Poor Lily goes flying across the room. I mean I pulled her off my neck and threw her. God…" Savannah pursed her lips hard to keep herself composed.

Savannah suppressed the giggle bubbling up in her throat. Then she just started sobbing. "I miss him so much. He was like my brother, my friend, and honestly Peggy the best lover." This thought made Savannah close her eyes and just savor their happiness for a few seconds. When she opened her eyes, Peggy was looking at her with warmth and tenderness and infinite patience. "He was in trouble and – you know – so was Amelia. God, what happens to people? My mom and dad drink themselves into oblivion. I mean what kind of pain drives these people to their own destruction?"

A rhetorical question, Savannah didn't expect an answer from Peggy. "Probably the kind of pain I've felt since Tommy's death. Peg, I tell ya, I truly understand why people go off the deep end. This is a nightmare that I sometimes think will never stop." Savannah reached over to the box of tissues on Peggy's desk, took out a couple, wiped her eyes and then blew her nose. Her face was red and sore from crying, but her stomach and chest suddenly felt so much better. She actually could take full breaths, talk to her friend and let the tears flow. She took a sip of her brandy and just sat back in her chair and sighed.

"I really thought Amelia was going to make it," Peggy admitted as she grabbed a tissue and wiped her own tears. "I used to watch Tommy and you and think that is the way a loving couple is supposed to look. You and Tommy were so obviously meant for each other. He adored you, Savannah." Peggy blew her nose and continued, " He still flirted with you like he was a kid at the dance trying to get your attention. Remember the time he came here with a different flower each day of the week just to make up with you for the grief he'd caused when he got drunk at the Christmas party. He was so sorry he'd hurt you, and I swear he would have brought you flowers the rest of his life if he thought it would get your approval." Peggy had always liked Tommy; but she, like everyone around him knew he was up against demons to big for earthly solutions.

Peggy continued, "That's good old passion for you. I think it is strongest emotion in the world." Peggy took another sip of her brandy. "Anyone who has ever had it aches for it again, yet realizes only a few times in your lifetime will you experience that out of control feeling." With her glass still in the air, she says, "Viva la passion!"

"Look at it this way, Savannah. There are people who will never ever know that feeling." Peggy sat her glass down on her desk. "Lucky you, you got to take that wonderful wild trip with someone you loved. Can you imagine not ever having had that in your life?" Peggy waited.

"Even though the price was excruciatingly high, I would not have missed it for anything, Peggy. I really believe the worst thing would have been to have lost him and not felt like I'd ever had anything. You know what I mean? I wanted him to quit drinking. I wanted us to live a lifetime together... I "

As her voice trailed off, Savannah came to the realization that the rest of her life would be without him. For the first time, this was not an impossible thought, just a painfully deep loss that she would learn to live with. Savannah stood up and walked over to Peggy. She held her tight and hugged her for all she was worth. "You're a wonderful friend, thank you for letting me unload on you. It helped. I'm just about ready to kick ass again."

Peggy hugged her back reverting to her childhood habit of saying a Hail Mary. Mother of God, protect my friend. Guide her with your wisdom and grace.

*****

I's watchin'

Chapter Thirty-One

"Ruby," Savannah peeked her head into Ruby's office, "Could you come in my office a minute?"

Ruby picked up a pad of paper and her pen, stood up and followed Savannah. "I called that lady you told me to call, the Events Planner, she'll be coming' in at 4:00 today. I got all the centerpieces you told me to get. So far 60 donors are coming. The caterer…"

"Ruby, please sit down." Savannah said quietly but firmly as she walked back into her own office. "We need to talk."

Ruby sat down on the edge of the chair in front of Savannah's desk, her eyes narrow slits and her mouth tightly closed, "I was fixin' to get these phone calls made today." Ruby replied. She was tired. She hadn't slept in nights with Tremaine staying away more and more. Now this bitch all over her ass. She stared Savannah down.

Like a black funnel cloud, Savannah could feel Ruby's anger tear at her from across the desk. This time, she would not back down. "You didn't come in again yesterday. That is the sixth time you've missed since you've been here, plus you've been late- let's see – you've been late on 8 different mornings. I mean, significantly late, each time with all kinds of excuses." Usually, when there was a performance issue, Savannah would take the necessary time to delve into the reasons, but not with Ruby – she didn't have a millennium available to her to listen to her litany of excuses. "This is not acceptable, Ruby. In fact, I'm putting you on probation."
Ruby heard the word *probation*. She knew that word and she knew what it meant. Tremaine would kill her if she lost this connection to his girls. *I kills you first bitch. I kill anyone who make me lose my man. Auntie, she ugly…. she"*

"Ruby, did you hear me?" Savannah was stunned at the look on Ruby's face, like Ruby was at the door of hell visiting the devil himself. It was only for a second, but she definitely caught a glimpse of why Ruby's husband could be trying to get custody of the kids. Savannah didn't give an inch. She stared evenly at Ruby, "I said we are looking at your performance today, and I have to say that if it doesn't improve immediately, you are not going to be able to stay here"

"Ms. Hart, I don' understand." Ruby couldn't bring herself completely back. She needed to get out of there so she could breathe. "I work hard, Ms. Hart." *I slits dat scrawny ugly throat.*

"Ruby, any more absences or tardiness in the next month – unless there is a good reason – and you will be dismissed. I've written this up and am going to go over this with you right now. I will sign this and so will you." Savannah was determined to confront this woman. She could feel Ruby's hatred of her radiate across the desk. How could she have missed this?

Savannah reviewed the memo with her and Ruby signed it quickly saying, "Ya'll see, I won't be missing' anymore." Ruby got up and quickly went back into her office shutting the door after her.

Savannah stared at Ruby's signature; illegible. She reached into her file drawer and pulled out Ruby's file and compared it to her original application. The initial Ruby Ebota was written in nearly perfect penmanship.

The signature before her wasn't legible. Big loopy letters took over most of the signature line with the end of the names falling well below the signature line. The name was impossible to read. Whoever had been sitting in front of her only a few minutes ago was not the same woman who came in last March and sat in front of her earnestly wanting a chance to work and to provide for her daughters. It was like the woman had slipped out of her own skin and disappeared. Who was this woman? What was happening? *The next screw-up,* Savannah vowed, *this woman is history.*

Chapter Thirty-Two

Tremaine had pushed himself up inside of Ruby, who was pinned up against the wall. Taking her from behind ruled out any hint of intimacy and afforded him paramount control and superiority that he thrived on. Sweat shown on his shaved head and his lean hard body was drenched in moisture. He hated her more each day and heading north with his pretty little Nicky sounded better all the time. Nicky had a thing for him and had made a few noises about them going up north together. Normally he would get real mad and punish any whore who did any thinking of her own but she was so damn fine and sweet tasting. Things were starting to get too hot around this city. *My whores getting themselves killed and the cops hanging everywhere, trying to catch that motherfuck'n serial killer. Shit like this is real bad for business.* Tremaine was becoming more edgy each day. *Stupid bitch, so dumb she loves it when I bang her and beat her like this. Listen to her crazy ass moan'n.* He suspected she had been doing that *voodoo shit* again even though he had beaten her more than once. *Bitch so dumb she even digs it when I beats her.*

He pushed Ruby's face into the rough wall pretending he was caught up in the moment. "Yeah, baby." Slammed his cock as far as it would go into her, coming inside her, he jerked himself out and let the juice run out of her and down her legs. He grunted and walked away. He wouldn't need her or her contacts much longer.

Just staying alive had been a big deal in the housing projects in Chicago, and as a kid Tremaine was a fast learner and even faster on his feet. He learned quickly that life was as dangerous in his apartment as on the street. The man who planted his seed in Tremaine's Mama must have been brighter than most. No telling who that could have been. His Mama had a different man in the house so often he and his siblings didn't much bother learning the men's names. They did learn to stay out of the way as much as possible. The men were ugly mean, most on drugs and alcohol, none with a legal income. By the time he was eight, Tremaine was selling drugs and his Mama and her men were some of his best customers.

Tremaine was smart enough to know he didn't want to end up like his older brother, dead at 15 from an overdose so his own drug intake was limited to recreational use. His sisters were whores before they reached their teens. They were having abortions before they were middle school age, not that they went to school half of the time.

He watched the way the basketball stars dressed, talked and hung out. Although he was no athlete he was filling out fast. He had the cash to spend at the gym. At 16, he was muscular, over 6 ft. and still growing. The girls were fighting to lie down for him. Before long he had several girls working for him. He was an equal opportunity employer, who even included his own sisters.

As time went on Tremaine became more powerful in his neighborhood. He had several brushes with the law, but he could afford a good lawyer or a bribe, sometimes a little of both. He did a little minor jail time here and there. Then one day along came a bigger fish, one that wanted to eat all the smaller fish. During the territorial wars, Tremaine killed a soldier of the big man and even though the cops hadn't fingered him the big man had. Tremaine had plenty of money stashed and so he decided to head out for the time being. His kind of business was profitable anywhere.

Then a few months after he hit Atlanta along came Ruby. She was not only a fine looking whore, she was smart and her idea to take Amelia's old job had paid off. But now he was getting sick of her, trying to own him. *Nobody owns*

Tremaine. Ruby was keeping Nicky so busy he had a hard time getting to her. He suspected Ruby was doing it on purpose. He was going to enjoy messing the bitch up, real bad. No whore got the best of him.

*****

Ruby's man can't git enough of my sweet pussy, not since I sews that root in his coat. See Auntie? I do has the gift.

Chapter Thirty-Three

July

White hag bitch don't know what's going on. She only thinks about that no good for nothing man of hers. Ruby had heard the office gossip that Savannah's man had been a drunk and died from an overdose. *Of course the other bitches feels so sorry for her. He dead an in his grave, in his grave. She got no man to fuck, no man to fuck, only dead cold flesh in her bed, in her bed.* Ruby blinked at Savannah; *Did I say that out loud? No, bitch still going on and on about some damn silly policy.* Ruby pretended interest, as usual, while thinking *I gots to be careful, can't let white hag bitch know I has the power until I's done wid her. Ms. Nasty Ass Hart hasn't heard about my man. My man, Tremaine, tall and oh so strong and oh so fine in his black leather jacket. Pants so tight I sees his delicious cock grow.* She clenched her fists, *just so it only grows for Ruby. Relax. White hag bitch watching.* Ruby made sure her Tremaine had the best of everything, a diamond earring for his ear and a gold chain for his neck, *he so fancy.*

Tremaine carried a .44 Magnum semi-automatic, *he a big man round this town.* Ruby herself preferred the personal contact with her victims, watching the warm, red blood burst from their throats as she slashed them. She did know how mean Tremaine looked with his big old gun in its smooth, black shoulder holster and how it made hot juices flow between her legs to see him in all his finery. Ruby knew how to provide for her sexy, conjure-man. She knew what had to be done and how to remove any obstacle in her way. Not like the old days when Ruby had to lay on her back and spread her bush wide for any man who came a long just to get a few little pretties. *Better listen a little to the white hag bitch, so I knows what going on. I gonna sees her blood soon.*

Chapter Thirty-Four

It was so hot and humid a person could hardly catch their breath. The office a/c had gone on the blink a couple of hours ago and the repairperson was due any minute. In the meantime box fans were pulled out of closets and windows and doors were opened to try and catch a breeze, not any easy task on a July afternoon in Atlanta.

To make matters worse Savannah and Peggy had been behind closed doors secretly reviewing resumes they had collected for the past two weeks. They had narrowed it down to three candidates. Peggy had set up appointments with them for this coming Monday afternoon. This time she and Savannah intended to meet with the applicants together based on the old two heads are better than one theory. If they struck out then it was "plan B", a temp, until a qualified replacement for Ruby was found.

"I feel like a fugitive sneaking around, keeping files in your office under lock and key, says Savannah, and working undercover every time Ruby goes out for one of her extended lunches. She's been gone for more than an hour and a half this time."

"Yeah, well the environment in this office will be a lot less stressful once she is out of here. You know we're doing the right thing. Ruby has been playing her little voodoo tricks on you and the rest of the staff for months now and we know she has actually scared some of the girls. I don't really believe she is harmless, she's off the wall and scary as shit. The staff is a great bunch with the exception of Ruby. The stress of Amelia being murdered by a serial killer and Ruby and her antics are beginning to make all of us jumpy." Peggy's face slowly changed from schoolmarm to a forgiving mother as she realized Savannah's own disappointment in her mistake.

"I'm so sorry…"

"You should be, hooking us up with Marie Laveau Voodoo Queen reincarnated," Peggy teased. "Okay you did the best you could at the time and Ruby sorta fell out of the sky. I'm still puzzled how that happened."

"Me too, and I was there," Savannah pushed her hair out of her eyes and sank a little lower in the comfortable old chair Peggy had beside her desk. "I know I was a hell of lot more vulnerable then, just grasping at straws. I don't take this lightly but I'm damn sick of her bullshit. One ridiculous story after another, the sick attempts at her hexes and intimidating the staff has done it for me."

"How about the little blue root you found under your chair pad? That was a kick. It would have been funnier if you had pulled it up in front one our fancy big bucks donors. We all want to help women, especially with kids, but you know as well as I do, this gal has to go."

"You're right, of course. The paper work is all completed and I'll pull Ruby into my office first thing on Monday, with you as a witness and we'll get on with it. I just wish it was over with, but we can't fire her on a Friday."

As Savannah started to pull herself up out of the chair, she glanced toward the open window. There was Ruby's sweat streaked face staring back at her, eyes wild, hair disheveled, teeth bared and spit running down her lips. "Ah kills ya now fo sure. You a dead bitch. Black bitch dead too. Blood gonna run." Ruby screamed words and phrases jumbled together.

"Jesus, Peg how long has she been out there?" Savannah ran to the window and called to Ruby to come back. It was already too late. Ruby ran down the street to the parking lot still screaming and cursing Savannah as she went.

*****

"Well at least the a/c is working again and you were smart to send the staff home early," Peggy reflected. "It was too hot and they were all shaken by Ruby's insane behavior. Having the locks changed and increasing the security for next week was the right thing to do. I'm too old for this shit, not that I really believe her threats, but it's sure took its toll today."

"I'd feel a hell of a lot better, Peg, if we would have been able to get her to answer her phone. I don't want things to end like this. She even heard us making fun of her too. What the hell was she doing outside the window in all this heat?" It was, of course, obvious there was no real question to what Ruby had been up to. When she had seen the two women behind closed doors, even with the a/c broken, her paranoid mind had to know what was going on.

"We've done all we can for now, let's go get a bite to eat and forget it until Monday. This has been the summer from hell. Taking a deep breath and realizing what her empty tummy craved, Peggy suggested, "How about Mexican? I'm in the mood for salsa, chips and a cold Corona with no discussion of Ruby."

*****

The sun was gone and there was a hint of a breeze as Peggy and Savannah left the restaurant and headed up the street arm in arm to the parking garage. Things looked a lot brighter than they had that afternoon, in fact, better than they had all year. They were both looking forward to a much brighter office without Ruby's dark influence.

"Wait 'til Irish hears about Ruby. She'll come out here and take care of her personally." Peggy knew the extent of Irish's concern about this bizarre woman.

"Yeah, she's off at the Oregon coast right now, but when she hears how Ruby went psycho on us, she's gonna rub it in big time."

"It's not funny, Savannah." Peggy reminded her.

Behind them a shadow detached itself from the wall, headed their way picking up momentum the closer it came.

"Hey, you ladies got any spare change?" Both women jump in unison. "Didn't mean to scare ya." A bleary eyed bum asked as he stumbled out in front of them from behind a large van.

"You didn't scare us one damn bit, now stand aside," said Savannah. They had parked side by side and were at their cars. They jumped in, started their engines, backed out and were on their way like they had been goosed.

The shadow melted back against the wall.

*****

Dem hag bitches is dead. I'm gonna cuts dem bad. They won't be a laugh'n soon.

Chapter Thirty-Five

Fast car, top down, wind in her face and hot man in the passenger seat. What could be better at this moment in her life? Irish and Jack were on their way to the coast for two whole days. This was the first time in months they had both been able to get away at the same time and the anticipation of the hours alone together made it even more exciting. It promised to be a carefree, relaxing and sex-filled couple of days. They both were content to have this free non-committed relationship that they were in. She could hardly wait to see his muscular body in the nude. His curly dark hair was blowing in the wind and his gray eyes had that had the lust she loved so well and knew was also in hers. His long legs were stretched out and he was perfectly relaxed, happy to lie back and let her drive. Jack Pardue was a man who felt comfortable in his own skin and didn't have to prove his masculinity at every opportunity. His tight Levi's held the promise of delights to come.

They had reservations at a romantic inn high on the cliffs where every room looked out over the Oregon Coast. Irish thought, *back east they say, "going to the shore", here it's "going to the coast."* Either way she felt lucky to have escaped Ethel, who was on the prowl today, and she felt better about Savannah than she had in months.

As Irish had pulled her car up in front of the building to load up for the trip she could see Ethel peering out of her drapes. *Oh, nuts*, thought Irish, *I'll never make it by her. She'll have a zillion questions and I have to pick up Jack. Okay, try not to make eye contact.*

Irish tried to bolt through the lobby but Ethel was standing there in her open door way, ready to waylay her. Ethel always dressed up during her "business hours", no old landlady housecoats for her. Her hair was newly permed, colored and tightly curled. Today she had half of her jewelry box on and a filter tipped cigarette in her bony hand. "Hi dear, saw you pull up, nothing to unload? Does that mean something to load up? Going away with "that man?" Not being nosey but I heard Mary in 3-B was going to be caring for your sweet little cat Beau for two days." Beau the 20-pound cat could not, under any circumstances, be considered sweet.

"Ethel, his name is Jack and yes we are taking off to the coast for a couple of days." Better to confess and get it over with than to wait until she breaks out the rubber hose. Ethel should work for the Portland PD. Criminals would spill their guts within 30 minutes of being grilled by her.

"High class look'n woman like you could be married to a rich man by now. You're not getting any younger you know. Why by the time I was your age I was on my second husband. Each one paid off too, bless their souls. Now if you had a weight problem like poor Rosie, bless her heart, I could understand it. But look at you. Just no excuse for not hooking an older man with some money. Get a man that can set you up in style. Big home in the west hills. How do you think I got this building, played my cards right I'll tell you that's how."

"Ethel we have been over this before, I am entirely happy with my life. I'm not looking for a husband or ready to start a family. I just love living here in this building and...."

"Don't try to change the subject by buttering me up. Go on then and have fun since your going anyway."

"Thanks, bye see you in two days." By this time Irish was half way up the stairs.

*****

Irish pulled up behind a slow truck and seeing there was plenty of room to pass she accelerated and went around him. She was a safe driver and did not take unnecessary chances but she did like to speed. "Will you fix my speeding ticket if I get caught?"

"Sorry, baby, you're on your own," laughed Jack, "Just get us there in one piece and don't get caught. Can ya hurry, please?" He joked, "I can't wait much longer. Let me tell you some of the things I'm gonna do to you." And he proceeded to do just that.

*****

As soon as the bellboy had pulled the drapes open to the view of the sunset and closed the door to their suite they began to undress each other. Shoes were quickly kicked off. They slowly savored each new area of skin that was exposed. They had waited months for a night like this and they intended to make it last. Irish stood still as Jack slid her top over her head and pulled her bra straps down with his teeth, then tickled her firm nipples with his tongue. She pulled his shirt off and ran her tongue slowly down his chest, around his nipples stopping to undo the buttons on his Levi's with her teeth. Jack let out a moan and picked her up, walked to the bed and gently put her on her back. He unzipped her jeans and slid them partway down her legs. He put his finger inside of her panties then fully inside of her, pulled his finger out and put it in his mouth. With his finger in his mouth, he tried to pull her jeans down the rest of the way, when he got them stuck, she raised her hips and slid them off. All the while their eyes were locked in a passionate stare. Eyes locked, Irish ran her hands down his chest and unbuttoned his Levi's the rest of the way.

As soon as Jack was free of his pants, his long, throbbing penis was in her mouth. Wanting to make it last, she was careful not to suck too hard. She pulled him out of her mouth and teased him with her tongue. Jack stopped her and straddled her until his penis was over her mouth and his mouth was parting the lips between her legs. Jack pushed his tongue in and out of her until she climaxed, then repeated and increased the intensity until she came several more times. When he could no longer withstand her lips on him without exploding he rolled them both over, turned and entered her. When he felt her about to come again, he let go and they climaxed together.

They lay panting, wet with sweat and smiling from ear to ear, like two kids in the backseat of '55 Chevy. After showering together, a long shower with more sex, they decided to order room service and eat on the balcony. It was a clear night, moon and stars made to order. Almost like being in love, *better* thought Irish because there were none of the worries about what comes next. This was as good as it needed to get for now.

Next morning they were up early walking on the beach. The morning was perfect, sun coming up over the mountains to the east and sandpipers running along the wet sand. Jack had brought the plastic ice bucket from their suite and they gathered shells, agates and sand dollars like children. The prior winter had washed up a huge supply of driftwood along the beach. There were several forts built by lovers or children as far back from the waves and as close to the cliffs as the builders could drag the wood. Irish and Jack sat out of the wind and rested for a while in one of the forts. "Hungry?" asked Jack, hoping she would ask for what?

"Starving for pancakes and bacon and all the trimmings," she replied pretending that was the answer he wanted. With that she crawled out of the little fort and sprinted back the way they had come. "Beat you back."

It was a perfect holiday. To celebrate the fact that it didn't rain they had sex. They visited tourist shops, had sex, walked on the beach, had sex, ate the local clam chowder for lunch both days, had sex, had dinner at one of the finest restaurants with an ocean view, had sex, packed their suitcases, and ...had sex.

Chapter Thirty-Six

Nicole stretched her arms and perfect little legs out as far as they would reach then wiggled her tiny pink painted toes. Pink was in style again and Nicole was using it to her advantage as the guys said it made her look like a "baby doll." The old guys just ate that up and they paid the highest price for the youngest girls. She wanted to make the big bucks and please her boss man.

Too bad Tremaine couldn't spend the night; I'd like to wake up to more of his big body on mine. I know he really cares for me. Tremaine had been spending more and more time with Nicole the past few weeks and that suited her just fine. Whenever she had free time, he just happened to call or drop by. When they first started getting together she knew he just wanted a quick lay. Now each time they met he acted more like he really cared and he took her slow and easy. Tonight, after they had fucked like there was no tomorrow, he lay beside her looking her up and down as if he had never really seen her before. Running his fingers through her silky hair and he even kissed the end of her pert little nose.

She told him tonight she was scared of Ruby, but he said "Don't you worry your pretty little self about that gal, I'm the one who run's things. I'm about to get tired of her stickin her nose in my business. You're just a little jumpy 'bout them whores getting themselves killed, but your Tremaine gonna take good care of you." Any concerns he had about his business, he wasn't about to share with Nicole. Last thing she needed to know was how badly everything really was going. He didn't know how he was going to get rid of that stupid bitch, Ruby, but he had to keep her until he didn't need her anymore.

It would be fine with Nicole if Tremaine got rid of Ruby and they could hook up full time. They could go up north, maybe New York City or Chicago and start an operation with some real class. Not a bunch of losers from a work center, but some girls that looked and acted like models. She had developed ambition in the few weeks she had known Tremaine. Funny what the right guy could do to a girl. Nicole had been buying all the latest fashion magazines, *Vogue, Elle,* anything *s*he could get her hands on. She was studying how the high priced models dressed, the way they applied their makeup and wore their hair. When she knew Tremaine was coming over she made herself up just like a model and believe me he was taking notice.

This town made her skin crawl lately anyway. The news was full of scary stories about serial killers, and she felt like there were eyes watching her. A week or so ago she had felt like someone had been in her apartment. There was no one thing she could put her finger on, but she was scared. *Maybe its just cause I got the hots so bad for my new man that's making me want to blow this town.* Nicole had begun to think of Tremaine as her man and she figured Ruby would freak if she found out. *That's one good reason to head on out,* she thought.

Speaking of heading on out, I'm outta fuck'n cigs., again. Damn things are gonna be the death of me yet. Shoulda asked Tremaine to leave me a few. Crap, I'll just throw on some cut offs and run to the corner market real quick like.

As Nicole exited her building, she looked up and down the street. It was unusually quiet and peaceful as she started walking quickly up the street.

Chapter Thirty-Seven

Before daylight Saturday morning after tossing and turning all night, Savannah had finally given up trying to sleep and headed for the kitchen to put on a pot of coffee. Once during the night she had thought she had heard a noise outside. Lily had sprung off the bed, the fur on her back and tail stood straight out. Savannah had turned on all the lights including the outside flood light but there was no one there. "All this damn spell and hex crap of Ruby's is getting to me, too, Lily." She returned to bed. By now Lily had given up her place on the bed for some peace and quiet in her favorite chair in the living room. Lily stretched, yawned and curled back up as she heard Savannah in the kitchen so early.

When Savannah had arrived home last night, after having dinner with Peggy, she had tried repeatedly to call Ruby. She had given up after midnight and gone to bed. As concerned as she was about the fate of Ruby and her children it was going to be a bright new beginning without Ruby's presence. The atmosphere had become dark and dismal during the past few months. One had to step away from it to realize how unhealthy Ruby's antics had been to their mental well being.

Screw this crap, though Savannah. *I'm getting out of here for the rest of the weekend. What's the use of having filthy rich parents if you can't cash in occasionally?* Her parents had a summer place on The Isle of Hope just minutes from historic Savannah and a few hours drive from Atlanta. The only reason she actually considered going over for the weekend was she knew her folks wouldn't be there. Laurel had called her daughter the week before and asked if she wanted anything from New York. Laurel's attempt at loving Savannah was to lavish her with gifts. The price of hearing about the cost of the gift for years to come was always too high. She usually declined all offers, but since she wouldn't have to actually see them she would make an exception. Laurel had said Savannah's father was off putting together a high stakes real estate deal. Savannah shuttered to think who was losing their family's holdings now. Each conquest gave him a bigger bank account and a surge of power. It was short lived and soon his feelings of inadequacy returned. Soon he would ferret out another fine old southern family, his favorite prey, and steal away their heritage with his money.

Savannah filled Lily's self-feeder to the top with dried cat food, put down an extra dish of water and cleaned the litter box. "There you are baby, all set until I get home tomorrow. Be a good girl and don't scratch the sofa." Lilly gave her a dirty look and stalked off. She knew a snow job when she heard one. Ha!

In less than an hour Savannah was showered, packed and ready to head out the door. Knowing Irish wouldn't be back from the Oregon coast yet she still decided to leave her a message.

"Hi, it's me. You can give me crap and all the "I told you sos" tomorrow night. It's a long story but Ruby overheard Peg and me getting ready to let her go on Monday. Our a/c was down and Ruby was listening outside the office window. She jumped up looking like a witch and scared the hell out of both of us. She ran off screaming and cursing us before we could catch up with her and talk to her. Anyway I'm heading down to my folks place in Savannah for the night. Talk to ya tomorrow. Love ya."

Chapter Thirty-Eight

Peggy was also up early on Saturday. She had gone to bed saddened by the events of the prior day but firm in her belief the termination of Ruby's employment had been inevitable. From a standpoint of office morale, it was not a moment too soon. The staff had a difficult enough job, dealing with the level of need their clients required without internal conflict. *The office should be a lot brighter this coming Monday,* thought Peggy. *Life without Ruby's constant dramas will be a major improvement.*

It was Peggy's habit to rise early even on weekends. At sixty, your body became a creature of habit and routine the same as your mind. It was also her ritual to have a little pot of tea on the patio of her townhouse on weekend mornings and plan her day. Peggy had bought into this community of townhouse style condominiums several years ago and it suited her lifestyle just right. The gated property off of Ashford-Dunwoody offered a sense of security she appreciated. She often worked long hours and found she had just so much energy to spend each day, so the upkeep of a larger home was out of the question.

Gardening had always been a favorite of hers but a large yard was too much to handle these days, so her tiny walled in garden and patio were the perfect size. *It's going to be a hot one today, so I'll get an early start. Let's see, today I'll go to the nursery and pick up some plant food for the camellias and...* so on went the list.

Peggy went back inside to prepare a croissant or maybe two, with real butter, to go with her tea. *Don't tell the diet police,* she thought. As she waited for the toaster oven to warm the croissants, she turned on the little television on her kitchen counter. She flipped to a local channel for a weather report and a well-known Atlanta newscaster was giving an on the scene report. There was a "Breaking News" banner at the top of the screen and Peggy leaned across the counter to turn up the volume. "...the third victim of the suspected serial killer being dubbed the "Call Girl Killer," he said. "To recap, the body of Nicole Williams was found in an alley right in the heart of Midtown shortly before daylight this morning. Our source revealed William's throat was slashed in the same manor as the prior victims, Amelia Brown and Estelle Marshall. This has not been confirmed nor denied by the police at this time. There is also a unconfirmed report of a possible person of interest being sought in connection with the case."

As the newscaster talked on, Peggy grabbed her portable phone and dialed Savannah's home only to get her recorded message, "Hi this is Savannah, please leave your name and number at the beep."

"Savannah, Peg here, call me as soon as you get this message. I just turned on the TV and there's been another murder. This time it's Nicole Williams, remember her? Listen I don't know what all this means but I'm getting a very, bad feeling about it. This can't be a coincidence, two dead girls we knew and Ruby flipping out on us – well this just *has* to be connected somehow. If you don't reach me at home try my mobile. I'm trying your mobile right now."

The weather report was on by the time Peggy hung up from leaving a message on Savannah's mobile phone. She turned off the TV and headed for the bedroom to throw on some clothes.

*****

Peggy pulled into the parking lot at the office and fished in her straw bag for her keys. Savannah had increased the security temporarily due to Ruby's reaction yesterday, but it didn't include weekends. They had also recently installed a new alarm system that was monitored 24/7. She punched in the alarm code, unlocked the door, reached to the right and turned on the lobby lights. The office had an eerie feeling about it today. *There have been too many strange happenings around here to suit me. I'm going to go through Ruby's office right now and see if I can figure out what the hell has been going on. It all started when Ruby arrived here. I'll bet my bottom dollar that girl is at the root of all these troubles.*

Peggy headed straight for Ruby's old office flipping on all the lights as she went. *Screw the taxpayer's electric bill*, she thought.

*****

About an hour later Peggy sat in Ruby's office, in Ruby's chair with a stunned look on her face. Her curly hair sneaking out of its bun a little more than usual. *It's amazing that she could have held together as long as she did and equally unbelievable we missed it for so long too.* Peggy had been through the desk, files, and storage closet and was still working her way through the files and e-mails on Ruby's computer. There was a bag of children's clothing that Peggy specifically remembered Savannah bringing for Ruby's girls. Only now all the little outfits, headbands and socks were cut to shreds. The desk drawers were full of small tins and jars of powders and disgusting little bits of what appeared to be frog legs. There was a dead blackbird with its feet pulled off and one tin contained the eyes of a dead animal, possibly a cat.

Little scraps of paper had Ruby's scrawled version of curses and hexes, many of them directed at Savannah. Peggy's hand shook as she studied the slips of paper. There was a warning to each of the murdered girls to stay away from "her man."

Ruby had continually searched the web for information pertaining to her obsession with voodoo, black magic, spells and conjuring. She had saved the information in her word processing program. It was amazing to Peggy the woman ever had time for her job, especially taking in to account the number of days she had missed work.

Fear crept into Peggy's being and she tried again to call Savannah at home. She dialed Savannah's mobile and as it began to ring she heard a phone ringing in the office. Following the sound she walked into Savannah's office. There on the credenza sat Savannah's mobile in the charger. "Damn it to hell," shouted Peggy, "No wonder I can't reach her." She thought for a minute then grabbed Savannah's Rolodex and found Irish Sullivan's number in Oregon. She was praying Irish was back from her trip to the Oregon Coast by now. Voice mail.

"Irish, this is Peggy Langtree and I need to talk to you as soon as possible. It's a long story but I think Savannah might be in danger. There's been another murder, another woman who came to us for counseling awhile back. I've just been all through Ruby's office and I think Ruby might be involved somehow. I know for sure that she has it in for Savannah. She overheard us preparing to fire her and she went nuts, threatening and cursing us. I'll leave you my mobile number. Please call me as soon as you get this message."

Peggy searched again in Savannah's Rolodex and found a card for Detective Al Benson. She quickly dialed the number. "Atlanta Police Department," said the abrupt voice of a no nonsense woman.

"Yes, I'd like to speak to Detective Al Benson please."

"I'll put you through to Homicide." Click went the line.

"Homicide, Sergeant Martinique."

"This is Peggy Langtree, and I would like to speak to…"

"Hold the line…You need to see the victim at the hospital. Name's Tyrel Jameson, yeah, he says he was shot by …what?" Peggy realized she had not been put on hold but was listening to a real life homicide department in action. There was so much going on at once that it was difficult to hear let alone keep track of it all. She did her best to follow. "What's your guys name? He's saying Jameson was the shooter of the woman in the market holdup?"

Another even more authoritative voice cut in, "Sergeant get the name of the guy Officer Reynolds is holding. Tell them to bring him on in. Get the officer at the hospital with Jameson. Who's at the scene?" Peggy couldn't make out the answer, as there were so many overlapping conversations. "Yeah, get him to take Jameson's statement and find out if the woman victim can talk yet. Bring in everyone else able to walk and we'll get to the bottom of this mess." These conversations went back and forth for several minutes as Peggy held the line. She was just about to speak when a new voice, a woman's entered.

"Sergeant, there's a lady downstairs says she's that kid Eddie Sanchez's mother. Wants to know if she can see him."

"Yeah, thanks Elaine," under his breath, "that little fucker Sanchez."

"Hello," ventured Peggy in a small voice.

"Oh my God ma'am, I didn't know you were on the line, I'm so sorry."

"No problem," chuckled Peggy, "I gotta tell you it was pretty exciting, sounded just like NYPD Blue. What I call for was to speak with Detective Benson, I might have some information regarding the…"

"He's out of the office right now working on a case. Give me your name and number and I'll have him call you back."

"That's not acceptable I need to talk to the detective as soon as possible. You don't know what has been going on around here. We had a crazy woman working here and she has made threats and…"

"Do you want me to send a officer to help you right now ma'am?"

"You are not listening to me or letting me finish what I'm trying to tell you. We had a crazy woman working here, we fired her, she made threats against us and now I have found information that I believe Detective Benson will be interested in. This woman could have a connection to the murder of Amelia Brown that was also our employee. I believe another employee is in danger. Now do you understand how important it is that I speak to Detective Benson?"

"Yes ma'am and I will give your message to Detective Benson. You have to realize ma'am that we have hundreds of leads and only so much manpower…"

Peggy decided while she's waiting for callbacks from her messages she'd keep looking through Ruby's office for any additional information. *It's slow work going through the ramblings of a totally insane person. I'd feel a lot better if I could talk to Savannah. Where is that girl?*

Chapter Thirty-Nine

Savannah immediately felt better traveling out of Atlanta even if it was only an overnighter. The tension of the past few months began to lessen with each mile. Savannah was making good time as she cruised along I-75S to the city of Savannah and to her parent's summer home on the Isle of Hope. The drive was only a little over 4 hours if she didn't stop to eat. She'd pick up lunch to go, once she reached Savannah.

Savannah's parents had bought the summer place several years ago, during one of Randolph Hart's attempts to buy a little class. It never seemed to occur to her folks that sobriety might add some class to their lives. She didn't want to know what kind of a deal her father had spun to purchase their summer home. She knew it had belonged to the former owner's since before the civil war, so it must have been devastating to the owner to sell. Good old "let's take advantage of others' misfortune" knew a deal when he saw it, and was first in line with a bucket of money to snap up the home.

The Isle of Hope, discovered by the Conquistador Hernando De Soto over 400 years ago, was rich with history. It was common in days gone by for wealthy Savannah residents to build summer homes to escape the torrid heat of town. The Hart home was a smaller version of the Wormsloe Plantation, which was one of the very first plantations built at the Isle of Hope. Like most mansions of that day, it had a mile and a half driveway lined with live oaks. It was still a major tourist attraction.

The Hart's home had a main house that was over 4000 square feet and would be considered a mansion by most. The veranda alone stretched the length and both sides of the home. There was a small two- bedroom guest cottage in the rear of the property that Savannah's folks had "given" to her as a token of their love. She seldom visited, but truly loved the cottage. Three summers ago during a rare truce with her mother, they had chosen the furnishings and decorations together, making the cottage a cozy haven from the rest of the world. From her living room window, she could look out to Skidaway Narrows, and see the different piers where the majority of homeowners docked their boats.

By the time Savannah had reached Macon and was zipping along on I-16E she had begun to soften and feel guilty about Ruby and her children, regardless of the weird things Ruby had done - and the list was endless. The way she had almost driven Savannah nuts with that constantly running mouth, absenteeism and hateful conjure nonsense was way more than enough to make the average person say good riddance. Although Savannah had no reservations about letting Ruby go, knowing it was her only option, she was sick about the way it had all turned out. She had wanted to let Ruby go in a civilized manner, giving Savannah an opportunity to sit down with her and point her to some community resources, which she obviously needed. *Probably wouldn't listen, but I have to try for the girls' sake.*

Savannah reached for her mobile to call Peggy. She wanted to see how she was doing today. "Shit," exclaimed Savannah, "Where did I leave my phone? Must have been at the office when all hell broke loose yesterday. Oh well, I'll call Peg from the cottage."

An hour later as she drove along with the cruise control set at three miles above the speed limit, Savannah's mind drifted back to what she could remember and decipher about Ruby's family home on St Helena Island. The information was jumbled. Savannah was remembering what Ruby had droned on and on about. She focused on what Marla had told her, which was a lot. Marla could give a person more information in two minutes than three sportscasters combined. How could Savannah forget the farm was on Duckweed Lane? Ruby had carried on *ad nauseam* about how "fine" the farm was she had inherited from her old Auntie Ada. Savannah had heard the word Duckweed so many times that she actually woke up one night, in a cold sweat, running away from the alligators surfacing up through the scummy, green duckweed trying to eat her alive.

Now to hear Marla tell it all that was left of the once large farm was a shack and a small piece of land. *Well, it wouldn't be too difficult to find. I've been there tons of times growing up and our crowd had super pirate adventure on Hunting Island and it's just a skip from St Helena. We had a ball that weekend* remembered Savannah. A group of kids from college had eluded the Park Rangers and spent the night on Hunting Island. *We built a tiny fire and pretended we were in the Caribbean. There was a lot of lovemaking and a few joints to go around.* Savannah had tried some of both. It had been a fun and slightly dangerous weekend. Looking back the best part was that they didn't get caught. You could get your ass in trouble messing around in a State Park.

Anyway I know I could find Ruby's place with very little effort. I just have a hunch this is where she'd run to. I don't remember her mentioning that she had any family or friends in Atlanta. There's a surprise! She and the girls might very well have come down here. Maybe, for their sake she will listen. I'll see she gets help if that's what it takes, or if we have to remove the children from her home, we will. No more bullshit, the girls come first. Here comes the exit to Beaufort. After all, what do I have to lose?

Chapter Forty

Peggy grabbed the call on her mobile on the first ring. "Peggy? Hi, it's Irish, what the hell is going on down there," asked Irish trying to keep the alarm out of her voice.

"Am I ever glad to hear from you. I don't know for sure, I may just be concerned for nothing, but I can't find Savannah…"

Irish broke in, "I know where she is. She left me a voice mail. She went to her folks summer house outside of Savannah." She grabbed a pen and paper, "Okay, I'm writing this down. Tell me all you know about the latest murder, and why you think Savannah might be in danger."

"It's been less that 24 hours since all hell broke loose around here," Peggy explained. "To make a long story short the a/c broke down yesterday and Savannah and I were working in her office with the window open. We were going over our upcoming termination meeting of Ruby for next Monday. We just couldn't work with her behavior any longer. You know part of the Ruby thing."

"I do," Irish shuddered as she thought quickly of all the information she had gotten from Rosie.

"We thought that Ruby was still out of the office, on one of her extended lunch breaks, when she jumped up at the open window. Scared the shit out of both of us. You can't imagine how brutal she looked, wild eyed, hair on end, even saliva running from her mouth. She went from a reasonably put-together woman to a friggin' maniac," Peggy took a breath, "and Ruby ran off screaming, cursing and saying she was gonna kill both of us. It was kinda hard to make out all the 'mout'; that's Gullah for curse, she was trying to lay on us."

Peggy went on to explain how they had sent the staff home and tried to reach Ruby to try to calm her down. She told her how she and Savannah had dinner together last night and when they had parted how there was no mention of her leaving town. "This morning I saw on the news that the police thought there had been another murder by the 'Call Girl Killer'. It was another of our girls, Nicole Williams. I got worried, I left Savannah a message and things just weren't adding up, so I came down here to look at Ruby's office. Irish, I'm more than scared now. I think Ruby might be involved with these murders somehow. The news media said the police want to speak to 'a person of interest' you know how they always say that instead of suspect. The reporter didn't say if it was a man or woman."

"God, no wonder you're worried. Tell me what did you find in Ruby's office?" Irish felt the hair on the back of her neck stand up and wished Peggy would hurry and at the same time was apprehensive about what she'd hear next. Something told her that her best friend has her ass in a sling, big time.

"Ruby slashed up all the cute clothes Savannah bought her girls into a million tiny pieces. I think Savannah knew it was a mistake to give them to her. Ruby took it all wrong. Ruby's desk was full of conjure powders, small roots, dead animal parts, slips of paper with death threats to Savannah and the murdered women." Peggy went on until Irish was more than convinced that Peggy had every right to be concerned. "So, I called you and I even put in a call to the Detective that came here when Amelia Brown was murdered. Oh, and to make things worse, Savannah left her mobile phone here last night."

"Have you heard back from the Detective?"

"Not yet, but they said he was out on a case. This one, I hope. I gave that young man on the desk a piece of my mind."

"Do you think Ruby may have headed for St Helena?"

"Don't know, but she drove Savannah nuts going on and on about that farm of hers down there. There's no telling where she might be and dragging those poor little kids with her." They both knew the children could be in danger if Ruby had snapped the tenuous hold she seemed to have on reality.

"Good thing Ruby doesn't know Savannah is that close. You don't think? Shit! I know how her mind works. I bet you she's going over to talk to Ruby." Both of them know of Savannah's drive to help others, even if they don't begin to deserve it, especially when it involved kids. "That does it. I'm on the first flight out of here. Soon as I get a flight I'll call you back. I'll get a car. Peggy I'll need to see Ruby's office. By then you should have heard from the cops."

"Irish, I'd feel so much better if you were here," said Peggy, "If we've worried for nothing then tough, I just have a really horrible feeling about this whole mess. Soon as you get here I'll meet you at the office. Keep in close touch."

"Peggy, keep the doors locked at the office and your home and be careful," warned Irish. "It's also a good idea to try and get through to Benson again. If nothing else the cops know you're not gonna go away until they contact you back."

As soon as she got off the line with Peggy, Irish was back on the phone making arrangements for a flight to Atlanta. In less that twenty minutes, she had booked a flight out and rented a car. Next she called her old boss Gus Russo and asked him to cover her pending cases. They went through the details with lightning speed. She would leave a key for her office with Ethel for one of his operatives to pick up so they could access information on current files as needed. She only expected to be gone a few days at the most but she liked all her bases covered. Next was a quick arrangement for cat care.

Whatever Ruby might have in her sick mind to do to Savannah she'll have to go through me first, Irish vowed. There was no telling where this Ruby person was, but Irish would make sure Savannah had round-the-clock protection until her connection-if any-to the murders was investigated. Even if Ruby didn't have anything to do with the killings she had it in for Savannah.

Irish was mad as hell and worried to boot. She didn't waste a moment as she packed a small bag and headed out the door. Her flight didn't leave for a while, so she still had time to stop by the office and further line out her current case load for Gus.

Chapter Forty-One

The instant Delta flight 1723 taxied to a stop in the Atlanta Hartsfield airport, Irish was out of her seat, carry on baggage in hand and heading for the front of the plane. Most of the other passengers were a little groggy from flying all night, not Irish. She was ready to bite the ass out of an alligator. She was going to find her best friend, and God help anyone who got in her way.

Her long legs moved her quickly through Concourse D, where she raced down the escalator, caught the underground train, waited for four stops, her head ticking off Concourse, C, B, and A and finally the Terminal. Quickly she headed up what seemed like a never-ending escalator packed with saddled-down travelers. Finally reaching the center of the terminal, she found the South Parking exit and hailed a cab.

"Peggy, Irish, I'm on my way to the car rental. Did Savannah call? Can you meet me at your office? Thanks, see ya in a few."

*****

By the time Irish reached Peggy's office, Peggy had hot coffee, juice and breakfast sandwiches waiting. She had been careful letting Irish in and assured her that all the doors and windows were locked and that she had checked out everything thoroughly. She knew Irish wouldn't have thought to eat and she had a feeling they were going to need to keep their strength up for what ever was coming. Peggy didn't have "the gift" just her strong gut feelings coupled with the evidence of Ruby's madness she had discovered in the office. She was cold all over although it was already hot and humid outside, high 70s this early meant at least 90s or better later. The newly repaired a/c was putting out a little too well, so she grabbed an old shawl she kept in her coat closet for her shoulders.

There had been no news from Savannah, no call back from Detective Benson and no break in the murder investigation. According to the latest news broadcast the police were following leads on a male "person of interest." There was one of those unidentified information leaks that a man's wallet had been found on Nicole William's nightstand. The media went on and on, over and over every crumb of a detail. It was the hottest story in the city at present and they played it to the hilt. If the police had a male suspect it probably meant Ruby had nothing to do with the murders. That didn't mean Savannah was in the clear, Ruby could still be out to get her. She and Irish both agreed on that.

Peggy had uncovered more and more of Ruby's irrational behavior, additional evidence of her roots, charms and hexes throughout the entire building. She walked Irish around and pointed out the collection. She had left it all where she found it. Then she had led Irish to Ruby's office, at which point Irish stopped cold and howled. "Nice deco choice, that is truly a deadly shade of blue. Take a picture of this and the next time Savannah mentions letting staff decorate stick it under her nose. What was she thinking?"

"I've looked at it so long now I almost forgot how bizarre it is. That's the tip of the iceberg. When you see Ruby's desk, files and e-mails you'll see what insane looks like."

*****

Irish took I-75 to Savannah's house and let herself in with the key Savannah had given her several years ago. She had given Peggy a strong hug, told her not to worry. They had decided Peggy would keep trying to reach Savannah at the cottage and she would also keep trying to contact the

Detective. Most likely, there would be no reason to involve the police. Irish would check Savannah's house and then head out for Savannah and cottage at The Isle of Hope. She would call Peggy with any updates and Peg would do the same.

Lily was curled up on the forbidden sofa. "Where's your mama?" asked Irish. The cat just stood up turned around and laid back down. She called Peg from Savannah's little home office in the second bedroom and reported all was well there. What she didn't tell Peggy was that while on the phone to her she was using the letter opener to open the lock on the lower desk drawer. She knew where Savannah had stored the gun Irish had made her purchase on her last trip home. The box of cartridges was still in their cellophane wrapper. *So much for the target practice she promised oh so faithfully to do,* thought Irish. *Guess I should be damn glad she didn't get rid of the gun or stash it someplace else.* Moment's later Irish was on the freeway with a grim and determined look on her face.

Chapter Forty-Two

She tried to wipe the dirt out of her eyes but she couldn't move her hands. Her mouth was full of dirt too and she winced when she tried to lick her lips, tasting blood mixed with dirt. *Oh, God what's happened, where am I?* Slowly Savannah attempted to open her eyes, one was swollen almost shut and anyway it was too dark to see. But, where was she? *My hands are tied behind my back. What the hell is going on?* She felt her heart race as the weight of the darkness surrounding her pushed her deeper into the earth. *Okay, stop making it worse,* she thought, *get hold of yourself, take a deep breath,* as she tried to breath deep, she almost cried out with the pain. It felt like her ribs were broken, but something way in the back of her fuzzy, disoriented mind warned her to be quiet.

Struggling made her so dizzy she almost passed out again so she tried to lie still and think back. Everything was a blur. Oh, she knew who she was, but she couldn't bring back the immediate past. *I'll just be still and think...*and she drifted off again.

Chapter Forty-Three

Irish hoped to hell that the information she got from the old guy at the country bait store was correct. If not, she was wasting valuable time and time could be running out for Savannah and those little girls. She had checked Savannah's 38 out at least three times and although she knew it was loaded and in her bag, she reached over again just to make sure. She had put part of the box of cartridges in her purse but kept a few out and placed them in the pocket of her jeans. No point in going over and over in her mind how upset she was with Savannah for taking off on her own like this. To her credit Savannah obviously had no idea that there had been another murder, not to mention the fact that the murdered woman also had connections to the Center. Irish knew how Savannah's mind worked. After she got over her initial anger at Ruby she would have begun to get all sappy about the welfare of the kids. Savannah never stopped trying to save the world. This time she was in over her head. She would read her the riot act when she caught up to her. But *"get over it"* she said to herself; she had to stay focused if she were going to find her friend and the kids before that disgusting bitch went sideways again.

She was racing so fast down the dusty road the old guy had told her about she went straight past the old broken down wooden sign that marked the way to Ruby's old Auntie's. The road she was on was paved maybe twenty years ago and was so full of potholes she was sure she would total the rental sedan before she went much further. The car burned rubber and spun as she slammed on the brakes, threw it in reverse and screeched backwards. There was the old wood sign, cracked, half-hidden by swampy undergrowth and lopsided to boot. Painted letters that had once been white so faded she could barely make out the name "Ebota."

"Hey, Peg. I got lucky fast. Got directions from a bait store owner. I'm at the driveway to the Ebota place," Irish informed Peggy. "Any news from the cops? Yeah, I'm sure they got hundreds of calls so I'm not surprised. That may mean they caught the killer. Yeah, I'm always careful. Don't worry."

Irish turned into the dirt road and proceeded cautiously not wanting to get stuck in the sandy soil or give away her presence to Ruby and who ever else she might have with her. The old driveway curved around the ancient oaks that lined both sides making it impossible to see very far ahead. Spanish moss hung from the trees so low it blended with the swampy growth below the trees. Daylight was filtered in through the trees and there was only breeze enough to make the wisps of moss move with an eerie and macabre motion. *This doesn't feel right,* thought Irish. *I'm going to pull over and check out the road on foot, that damn house could be right under my nose, and I wouldn't be able to tell until I was right on it.*

Irish stopped the car before the next upcoming bend in the driveway, grabbed her bag, got out and quietly closed the car door. She put her long strapped bag on as if she were shopping in the city, over her head and across her body. Moving to the right side of the driveway as close to the edge as possible without slipping into the swamp Irish crept up the road. Sure enough, her instincts were on track, the dilapidated old house was in sight as she rounded the next bend in the driveway. It was a small two-story house on stilts with a roof that sloped down over the front porch. The porch covered the entire front of the house that was not saying much as the front couldn't be more than twenty-feet wide.

She spotted a window on each side of the front door, an attic window and two windows on the side of the house. The house was slowly being drawn back down into the swamp, broken steps, hanging screen door and broken windowpanes were but a symptom of the disrepair of the entire structure. Moss and broken tree branches covered the roof and it looked as if it could topple into the mire at any given moment. Irish stared, *Can hardly tell the house was once white the way the paint has peeled off.* Irish's stomach sunk and thoughts returned to Rosie's conversation when she saw the indigo blue paint. *There's that blue paint again.* This time it was on the front door, on the rickety posts barely holding the roof to the porch and on what was left of the shutters.

A crow gave notice of her presence; however, the house was still, no sign of life and no movement. Irish felt the hair rising on the back of her neck. What little sunlight filtered through the oak trees was diffused and it was as if she were looking at the house with a veil over it. Moments ago she had sweat running down her face. Now she shivered and shook her head saying to herself, *Don't you start believing in this root magic now, girl.* It was difficult to tell how far the driveway continued past the front of the house from where she stood and she suspected it lead to a barn. If so, Ruby could have her car concealed there and she could be hiding anywhere waiting. No sign of Savannah's car either. Irish still could not hear or see any activity from within the house. *I hope to shit crazy Ruby hasn't killed those kids. Where the hell are they? Don't kids run around and play these days?*

*****

Here come another white hag bitch think'n she gonna get ma man. Hag her white ass. Gonna hex that bitch. Don puts a root under the porch for all dem bad gals. Cuts her too, Auntie you sees now. Gotta cuts em.

Chapter Forty-Four

Savannah had slowly regained consciousness again, this time she began to piece her memories back together. She remembered pulling up to the front of the old and seemingly deserted shack that had once belonged to Ruby's Auntie Ada. *So, this is Ruby's "farm house,"* it may have been so once but now the swamp was reaching up to claim it's own. Savannah had stopped so quickly she stalled the car, flung open the door and jumped out. She stumbled as she tried to run up the rickety old steps, caught herself and ran across the porch calling out Ruby's name. Savannah almost ripped the broken screen door off the rest of the way. When she discovered the door was locked, she knocked on it. Then she pounded on it, calling, "Ruby, Ruby are you in there. Open this door right now. Where are the girls? Ruby."

Just as Savannah was turning around to find a tree branch or anything she could use to force the door open the door swung wide and there stood Ruby. "Why Miss Savannah ma'am you all do come on in. So nice of you to visit." Ruby's eyes were dilated and she shifted them from side to side, her clothing was slightly disheveled and she was aware of it because she was trying to smooth out the wrinkles. Savannah had never seen the dress Ruby had on before; this was no outfit one would wear to the office or for casual wear. This was a dress that could have been worn in the best of nightclubs that is before it fell into its present condition. It was artfully designed, low cut, tight waist, and deep fiery red silk. Very short but still tasteful with tiny little straps, one of which was hanging off Ruby's left shoulder.

Ruby pushed the screen door open and moved aside giving Savannah room to enter the house. As Savannah stepped forward into the living room she felt strange as if she were walking through a portal of evil. Ruby gestured to a broken down flowered sofa; however, Savannah remained standing.

"Ruby, I came to talk to you about what happened yesterday at the office. We, Peggy and I that is, never meant for you to over hear us. Now that you've had time to think it over you can see it was all for the best." *Right.* "If you'll let me I'll see that you get some help to get started again. Where are the girls? This must have been upsetting for them?" Savannah knew she was rattling on but she hoped to keep Ruby busy until she could find out what was happening here.

"You hush now and be a good girl, I won't have to cuts you none." Ruby grinned, more to herself than to Savannah.

*****

White hag bitch comin down here to take my man, Gonna cuts you too. I knows, I knows Auntie.

*****

"What the hell do you mean? What's going on here?" Savannah was stalling for time, trying to think of a way to find the children and help them. It was obvious that Ruby had lost her mind. She had to measure each word and do nothing to upset her any further.

Across the room on the floor there were a couple of sleeping bags and blankets piled up to form a bed. *Oh God, the girls are here* - there was the large beach bag decorated with farm animals that Savannah had given Ruby for the girls. She had thought it might be fun for them to carry their things to daycare in such a colorful bag. Savannah slid her eyes away, but Ruby had not missed the fact that Savannah recognized the bag. Ruby grinned to herself again and she knew she had control over Savannah because of the girls. "You wait right here while I go up and make sure your banging on the door didn't scare the girls. It took me an hour to get them down and now you come along making all that racket."

"Yes, go see to the girls, I wouldn't want them to be scared either." Savannah is so damn glad to hear the kids are alive. *While she's up there I'll figure out what to do next. Damn, I just can't leave the kids-or should I, and go for help?*

"Shall I go with you and help? I'm good with children." *I have to make sure the kids are okay before I do anything else.*

"No ma'am I'll be right back," says Ruby in a more friendly voice.

Savannah can hear as she climbs the stairs and talks to the children.

"Hush, hush babies."

"Mama I scared,"

"Okay that must be Faith." Savannah was relieved. She sounded sweet, innocent and, Thank God, alive.

"Can we get up now Mama," said the older girl, Jasmine. She sounded like the big sister. Good to know both were alive.

"Not yet babies," said Ruby tenderly, "you be good girls and mama will bring you a treat. Hush now."

After it was quiet for a few moments, Savannah decided to go see if she could help anyway. As she rounded the corner from the living room to head up the stairs, Ruby came quietly down the stairs with her finger over her lips. "Shush, lets go back to the living room before you scare them again." Ruby grabbed Savannah's arm in a viselike grip and propelled her back to the living room.

"Ya'll down here fixin' ta take ma man?"

"Ruby I don't have any idea what you're talking about. I told you why I came, just to try and see if there was any way to help. I've never even met your man."

"You better be a good girl or I'll cut those babies and you." Ruby grinned at Savannah.

"Now look Ruby this has gone on long enough. You need to calm down and stop talking about cutting anyone." *I've got to figure out how to grab the kids and get the hell out of here.*

Ruby's grin froze on her face and she spun around towards the old rock fireplace. She held up her hand as to shield her eyes from the light.

"Auntie, I is a good girl, I 'member you taught me how to do the magic. Auntie I does it good like you teaches." Ruby's voice whined like a young girl, then changed as fast as it had begun. "White bitch," she directed towards Savannah, "I don't care what Auntie says about white folk, she *all* the time say.

"Now, Ruby you knows God say we all his childs. Be no good to hate any peoples cause their skin different than you is. Come sit by the fire and Auntie tells you the old ways. Why when I little there be no cars on da island, we was rowboat folks. Come here girl let Auntie hold ya close." Ruby's voice now had a singsong tone as if she had chanted Auntie's words over and over and over.

Ruby's voice turned cold and hard again, "Auntie old, she don know what dem nasty ass white girls does to Ruby. They pretend to be oh so nice, but I know they laugh'n behind ma back. They is *so* jealous cause all their men likes Ruby mo. I show them, like I show dem bitches come to take my man in Atlanta. Now you come clear down here try to take my man." Spittle was gathering at the corners of Ruby's mouth, her face glistened with sweat and she was beginning to pant heavily. Savannah had already began to back up slowly hoping to reach the door, but Ruby sprang across the room like a wild creature and slapped her full force in the face. The large ring Ruby always wore caught Savannah just below her left eye and it began to swell instantly. Savannah bent over from the nausea that accompanied the pain. The last thing she remembered before she woke up wherever she now was being held was turning her head at the sound of a car motor approaching.

Chapter Forty-Five

Can't stand here all day, thought Irish, *I've got to make a move.* It was still much too quiet to suit her. *Maybe Savannah was here yesterday, found the girls, talked Ruby into letting her...yeah right, that crazy ass bitch could have killed Savannah, the kids, dumped Savannah's car and be halfway to Mexico by now.* Sweat ran down Irish's face in rivulets and her clothes were wet enough to wring out. The white sleeveless top she had on felt like a dishrag and her jeans were plastered to her legs. She reached into her purse and drew the gun out, then began to move forward one slow step at a time. Irish walked in a crouched position, both hands on the gun, arms stiff and swinging first one way and then the other covering the territory ahead. Her eyes probed the area, still no movement. Advancing around the yard in front of the house the afternoon sun almost blinded her and then the barn came into view.

The old weathered barn was in as poor condition as the house; however, its size gave an indication that this was once a fairly prosperous property. The large door was closed and the structure was beginning to lean, if there ever had been paint on the wood it had long since faded away. Irish approached from the side being careful not to step on any dry grass and attempted to peer in through the cracked and splintered siding. It was too dark inside and too light outside to make out anything other that what appeared to be the shape of a large car.

Chapter Forty-Six

He had paced back and forth trying to figure out what to do next. Tremaine had known he would have to kill that ugly bitch and soon. *Bitch is gett'n on my last nerves.* He had never killed a woman before, but that was going to change as soon as he got all he needed from that bitch. She told him they could hide out here a few days until they had their new I.D.s and then get the hell out of the country. Tremaine had plenty of cash with him and unknown to Ruby a nice account in the Cayman Islands. He had been sending money down there since his days in Chicago. Tremaine had a lot more going on than he'd ever let on to a whore like Ruby. Sweat shown on his shaved head and his lean hard body was drenched in moisture. He hated it here in this goddamn swamp *Ain't nobody gonna find me here,* and he hated her. Everything had changed last night.

After he had left Nicky's last night, he had stopped on Piedmont for a couple of drinks. He had wanted to think about getting rid of Ruby and taking off with Nicky. The idea had sounded better all the time. He had never loved anyone in his life and he damn sure didn't love Nicky but she was soft and sweet. Nicky had some class for a young gal and some good ideas for making some bucks. Besides the cops were all over the place looking for the serial killer. He couldn't afford any close scrutiny by the cops. Tremaine was beginning to think a rival was setting him up. *Some motherfucker after my gals.* He had put the word out on the street and the street was quiet. Eerily quiet. No one was talking.

Then he went to pay his tab and discovered he left his wallet at Nicky's. No problem his man Jake the bartender knew he was good for it. Tremaine had cruised back to Nicky's to pick up his wallet. As he rounded the corner he had seen cops all over her street. The medical examiner's van had been backed up to the alley next to Nicky's building. Traffic had been jammed up in between all the emergency vehicles. He decided to double park with the rest of the crowd and walk up the half block to Nicky's. He could have been in and out of there in less than five minutes. The entrance to the alley had been taped off with all too familiar yellow tape. As Tremaine had walked by, they had been wheeling out a gurney with a black bag on it.

Tremaine had stopped for a second and some old woman stood on the sidewalk in her bathrobe, her hair in curlers rattled on to no one in particular, "She was such a sweet girl. Goddamn shame that's what it is. I knew her since she moved in the building. Her name was Nicole, but we all called her Nicky. Hope they catch the murdering bastards." Tremaine turned on his heels and eased back the way he had come.

Somehow he had slipped back to his car and got the hell out of there without being stopped. It was only a matter of time before the cops found his wallet. They would be all over him in nothing flat. *Man I gotta think what to do. Police gonna have my black ass in jail and I ain't never gonna get out, except'n feet first.* He had grabbed his mobile and punched in the numbers, "Listen Ruby, gal, I needs your help and now. Throw a few things together. We gotta get out of here for a while. I can't talk now. I'll be there in a few." It was too bad about Nicky but he had to get the hell out of here now. Who ever had set him up had done a good job of it. His balls were in a vise now. He had to lose this town tonight. When he had met up with Ruby back at the apartment she had everything ready to roll. He had filled her in on what had happened, how he had just stopped by Nicky's to see if she was tending to business. He had a quick drink and some how left his wallet. "Course that whore mighta stole it too." Tremaine had needed to keep on Ruby's good side right now, until he got her help. She had a plan put together to get them out of the country so goddamn fast he almost wondered....

Then late this afternoon Tremaine had taken a chance and driven to the package store for a bottle of vodka. He had been gone only a short time and Ruby had that fine piece of ass laid out cold when he got back. "Dumb bitch." He had only seen this pretty little gal Ruby had knocked out unconscious so far, but he intended to have some of that. Ruby said she came up the road looking for her old Auntie Ada's kinfolk, this gal's family had a farm close by or some shit. Ruby was afraid this gal might go back and tells someone we was here. She said the gal had told her she was from out of state so they wouldn't miss her anytime soon. *Havin' a hostage might not hurt, I'm in so deep now an' for something I fuckin' didn't do!* He thought. He had helped Ruby dump her in the barn, but it was up to Ruby to take care of her until he said different. He had made Ruby pull the gal's car to the far side of the barn. She had been forced to climb out fast because the car sunk in the mire down to the hubcaps. He had snickered about that one.

"Tremaine baby, come let your mama make you feel fine. You know I do it better than any gal you ever had. Let me love you fine." Ruby tried to rub herself on him and as she reached to undo his pants he shoved her roughly away. He no longer desired her for she merely enraged him. He was having a difficult time waiting to do away with her as it was, without having to touch her. *Soon as I gits what I wants, she one dead whore.*

*****

Ruby's man fuck her so fine, see he don't miss dem bad girls Ruby cut. See Auntie?

Chapter Forty-Seven

Savannah couldn't see who was coming but she smelled her, the scent of Ruby's perfume mixed with sweat was all over her and Savannah did all she could do not to retch. Ruby was on her now, her switchblade at Savannah's throat cutting her neck just deep enough to start a thin trickle of blood down between her breasts.

"You better be a good girl, you make any noise, any trouble and I'll have to cut you bad. Then I'll cut my girls and it will be your fault. You tell my man who you are and I kill you then my girls and it will be your fault, you got that? Just say your name and it's over, you understand all that?" Savannah didn't understand "all that" but nodded her head and before she could say a word Ruby slapped tape over her mouth. She bent and cut the tape that had been around her ankles. "You remember what I just said, I'll kill those girls and be on my way with ma man."

"You have to pee?" Savannah nodded again, eyes wide at Ruby's quick change of direction. "Okay," she pulled Savannah up by her hair and when she was standing Ruby shoved her along until they were outside structure they had been in. Savannah could see shapes in the faint light of the moon but nothing definitive. She already had tears in her eyes from having her hair pulled so hard. When she stumbled and fell on the rough ground Ruby grabbed her hair again and pulled her upright. The searing pain in Savannah's ankle made her almost vomit. Now she could barely walk and Ruby was forced to help her along. They had both almost fallen together when they had crossed an old rock bridge. Just when she thought the trek would never end they reach their destination, an outhouse so old the very idea of what could be inside made Savannah shudder. Ruby swung open the door and a nasty odor flooded out. "Think your white ass to clean to sit on that old hole? It's that or piss your pants."

Savannah eyed the huge furry black spider hanging from the corner and stumbled inside. Right beside her, Ruby undid her once clean shorts. Her soft yellow tee was ruined as if any of that mattered now. *This is disgusting.* Ruby was pulling her panties down and pushing her down on the old wooden toilet seat. *Even if I make it through this, I'll die of some dreaded disease.* She closed her eyes and peed, no telling when or if she would get another opportunity. The old outhouse had been deserted for years and used to dump trash in. Someone, probably Ruby had cleared the way to the seat. The place was full of papers, tin cans, and broken glass in fact Savannah cut her butt sitting on a piece of old glass. She leaned back as far as she could and clutched the small piece of glass in her hand just as Ruby spoke again.

"Sorry Miss Fancy Ass there is no paper for you to wipe your stinky crack on."

Ruby didn't sound a bit sorry. *When I get out of this mess, and I will, I won't think twice about strangling the shit out of you.* She was madder than hell now. *Speaking of stinky cracks.*

The return walk, more like a stumbling match, was a repeat of the trip to the outhouse. The only difference was she had not fallen down this time. The moon came out just enough for Savannah to get a quick look at the building she was headed back towards. Judging by the size it must be an old barn, besides the floor had all been hard packed dirt like most old barns. It must have been a side door they use as she could tell it was not the size one expected on a barn. When they stopped walking Ruby jerked the tape from Savannah's mouth as roughly as possible and held a small bottle of water to her lips. Savannah gulped down the entire bottle less

Ruby pull it away. Smack! - The tape went back on her mouth. After that Ruby had slapped her face smiling as though it were just for fun. Ruby pushed her back down on the ground re-taped her ankles and this time cut off a long hank of her golden hair. The pale moonlight filtered in through the cracked sides of the barn and lit up the hair just long enough to set Ruby off again.

"White hag bitch with her white hair a bad girl. Gots to cuts her. I knows Auntie. You sees all dem faces? Dem faces follows me. No, you jus don knows how bad I tries to be good. Bitches comes for ma man, I got to cuts em. I gotta make a spell with this white hair. Bitches can't gets ma man. Gotta conjure up a curse."

Ruby ran off and Savannah knew she had very little time to find a way out of here. She had to focus on several things she learned during Ruby's *visit*. She knew now that there was a man here somewhere and she hoped to hell that he could control Ruby. *Can anyone control her? She is insane, maybe a killer, who knows the way she keeps talking about cutting girls. What the hell does that mean? She has no conscience unless you could call her dead Auntie one.* Savannah felt she must be going insane herself, no wonder a little more time with Ruby and she would be. Still, she could have sworn she saw a pale light in the corner where Ruby spoke to who she believed to be her dead Auntie. *Listen to me now I'm seeing spirits too.*

Savannah tried to move around into a more comfortable position but it was hopeless. Rocks protruded from the hard packed earth beneath her. *Why is Ruby keeping me alive? She obviously hates me, but something or someone is holding her back.* Savannah wasn't sure what was going on; there was certainly a lot more to this scenario than she knew. *What made me think I could help Ruby or her girls? This is just great, no one even knows where I am and twisting my ankle certainly doesn't help matters.* Tears formed in her eyes and she was filled momentarily with despair. She had been compelled to check upon Ruby, and now she realized that the girls were in danger.

That's enough. Think. There's got to be a way out of this. What would Irish do? Man, do I ever wish she were here right now.

She held tightly to the small piece of glass and began to try to cut through the tape binding her wrists. Thoughts swirled in her mind all night and at times she almost lost consciousness. It was almost dawn when she drifted off into a fitful half sleep still clutching her piece of glass.

Chapter Forty-Eight

Ruby had tried to climb back on the pallet without disturbing Tremaine but he was wide-awake and furious. "You hurt that bitch?" he asked.

"No, baby, I does jus like you tol me."

"Don't use that old talk, didn't I tell you how I hate it? Don't you fuck with me none. You hear?"

"Yes, baby." She tried to move up close to him.

"Yes, baby, my ass. Ya better stop with all that voodoo shit and do like I tells you. Who the fuck you think is running things, not your dumb bitch ass that's for sure."

With that he threw her against the wall, got up and began to pace the floor. "You better get on the mobile and find out first thing tomorrow what the fuck'n hold up is with my money and my I.D. You got that? We can't fuck'n stay here much longer. Somebody be look'n for that bitch an I fuck'n hate it here, fuck'n ass country. You hears me bitch?" By now he was so furious his own grammar was taking a turn for the worse, and it was all he could do to keep from blowing Ruby away. He pulled his .44 Magnum from its holster and aimed at Ruby. It was too dark for her to see him but it made him feel more powerful. Even though he'd stripped to the waist he kept his shoulder holster on. He'd begun to feel the loss of control, this compounded his anger and he had steadily become more dangerous.

"Yes, baby."

*****

See auntie how big and strong ma man is? He take good care a Ruby, he needs his Ruby. He don wants no other gals. No, tole you before I is a good girl. Auntie, dem faces follows me. Please make dem go away.

Chapter Forty-Nine

Once Irish spotted the car through the cracked siding of the barn she figured since there was no door on this side of the barn she would have to go through the front. *Damn, I don't like to be in full view of the house, but guess I'll have to chance it.* With that she crept slowly around to the front staying as close to the barn without touching it as possible. The ground was uneven and she was careful not to slip and fall against the barn. It seemed to be getting hotter and not a whisper of a breeze stirred. She made it to the large door, pulled on it and as it came open she peered inside.

Sitting up against the front end of a new black Mercedes was a large dangerous looking black man holding Savannah with his left arm around her waist and a .44 Magnum in his right hand. "Come on in and join the party, baby," said the man. "Lay your gun down on the ground real easy like. Two pretty gals dropping in like this, too good to be true. Even if you is a police officer you too fine."

Irish's experience as an investigator quickly cued her into the thoughts of Savannah's captor. *This guy thinks I'm a cop, so he knows they're after him. Does he know who Savannah is? What's going on?* Irish was quick to process this but couldn't figure out why Ruby didn't speak up and spill the beans. Was she hiding and why were they still here? She was relieved to see Savannah actually alive although her condition didn't look too good. She appeared weak, left eye-swollen shut, duct tape over her mouth and there was dried blood on her neck that had run down onto her top. Her clothes and hair were filthy. Irish wondered if she could stand if this guy let go of her. It appeared there might be something wrong with her right foot or ankle. She was standing okay on her left foot, but only putting weight on the ball of her right foot.

As for him, he was an immense guy, way over six feet and had a hot build. His designer slacks were dirty, wrinkled and his once shiny loafers lacked their original luster. Sweat dripped from his shaved head and trickled down his bare muscular chest. Besides slacks and shoes, he was stripped to the bare necessities, gold neck chain, diamond earring and shoulder holster, *Just your everyday gangster apparel. He's gotta be the guy the cops are looking for. This is just great. He sure as shit doesn't fit the cops serial killer profile.*

"Close your mouth bitch and do like I tell you, real easy like, put your gun on the ground and stand back up slow and easy, you hear me bitch?" he said.

Fast change of tone here, thought Irish. She glanced at Savannah and her eyes pleaded. They had used eye signals since they were kids and their folks never had caught on. It was about to pay off. Irish caught on that she meant for her not to do anything to get the kids hurt, *I understand.* Irish's eyes replied looking directly at Savannah. Savannah blinked and Irish realized that like always they understood one another. Irish also caught a spark in Savannah's eyes and hoped that meant she was not as weak as Irish had first suspected. She tipped the barrel of her gun up, slowly squatted and set the gun on the ground. As she began to stand back up she saw a slight movement from the dark interior of the barn.

"Okay, baby, start walking to me, nice and slow. Easy does it. That's a good girl," he crooned as Irish moved forward. "Stop there."

"Ruby," he called roughly.

"Yes, baby?"

"Get up here and get me that goddamn gun. Don't get between my new baby or my line of fire, you hear? This here po'lice officers a dangerous lady."

"Yes, baby," Ruby moved forward, and Irish got a look at her for the first time. She tried to cover her reaction. Ruby fit the picture of the wild woman they had suspected she was.

Ruby stood before them, her hair untamed, on end, mascara running the length of her face, and eyes glazed, almost lifeless. Irish had quickly sized up Ruby as she approached her. The moment they made eye contact Irish saw the fury in her. Ruby had a switchblade in her hand and pointing it right at her. She moved behind Irish and retrieved the gun from the dirt. As she turned to walk away with the gun, she stopped, ready to plunge the knife into her. A ray of light shining in through a crack in the old barn's siding bounced off the blade of the knife. Ruby's eyes dilated and she smiled at the knife as if she were spotting her lover across a crowded room. During that split second in time Irish recognized the face of the killer.

"Get back over here with that damn gun you hear me," called Ruby's man. Ruby turned reluctantly and walked with an exaggerated sway over to her man to give him the gun. His full attention was on Irish, "Where's your partner? Don't lie to me bitch. I knows you didn't come out here by your little bitch self." Ruby starts to hand Tremaine the gun, "Hang onto that motherfuck'n gun. Can't you sees I got ma hands full?"

"But..."

"Do what I tells ya and put that goddamn knife away, dumb whore," he tells Ruby. He clearly expects her to obey him without question. Ruby pushes the blade back into the handle of the knife. Trying to get her man's attention she squirms her ass around. Failing that she slides the knife down between her breasts. He ignores her. She shoots him a look of surprise and then intense anger.

Irish was increasingly aware that this guy was out of his element out here in the swamp. The fierce heat and insects bothered him. *I'm sure he hates his expensive clothes being so dirty, what he has on that is.* Irish saw he was about to unravel. Concentration did not appear to be his strong suit at the present. She would bet underneath he was scared shitless. Not to mention Ruby's a homicidal manic. *"How the fuck do we get out of this?"*

"Ruby."

"Yes, baby?"

"Get on the goddamn mobile and find out what the fuck'n holdup is? You says there is another delay and I'm gonna beat your dumb bitch ass, you hear?"

So that's why they're still hanging around here. They're waiting for their contact to bring money, passports, new I.D.s. Now Irish figured she was closed to having figured out that part of the puzzle.

Irish was trying to keep her eyes off Savannah, so she wouldn't give away the game, whatever that may be. As Irish watched Ruby's man's every move, Savannah moved closer to the guy, slowly raised her right leg and rubbed him ever so slightly. He frowned, momentarily confused by her actions. "What cha up to?" He asked.

Savannah shrugged and moved closer yet. He responded by dropping the arm he had around her and when his hand was on her butt he gave it a playful little squeeze. He leaned over and whispered something in her ear. As his eyes moved to Savannah, he grinned and Irish stole a look at Ruby. Ruby was still talking softly into the mobile phone but she hadn't missed the encounter. Ruby began to tremble with rage, meanwhile Savannah's plan was conveyed to Irish.

His attention shifted back to Irish, "Didn't I ax you where your partner was?" Since she didn't know the entire scenario, she decided to keep it simple. Maybe she can get him to calm down and buy a little time for them to implement their plan. *It doesn't look like he's big in the multi-tasking department.*

"I came alone, I don't need any back up." She raised her eyebrows and gave him the beginning of a smile, then slowly ran her tongue over her lips. Irish tilted her head and let her long, red hair fall over the side of her face. "Maybe now I'm kinda glad I did." Irish looked up at him. "Looks like you're doin' okay for yourself. That's fine a look'n ride you got there." Irish nodded her head toward his car. "Can't get a car like that on my pay"

"You not so dumb, baby, maybe you jus wanna make some real money?" Irish moved her eyes from his eyes down his body to stop at his crotch and back up again. Meanwhile Savannah was cuddling him as best she could with her hands behind her back. He was really working his hand on her ass now, all the time looking into Irish's eyes. "Come on over here, baby, an say a real hello to Tremaine."

"That's your name, Tremaine?"

"You like it, baby?" He asked Irish as he's rubbing Savannah's ass.

"I like it and I'll bet it *fits*," said Irish, moving slowly forward, eyes on his crotch. When she was directly in front of him he reached out gun in hand, and with the gun barrel carefully moved her hair from her eyes.

"You might have ta come along with Tremaine. I could turn you on to some real big bucks. Course you'd be work'n under me, if ya get my drift." *Bitch might help me gets outta here, she's want'n moneys. Gotta gets the fuck outta the country or the cops is gonna kill my ass. Soon as my money and paper's is here fo sure I'm gonna kill this motherfuck'n Ruby whore.* Tremaine's mind was racing as he tried to figure all the angles.

Suddenly, a blood-curdling scream tore from Ruby's throat, she dropped the mobile phone and started toward them gun in hand. Saliva running from her mouth as she cursed and screamed "White hag bitches not gonna take ma man." She was moving fast, closing the gap between them.

Tremaine was completely taken by surprise with Ruby's outburst, and Irish took that moment to knee him in his crotch and grab for his gun. She didn't connect because he bent to clutch his crotch. He dropped the gun and it slid under the car. At the same time, Savannah snapped the final scrap of tape around her wrists and grabbed his left arm with both of her hands. She bit his arm, sinking her teeth in as hard as she could.

Ruby was incoherent, as she stood in front of Tremaine pointing Irish's gun directly at him. It was as if the other two women no longer existed. Tremaine straightened back up slowly and then froze. Aware at last that she had completely lost her mind; he tried to sweet talk her. "Come on, baby. Ya knows I don mean anything by it, jus trying to get us some new gals. We gots to have some gals to get started with again. Right? Ya knows it's you and me all the way. Baby, you is the onlys one for your Tremaine," as he looked into her eyes begging now, "Please, baby, please."

Ruby stood rigid before him, jaw clenched, her eyes blazing with hatred. Sweat ran down his face in rivulets, and his voice trembled as he kept trying to appease her. He had no weapon and he was holding his arm where Savannah bit him. Blood was oozing from the wound.

Ruby ignored him, couldn't hear his pleas, she was in her other world now, back with her Auntie. Broken words and phrases tumbled from her lips. "Auntie, they comes from all over now to get ma mans, now he no good, he done took up with um Auntie. I keeps tell'n ya I is a good girl, dem hag bitches made me cut em. Now ma man bes bad too, jus like dem. He kilt ma babies, yes he did Auntie, he did so. I gotta hex him. I make more potions, make him mind me now, no it won work he no good for noth'n now. Auntie please make dem faces goes away."

Ruby was now down on her knees, directly in front of Tremaine. She was moaning, and the gun was pointed straight at Tremaine's face. She's shaking as she held the gun with both hands. No one moved or exhaled. He was crying now, begging faster. Ruby's once stunning, red dress split up the side when she slid to her knees. She had lost her high heels somewhere.

Tremaine slid down to his knees and all he could say was "Please, baby" over and over again. He was so terrified he'd urinated in his slacks. Ruby's eyes suddenly cleared and she really noticed him for the first time. She looked him directly in the eyes. In what Irish thought must have been Ruby's most normal voice she said "I killed them all for you, Tremaine," With that she pulled the trigger. The sound echoed within the barn like a cannon shot. Tremaine fell forward, head in Ruby's lap.

There was a gaping hole where Tremaine's right eye used to be and his blood and brains covered the front of Ruby's red dress. Fragments of his skull lay on the ground around them. She rocked him and crooned to him like a small child. The hair that she had always so artfully arranged was a tangled mess. Her eyes were vacant and saliva bubbled from her lips. She opened her mouth and emitted animal-like screams of pain. A beam of sunlight flashed in through a crack in the old barn and as it hit Ruby's face it seemed to glow. She suddenly stopped screaming and her right hand stretched out with the gun in it as if she were handing it to an unseen entity. Ruby smiled softly as Savannah gently took the gun from her hand.

EPILOGUE

Catherine Sullivan slowly opened the door to Savannah's hospital room and peeked around the corner. Tears sprang to her eyes and she stood still a few moments to recover her composure. There were her two girls safe and sound. As a mother it's one thing to be told they were both fine as Irish had told her in her call last night, and it was another thing to see for yourself.

Savannah was still in her hospital gown propped up with several pillows. Perched on the bed beside her was Irish. They were giggling and laughing like old times. Savannah had a small bandage on her neck and her left eye was swollen, puffy, black and bluish green. Aside from a badly sprained ankle, scrapes, bruises and minor dehydration the doctor had said she would be fine in no time. In fact, he was releasing her today, in Catherine's care, as Savannah's parents were unable to come for her. Normally Catherine would have been angry at their lack of concern, for anyone except themselves, of course. Today, however, she was happy to have the girls to herself.

Irish had called her from the police station last night and filled her in on the events of the past few days. She said that Ruby Ebota was locked up where she couldn't harm herself or others. The authorities had yet to unravel how many people Ruby might have killed and there were legalities regarding jurisdiction, crossing of state lines and so forth. It did appear that besides killing her boyfriend and the two women in Savannah's office, that there was evidence now that she may be responsible for another murder the police had previously believed was committed by the "Call Girl Killer." Irish had attempted to play down how much danger she and Savannah had been in, but Catherine was not buying it for a second. She planned to read them both the riot act, just not today, wait till they were all a distance from the horror of the ordeal. Evidently there were to be more meetings with the police before they would be able to leave, and so she had reserved rooms at a lovely Bed & Breakfast in Beaufort. The girls could enjoy the waterfront restaurants and marina for a day or so before returning to what ever came next. Catherine wished she could stay with them but she had to get back to care for John.

"No need to ask how you two are, chattering like little magpies."

"Mom, boy it's good to see you," says Irish as she slid off the bed to give Catherine a big hug.

Catherine held her a bit longer than she normally would have. The thought that she could have lost her only remaining child was more than she could bear to consider.

"Doesn't Savannah look like the walking wounded? A real heroine." Irish asked.

"She looks like a sight for sore eyes. Give me a hug, sweetie," Catherine gathered Savannah to her, careful not to hold her too tightly and wiped her own tears away behind Savannah's back. "Savannah dear, I brought a few of my things for you to wear. They should do well enough for today and then you two can do some serious shopping tomorrow. I've made all the arrangements for a place for you girls to stay and all."

Savannah and Irish exchanged glances and smiled. It would be best not to talk about the clothes they had to discard. There had been plenty of Tremaine left to go around and Ruby had not been the only one splattered with his remains. Before Catherine had come in, they had been joking about Ruby's red dress. Irish had said " Think the dry cleaners can get that little number cleaned up for the Cotillion?" They were rapidly recovering from the horror of the past few days and in fine form. Savannah had rubbed in the fact that Ms. Private Detective had missed grabbing Termaine's gun in the melee and worst of all Ruby ended up with Irish's gun. She intended to get all the mileage she could out of that one.

"I appreciate you so much Catherine," says Savannah, "You're the best, always taking such good care of me."

"Why wouldn't I? You're my girl, too. Enough now let me get a chair. I want to hear all about this adventure you girls have been on and don't try to leave out what you think I shouldn't hear."

"Yes ma'am," came from both girls at the same time; however, they had no intentions of spilling all they knew. They themselves didn't understand everything that happened. Some events seemed surreal like the glow of light on Ruby's face just before Savannah had taken the gun from her hand. Savannah had told no one of the light she thought she saw in the barn when Ruby talked to her dead Auntie. Neither of them had cared to discuss or bring up those events, at least not yet.

"What puzzles me the most is where are Ruby's little girls? Have they found them yet? Are they okay?" Catherine looks from one of them to the other.

Savannah and Irish look at one another and finally Savannah says, "There never were any children."

*****

Auntie, whys ya not lets me kills dem bad gals?